## SPONTANEOUS CONFESSION

"Don't touch anything," Miss Withers warned. "That's for the police to do when they get here, if they ever do. It's too late to do anything for the man who's in the water. Anyone can see that he's dead."

Anyone could see that. Even Gwen Lester, who pushed past the shoulders of those who hid the thing she feared to look upon. It was Gerald, her husband.

Gwen's fingers clawed for the arm of her companion, but he too was staring into the tank, his face white as chalk.

Gwen felt her lips move, and heard words come forth that she would have given anything in the world to keep from saying. "Oh, Phil . . . what have we done!"

Damningly clear, the sentence rang through the high-arched room. . . .

Bantam Books offers the finest in classic and modern American murder mysteries. Ask your bookseller for the books you have missed.

**Stuart Palmer**
THE PENGUIN POOL MURDER
THE PUZZLE OF THE HAPPY
 HOOLIGAN
THE PUZZLE OF THE RED
 STALLION
THE PUZZLE OF THE SILVER
 PERSIAN

**Craig Rice**
HAVING WONDERFUL CRIME
MY KINGDOM FOR A HEARSE

**Rex Stout**
AND FOUR TO GO
BAD FOR BUSINESS
DEATH OF A DUDE
DEATH TIMES THREE
DOUBLE FOR DEATH
FER-DE-LANCE
THE FINAL DEDUCTION
GAMBIT
THE LEAGUE OF FRIGHTENED
 MEN
NOT QUITE DEAD ENOUGH
THE RUBBER BAND
SOME BURIED CAESAR
THE SOUND OF MURDER
TOO MANY CLIENTS

**Victoria Silver**
DEATH OF A HARVARD
 FRESHMAN
DEATH OF A RADCLIFFE
 ROOMMATE

**William Kienzle**
THE ROSARY MURDERS

**Joseph Louis**
MADELAINE

**M.J. Adamson**
NOT TILL A HOT JANUARY

**Richard Fliegel**
THE NEXT TO DIE

**Barbara Paul**
KILL FEE
THE RENEWABLE VIRGIN

**Benjamin Schutz**
EMBRACE THE WOLF

**S.F.X. Dean**
DEATH AND THE MAD HEROINE

**Ross MacDonald**
BLUE CITY
THE BLUE HAMMER

**Robert Goldsborough**
MURDER IN E MINOR

**Sue Grafton**
''B'' IS FOR BURGLAR

**Max Byrd**
CALIFORNIA THRILLER
FINDERS WEEPERS
FLY AWAY, JILL

**R.D. Brown**
HAZZARD

**A.E. Maxwell**
JUST ANOTHER DAY IN
 PARADISE

**Rob Kantner**
THE BACK-DOOR MAN

**Ted Wood**
LIVE BAIT

# The Penguin Pool Murder

Stuart Palmer

BANTAM BOOKS
TORONTO · NEW YORK · LONDON · SYDNEY · AUCKLAND

*This low-priced Bantam Book
has been completely reset in a type face
designed for easy reading, and was printed
from new plates. It contains the complete
text of the original hard-cover edition.*
NOT ONE WORD HAS BEEN OMITTED.

THE PENGUIN POOL MURDER

*A Bantam Book / published by arrangement with
the author's estate*

*Bantam edition / March 1986*

ISBN 0-553-26334-X

*Published simultaneously in the United States and Canada*

Bantam Books are published by Bantam Books, Inc. Its trademark, consisting
of the words ''Bantam Books'' and the portrayal of a rooster, is Registered
in U.S. Patent and Trademark Office and in other countries. Marca Regis-
trada. Bantam Books, Inc., 666 Fifth Avenue, New York, New York 10103.

PRINTED IN THE UNITED STATES OF AMERICA

O     0 9 8 7 6 5 4 3 2 1

To Melina

## Foreword

The teller of the tale claims an ancient right to choose setting, situation, and the framework of character from among those which possibly may be recognized by some of his readers, with the warning that no actual personages are herein designedly pictured.

S.P.

## Contents

# What the Penguins Knew

Two little black penguins were the first to know the secret. They became vastly excited, flashing their sleek black bodies through the water, and now and then coming to the surface to shriek Bloody Murder in a Galapagoan squawk. But for a time their intense excitement did not communicate itself to the greater world that lay outside the glass barrier of the tank.

Suddenly a woman's voice, reedy and shrill, rang against the ancient white-washed walls of the Aquarium. Even as its echoes died away, the figure of a frightened, rabbit-like little man scuttled past the dim corner under the stairs where the penguins were trying to blazon their secret. In his hand the fugitive clutched an oblong of black leather which all too evidently proclaimed itself to be a woman's purse.

His objective was a stair which led to the balcony above, but in his path there suddenly appeared the embattled bulk of a gray-clad guard. With a squeak like a cornered rat's, the little man whirled in his tracks and ducked back between the cases of stuffed exhibits, past the gaping and bewildered crowd. As he ran, there came from his bulging pockets a faint musical jingle.

The way to the main exit was clear now, though close behind him still pounded the heavy feet of the guard. The little man made a last frantic burst of speed—freedom was almost within his grasp—only to tumble ingloriously over a black cotton umbrella that dropped like a bar sinister across his path. His skull collided with one of the pillars, and for the time being the little man lay very still.

For a long minute there was a hush, and then Miss Hilde-garde Withers, whom the census enumerator had recently listed as "spinster, born Boston, age thirty-nine, occupation school teacher," dusted off her umbrella and restored it to its place under her arm with a certain air of satisfaction.

"Serves you perfectly right," she admonished her silent victim. Then she turned her keen blue eyes on the milling crowd. "Abraham!"

A small sepian lad detached himself from the little group of third grade pupils who stood, awestruck and admiring, behind Miss Withers. "Abraham, pick up that handbag and give it to the lady."

Abraham obeyed with alacrity. The leather bag was eagerly seized by the woman whose shriek had set the echoes ringing but a few moments before, and its contents found intact. "I saw him trying to cut the handle with a razor blade," she was eagerly explaining to whomever would listen, ". . . and then he jerked it right out of my hand, he did."

The guard, fat and perspiring from his unaccustomed chase, took a firm grip of the prisoner's coat collar and jerked him into a sitting position. As he did so, three gold watches slid from the pocket and clinked musically on the tile floor.

"A pickpocket, huh?" said the guard.

"Quite obvious, even to the most limited intelligence," pointed out Miss Withers. "I guessed it myself."

"Stealing watches, too."

"Do they look like grandfather clocks?"

"We've got him, dead to rights," the guard mused. "Yes, mum. A case for the cops, I shouldn't wonder."

"Or for the ambulance, anyway." Miss Withers shooed her chattering charges toward the door. "Don't stand there like a log, my good man. Do something!"

The guard let go of his prisoner's collar, and the man slumped again to the floor. "I don't just really know what the official procedure ought to be in a case of this kind," he observed doubtfully. "The Director is busy with guests, and I know he doesn't want any publicity of this kind. . . ."

"HEY!" A big bass voice boomed through the building like a husky fog-horn, clearing the crowd from the doorway like chaff before the wind. "Hey, there! What's all this fuss about?"

Six feet three of bone and muscle shoved its way belliger-ently through the crowd. "One side, one side, will you?" The policeman looked down past the two rows of shining buttons on his front to where the crumpled figure lay on the floor. Then he whirled on the guard, belligerently.

"Well, speak out, Fink! What is it? Alcoholism? Did you send for the ambulance?"

"Not yet, Donovan. And this is no alcoholism, it ain't. It's a pickpocket that I've nabbed." Fink held up the three watches as evidence. Immediately they were engulfed in the policeman's enormous paw. He bent over to survey the bruised face on the floor. Then he started.

Wetting his thumb, he whirled over the pages of a little black book that he took from his hip pocket. Finally he found a certain page, and read aloud with much puzzling over words. . . .

"McGirr, John—alias Chicago Lew—height five feet three, weight one hundred and two pounds, wanted in Des Moines, Detroit and Chicago for petty thievery and picking pockets—" He replaced the black book in his pocket with a flourish. "It's him all right. We've been looking for this guy for two months, we have." He bent over the prisoner.

"Just you hold on there, Mickey Donovan!" Fink, the fat guard, stuttered with eagerness. "What about the reward, I wanta know? Is they a reward for this Chicago Lew? Is they? Because I lay claim to it, here and now. I want these people to witness it, I do. If they is a reward, I'm going to get it."

"Suppose there is?" Donovan put his hands on his hips and stared at the other. "I'm doing the arresting, ain't I? I'm the cop here, ain't I? I got the prisoner, ain't I? I recognized him, didn't I?"

The big policeman moved toward his prisoner again, but Fink thrust his face between.

"That don't make one bit of difference," insisted the guard. "Just because you're the flatfoot on this beat, Mickey Donovan, is no sign that you've got a right to walk in and hog the reward for this prisoner. He's mine, I guess. I leave it to anybody here, I do. Didn't I chase him through the place? Didn't I nab him here in the doorway? Didn't I . . ."

"If there is any reward, I don't see why I shouldn't get it." Miss Withers left her little flock and strode forward, her umbrella held menacingly before her. Both Fink and Donovan drew back a step, as did the surrounding crowd.

"I stopped him with this umbrella, you know. He would have escaped if it hadn't been for me, and then this poor woman would have had to lose her handbag, besides the watches that were stolen from somebody. . . ."

Immediately loud voices from the crowd announced that most of the gentlemen present had lost their timepieces, and that they recognized their property among the watches in Donovan's hand. The air became filled with strangely vague descriptions of the property, until Donovan silenced them with a roar.

"You can get your property up at the Police Property Clerk's office, if you can identify it to the Captain's satisfaction. Some of you never saw a watch before except in a pawnshop window. Leave off your jabbering, will you?"

"But I tell you, this man doesn't get taken out of here until we come to some agreement about the reward," insisted Fink. "Half of it, anyway. That I've got to have, Mickey Donovan! Half of it, or he doesn't go to jail. There's nobody here to make a complaint against him anyway. . . ."

"Not a cent, Fink. You didn't know this guy was wanted anywhere."

"Half, I tell you. Why, do you think I'm maybe going to let fifty dollars slip out of my hands like nothing?"

"Not a cent, Fink. I saw him, and I knew him . . ."

"Stop quarreling, you two!" The sharp and commanding voice of Miss Withers cut in with unmistakable authority. "Stop it, I say! Don't you realize that this man is hurt? He ought to be on the way to the hospital, and you know it. Suppose he should die while the two of you fight over the reward?" Miss Withers gestured dramatically with her umbrella. "You can't leave him there on the floor——"

Her voice died out in a thin whisper . . . for he *wasn't* on the floor. . . .

The pickpocket had vanished!

The spot where he had lain, so lifeless and inert, was very very bare. The crowd moved uneasily, each man staring into the face of his neighbor, and the surprised eyes of Donovan stared into everyone's . . . but Chicago Lew had made himself scarce.

Somehow, while the two of them had wrangled over his body, he must have come to his senses and wormed his way, like the scared rabbit he was, out of these walls which had been his Happy Hunting Ground all morning. But nobody had seen him go.

Donovan reached the door in two great strides, upsetting an onlooker and several of the school children in his dash. But Battery Park stretched empty before him . . . empty of Chicago Lew, if not of the usual crowd of idlers.

"He's gone," observed Donovan. "Damned if he isn't gone."

"He's gone, and the reward with him," moaned Fink. He mopped his brow.

Miss Withers marshalled her thrilled and delighted charges into line. "We'll go now, children," she ordered. "Isidore, there's no use trying to make that policeman believe that you own one of the watches in his hand, because both he and I know that you don't. Jimmy Dooley, stop whispering. It's time to go home, and you can't play around here any longer. We came to see fish, not anything so exciting as this. I . . . ."

Her hand went, out of habit, to arrange the blue beaded hat which rested like the stopper of a bottle on her angular frame. And Miss Withers gasped.

"Children, my hatpin! It's gone!" Her fingers felt feverishly through her hair. "It's the most treasured possession I have, and I wouldn't lose it for the world. My mother gave it to me years ago, and it has a genuine garnet set in it. It's the pickpocket, that's what it is. He took it!"

Donovan, who had been standing disjointedly at the door, shook his head ponderously. "A pickpocket wouldn't go for stealing anything like that, mum. He couldn't hide it, you know, and it wouldn't go in his pocket. They don't bother with such junk as that, just watches and money. . . ."

"And a fine lot you know about it, to let one slip out of your fingers like that," Miss Withers pointed out acidly. "If the pickpocket didn't take it, I'd like to know who did?"

"Teacher!" A plump hand waved wildly above a dark bob. "Teacher . . ."

"What is it, Becky?"

"Teacher, I saw your pretty red pin when we were coming in this morning, and it was sticking way out of the hat on one side. . . ." Becky subsided. "Maybe you lost it?"

"Maybe I did," said Miss Withers. "Well, I certainly

wouldn't ask either of these gentlemen in uniform to find it for me. Because if they did, they'd lose it again in an argument. Children, you'll have to help me. Use your bright little eyes, and go on back over everywhere we've been here in the Aquarium and try to find it. And the first to spy it gets a prize!"

"What sort of a prize, Teacher?" The question came as a chorus.

Miss Withers thought a moment. "How about a brand-new dictionary?" There was a silence which denoted a certain lack of enthusiasm.

"Well then, if you'd rather, the prize might be a ticket to any play the finder would like to see," amended the wily lady. She knew her children. They scattered with a rush, but she called them back.

"That's not the way to look," she explained. "You must go, all together, starting just where we did when we came in this morning. Then we'll be sure to find the hatpin unless someone has picked it up." She cast a suspicious look at the crowd, which was already melting away. Donovan and Fink still eyed one another hostilely.

"At least you won't have to fight over the reward any more," she gave as a parting shot, and then the search began. The children went eagerly on ahead, while Miss Withers dropped back.

Slowly they moved across the vast circle of the Aquarium, stopping at each tank and showcase just as they had done on the first round of the place, when Miss Withers had given a brief lecture on every point of nature study which she wished to bring out. Past the eels, past the flaming tropical fish, past the tortoises, the crocodiles, and the flashing schools of minnows. Across the great circle of the room, up the stair, along the great half-moon of a balcony, and down again. . . .

Still no hatpin. No bright flash from the garnet stone which had once been given to the middle-aged teacher in the days when she was beginning to be a teacher and not even beginning to be middle-aged. No sign of the old-fashioned, beloved hatpin. A dozen pairs of eager eyes scoured the floor and the corners.

Down the balcony stairs again, with little black Abraham going on his hands and knees. Abraham had been stage struck ever since his mother's cousin played the part of the Lord God in *Green Pastures*, and he was determined to find the hatpin if it was to be found. It must be somewhere, and he wanted to win the prize.

Eureka! There it was, at the bottom of the steps! The dark-red stone was intact, the shiny steel undimmed. Miss Withers remembered, as she hurried up, that she had put back a wisp of her hair as they passed this way before. She made a mental apology to the absent Mr. Chicago Lew, who certainly hadn't picked her as a victim after all, in spite of appearances.

She graciously accepted the relic from the hand of proud Abraham Lincoln Washington and replaced it carefully in her blue beaded hat.

"Good boy, Abraham. The prize is yours," she announced. "And now we've got to hurry, children. It must be nearly one o'clock, and I'm getting hungry. . . ."

Rapidly she counted noses, and found a considerable lack. "Isidore!"

There was no answer. She heard the hum of voices and movements through the building, and from the main doorway the excited tones of Fink, still explaining to the departing back of Officer Donovan why he was entitled to the reward if there was one and if the prisoner hadn't escaped.

Miss Withers called again. "Isidore! Isidore Marx!"

"Yis, teacher." A piping voice sounded from behind the stair. Miss Withers peered into the corner.

Isidore was staring at the penguins again. "Come along, Isidore. We're half an hour late now. This nature study class isn't supposed to take all day, you know. Hurry!"

But Isidore didn't budge. His nose was pressed tight against the glass of the last tank in the line, the tank hidden in the shadow of the stair down which they had come.

"Teacher, dese ducks act so funny!"

"I told you before, Isidore, that those are not ducks, they are penguins. See, they don't look like ducks! Those are black penguins, from the Galapagos Islands down off the western coast of Central America. Now don't bother about them any more, come along. . . ."

But Isidore didn't move. "Look teacher how dese penguins hop up and down!"

Miss Withers was unusually tolerant, for she had just recovered a treasured keepsake. But she had arrived at the limit of her patience.

"Isidore Marx, you mind me!" she ordered in a voice that would ordinarily have sent any one of her group into tremors. And Miss Withers advanced, her umbrella held ready for action. But even as her hand fell on Isidore's shoulder, something caught her keen eye.

The little black penguins were swimming as they had not done when she pointed them out to the group of children an hour before. They were dashing madly around the tank, now and then leaping high out of the water to squawk and snap their pointed bills in the darkness of the hidden space above them. Miss Withers, peering through the glass, could only sense that something had excited them. . . .

She stared up through the water, into the obscurity of the inner chamber. As she watched, something happened which made her wipe her glasses furiously.

The two little black penguins were fighting something, snapping and biting viciously at something . . . something which was beginning to slide down upon them. . . .

A dark and shapeless horror lowered itself with a rush, amid the frightened squawking of the frantic birds . . . a dark horror which crashed into the water of the square tank like an awkward diver . . . a twisted, nameless horror that made the water boil and the penguins scramble madly up the steep sides of the tank. . . .

The water subsided and became clear again. Miss Withers realized that her lips were very dry, and quick as thought she pushed Isidore behind her. For she realized that she was staring into a human face . . . a face in the water. . . .

That face had something wrong with it. Something very wrong with it, she knew. It was the face of a dead man, and it was upside down. From the right ear a blur of blood, like a misty coral earring, was dissolving slowly. . . .

# 2

# Behind the Glass

THE office of Bertrand B. Hemingway is on the left side of the main entrance of the Aquarium as you come in, just beyond the little cubby-hole sacred to the guards, Fink and his mates. It conforms to the general circular shape of the old building, with two high windows that open out, one toward lower Manhattan and one to the docks of the Battery. There are also two doors, half leaded glass, that open into the big auditorium itself.

Within this office were three people. Gwen Lester comes first. Gwen had always come first, even as a child. It was mainly a matter of appearance. Even as a baby, Gwen had been a beauty. Now, as a woman, she was possessed of an uncomfortable sort of magic, compounded equally of figure, face, hair and bearing. A cynic would have said that Gwen Lester was sex-conscious, though she would have been offended at the words. However that may be, nature had produced in her a creature eminently fitted to attract. Women hated her, and wanted to be her friend. Dogs and children adored her, even when she was admittedly bored with them. Men's eyes clung to her whether she wanted them or not.

The eyes of two men were on her now. But she sat there on the very edge of her chair, only making the faintest little pretense of listening. Her fear-numbed brain side-stepped the problems that were before her. Idly she spelled out the inscription which showed in reverse on the door. "Bertrand B. Hemingway, Director . . ."

Then this fussy, pompous, excited little man must be Hemingway. Where in the world had she met him, and why had it been her luck to be remembered, as she was always remembered, and pounced upon by this impossible person?

Probably at one of Athelea's teas or dinners . . . Athelea

was always having impossible grubby people at her house, people who climbed mountains or swam through the Panama Canal or wrote senseless verse. She did not remember his face, but that high, nervous voice sounded a little familiar. Only it was so hard to think, so dangerous to think, now. She only wanted to run away, and that was the one thing that she could not do.

It was just as bad for Philip, but he was a man. He was watching her now, pretending to listen to Hemingway just as she was pretending. But his gray eyes were narrow. Philip was getting off with it better than she was, but then he was more of an actor. He looked almost interested.

"Now this just arrived yesterday," Hemingway was saying. "This is the famous Gyppi fish, Mrs. Lester. Notice the delicate coloring of the caudal appendage. Notice the long trailing fins, and the superb canary yellow of the belly. . . ."

"How perfectly lovely," Gwen found strength to murmur. She crossed and recrossed her slim silken ankles. Her pink-tipped fingers held one Camel after another. The blue-gray ash spilled like snow in her lap. Her kid slipper was pressing hard against the Scotch-grain oxford that was Philip's.

"Perfectly, perfectly lovely," she murmured. "But really, we must . . ."

"Notice, if you will, how the little Gyppi swims around and around," went on Hemingway, wrapt in his subject. "Of course, you think that she is lonely?"

With a mighty effort, Gwen focussed her attention on the small square tank of glass in which one sad-looking, goggle-eyed little fish swam in a grimly monotonous circle.

"You think of course that she is lonely! You think that perhaps she longs for her mate, far away in some distant tropic river? Then you are wrong!"

He tapped the glass with a triumphant forefinger. "It is the end of the mating season, and she has no use for her mate. Only this morning he was swimming happily with her. Now she is alone. She may regret him, but I doubt it. For this morning, while I was preparing a separate tank for him, she killed and ate him, bones, fins and all. Nowadays the bored wife, here in New York, gets a divorce or uses a revolver. Among the equally enlightened Gyppi, the little lady uses her teeth to get rid . . ."

Hemingway tittered at his own joke, but Gwen rose unsteadily to her feet. She knew that her face was white as death, but she tried not to cry out. Philip caught at her hand warningly.

The goggle-eyed fish was making fervent if abortive attempts to make away with the tip of the Director's stubby forefinger. Hemingway looked up.

"You're not going? And it's only one o'clock. Must you really tear yourselves away? It is such a pity. So seldom do we scientists have an opportunity to show our work to anyone really sympathetic. If I had only known that you were coming, I would have arranged to take you through the place, behind the tanks and everywhere."

Philip Seymour started slightly at the words "behind the tanks." Hemingway was to remember this afterward.

But now he went on. "Do come again soon, Mrs. Lester—and you too, Mr. . . ?"

"Seymour is the name," said Philip bluntly. Their host dried his finger on a towel and moved toward the door, the glass jar still in his hand.

"Remember, Mrs. Lester, to tell that busy husband of yours that I haven't heard from him in weeks and weeks. Ask him when he is going to pay me that visit he promised me. Though ever since I met you, Mrs. Lester, I've understood why Gerald has neglected his friends during the past few years."

Then this persistently babbling person was a friend of Gerald's, Gwen thought. "So happy to have seen you," she lied.

Then the door flew open, and Fink, the guard, burst in. He was babbling, and out of his breathless incoherencies gradually one sentence made itself clear.

"A man . . . a man in the penguin tank!"

"Didn't I tell you never to bother me when I have visitors? What's a man doing in the penguin tank? Who let him through the door into the runway, anyhow? Make him get out, at once!" Hemingway raised his voice. "I won't have men in the penguin tank!"

Fink gulped twice. "But this man is dead."

The Gyppi crashed to the floor, bowl, water, and all. A miniature tidal wave scattered toward the four corners of the room.

Hemingway fumbled for his glasses, and then got into action. "Come on," he shouted, and shoved aside the dazed Fink. For a moment, a long moment, Gwen Lester searched the eyes of the young man who faced her, and she did not like what she saw there. Then the two of them ran out of the office and down the corridor after the fleeing Director. It was but a step past the stair and across part of the rotunda . . . back to the corner under the stair, the tank of the penguins.

On the dampened floor of the office, neglected and annoyed, a goggle-eyed little fish made the supreme atonement for its cannibalistic habits.

The bulk and nervous energy of Bertrand B. Hemingway cut a swath through the gathering crowd. "Get this mob back," he was shouting. "Get all these people out of here, send for an ambulance, somebody. . . ."

"Stop shouting, young man." He came suddenly face to face with a tall, bony woman who glared at him from beneath a hat faintly reminiscent of those created for Mary Queen of England. An authoritative voice issued from firm, unrouged lips.

"The police have already been sent for. And instead of trying to get this crowd out now, young man, you'd better have somebody shut the front doors, so that every Battery Park loafer doesn't drift in to see what the shouting is about."

Dazedly, Hemingway turned to obey. Fink was dispatched to the door, with orders to allow only the police to enter. "What's next?"

Miss Withers stared at the melee of chattering, gasping people who blocked the way to the penguin tank. "How does one get back of that tank?" she wanted to know. "Where is the entrance?"

Gwen Lester stole a look at Philip, but he was not watching her. His eyes were wide open, and he was staring at the door.

Hemingway's finger pointed it out. There was a large sign, lettered "Public Not Admitted Here," and it was ajar.

"That is the only way in," he said slowly. "It's always kept locked except when somebody is working back there. But do we have to go in there now?"

Miss Withers shook her head as he moved toward the door. "Don't touch anything," she warned him. "That's for the police to do when they get here, if they ever do. It's too late to do anything for the man who's in the water. Anyone can see that he's dead.''

Anyone could see that. Even Gwen Lester, who pushed past the shoulders of those who hid the thing she feared to look upon.

The two little black birds had battled their way up the sides and out of sight, although their hysterical protests still sounded from somewhere in the rear. But their tank was not empty. The body moved in the circulating current with a faint and horrible suggestion of piscine life, and the face showed itself as that of a fattish, well-kept man of about thirty. His brown hair floated in the water like clipped seaweed.

It was Gerald, her husband. But the pale face bore an expression of mild wonder, almost ludicrous in comparison with the way he had been staring at her ten minutes or a century ago.

Gwen's fingers clawed for the arm of her companion, but he too was staring into the tank, his face white as chalk.

She felt her lips move, and heard words come forth that she would have given anything in the world to keep from saying. ''Oh, Phil . . . what have we done!'' Damningly clear, the sentence rang through the high-arched room. The crowd surged closer, nightmare fashion, and then blurred out. Gwen felt herself slipping. Her hand grasped at the smooth glass for support, and then drew back as if it were itself sentient of the thing that lay just behind, staring out with eyes that saw nothing. The blurred phantasmagoria of light and shade became darker . . . darker. . . .

Gwen came to herself lying at full length on the floor, her head held by someone . . . she was choking. . . .

She opened her eyes and stared straight up into the smiling face of the handsomest man she had ever seen . . . a total stranger. He was pouring something between her clenched teeth, something that stung her throat. . . .

''And now be easy, darlin'!'' It was a silver flask, heavily chased, that pressed against her lips. ''Just one more swallow. There, now. Just lie quiet. . . .''

There was something warm, something intimately caressing, in the slight suggestion of Irish brogue which colored the speech of this dark-haired stranger who had stepped out of the crowd. This good Samaritan had bright blue eyes, and a forehead covered by rebellious black curls.

It was very pleasant to lie there, and not to think. But a voice rose above the hubbub of many voices. "Young man, if you don't stop pouring those nasty spirits down this girl's throat, we'll have two corpses on our hands."

Gwen looked up and saw for the first time the stern face of Miss Withers. Behind her a policeman was pushing his way through the crowd, a broad blue policeman in tow of a small black boy, like a tug with a liner attached, or an ant with a piece of biscuit. Donovan was here again, a strangely self-important and quiet Donovan. He came straight to Miss Withers.

"An Inspector is on his way here from Headquarters," he announced. "Till then, I'm in charge. The boy here says there's been a killing. Where's the stiff?"

He looked toward the display tank, and was dumb for a moment. Then . . . "In the water, hey? Quick, somebody show me the way back there. I'll need a man to help me, too. Maybe there's life in the corpse yet, if he's only fell in the water. . . ."

His eyes wandered through the crowd, which was being slowly forced back by Hemingway. No one volunteered, but then he caught sight of the man who still knelt beside Gwen Lester. He caught the glint of the silver flask, and an answering gleam came in Donovan's eye.

"You'll do," he decided. "Follow me."

The stranger helped Gwen to sit up. "You're feeling fine now," he assured her. "I'll be running along now. But remember, I'm at your service, ma'm. Barry Costello is the name." Her eyes thanked him, and lingered as the big man rose lightly to his feet and passed through the door after Donovan.

Somehow Gwen struggled to her feet and pressed forward with the rest of them. Miss Withers was beside her, and Bertrand B. Hemingway was trying to get through. She looked for Philip, but he was still staring at the tank as if turned to stone by the hollow glare of those sightless eyes.

Inside the door marked "Public Not Admitted Here" there was a sharp turn to the right, and a flight of three steps up. Donovan stood at the top of these steps, facing the darkened runway ahead of him, a long curve of cool obscurity. Here were the open tops of the exhibition tanks, here were the thousands of criss-crossed pipes that made up the circulation system of the place. A narrow cat-walk, about ten inches wide, ran along the tops of these tanks, and on this walk two black penguins complained bitterly at the turn events had taken . . . complained above a six-foot square of water on which floated a man's hat.

Donovan craned his neck along the tanks, and up toward the higher level, reached by an iron ladder. But there was no one in sight. He bent gingerly over the tank, and Costello came up beside him.

Hemingway was making voluble explanations from the doorway. "This door is always kept locked," he was protesting, "except when we are working back here in the runway. It just happened that today workmen were supposed to come to clean out the big central pool, and so my assistant Olaavson put the penguins here in this spare tank, temporarily, as he always does in such a case. He must have gone off to lunch and forgotten to lock the door."

Donovan was rolling up his sleeves. "Here's for it," he said slowly. "Come on here, Mister, and grab hold of him."

Costello hesitated, and then nodded. They lifted the dripping body out onto the runway, while eager faces packed the doorway. "Looks sort of cold, doesn't he?" Donovan shook his head. "Let me have that flask of yours, mister."

"I could do with a swig myself," agreed Costello. "But you're on duty, aren't you?" He looked toward the doorway. "Can you get away with it in front of all the audience?"

"Sure I'm on duty." Donovan took the flask and forced its neck between the blue lips of the body which lay between them. "It's not for meself." His effort was not a success, and he returned the flask to its owner, who seemed to have lost his thirst.

"Well, orders is orders," said Donovan. "We'll have to do what we can. You'll take turns with me, mister!"

"Take turns at what?" Something of the joviality had gone out of Costello's voice. "Sure, I'd better be running along now, officer."

"You'll stay here with me," said Donovan. He shook his little black notebook in the face of the other. "You'll stay and do what I say, mister. Here it is in the little book, in black and white. In case of drowning, it says to apply artificial respiration. That means to turn him over on his face and pump his ribs. We learned all about it in police school, and I'm going to try it. Sometimes men have been brought to life after an hour in the water, with a lot of pumping. That's why you've got to stay right here and take turns with me.''

Costello showed a certain not unnatural reluctance. He would rather have been outside, murmuring polite words of comfort to the young lady who had fainted, and he made no bones about it. But at last he nodded. "I'll stay," he agreed. "If you think we ought to pump this guy, sure we'll be pumping him.''

He looked down at the pallid face of the man who lay beneath them, and then looked quickly away. "Sure I'll stay. . . .''

Miss Withers shook her head as the two men knelt in the iron runway, and Donovan began the monotonous refrain . . . "One-two-press . . . one-two-press. . . .'' Her mouth was set in a grim line.

Then someone pushed lazily through the press about the door, a tall gaunt man in a loose topcoat. He looked like a newspaper reporter grown gray in the harness, and Miss Withers took one look at his protruding lower lip and thought it was like a sulky little boy's.

But the voice that broke the tension was not a little boy's voice. "Donovan! What the merry hell do you think you're doing?''

Donovan left off his life-saving activities, and saluted. "Good afternoon, Inspector Piper. I was just trying to bring this man to life, Inspector. According to regulations. . . .''

"Never mind." Piper mounted the three steps and bent over the body. He viewed it from every angle, and then turned it over carefully. "Drowning, huh? What a funny place for bathing." He looked without enthusiasm or visible interest at the fishy tanks beneath them . . . at the tangles of water piping above . . . and finally at a thin ray of light that slid in through a window high in the wall toward the bay.

"Who's the stiff?" He turned to Donovan, but Miss Withers answered him from behind.

"The Director here identified him as a Mr. Lester, a stockbroker," she said. She pointed out Hemingway.

"Yeah? And who are you?" The pale tan-colored eyes focussed themselves on the official. "Boss of this fish house, I suppose?"

"I'm Director of the New York Aquarium," gurgled Hemingway. His face was red. "The man must have been drunk, and fallen into the tank. . . ."

"You've got it all figured out, haven't you?" Piper touched the body with his foot. "Friend of yours?"

"I've known Gerald Lester for years, but never intimately," explained Hemingway. "I didn't know he was here today until I recognized his face."

"Well, Mr. Lester appears to have a bruise on the point of his chin," said Piper slowly. "And a bump on the back of his head. It would seem that there's something a bit fishy here."

"I knew that a half an hour ago," said Miss Withers acidly. "That's why I sent one of my pupils for a policeman, and to call somebody from Headquarters, Inspector."

"Hmm." Piper nodded gravely. "Mr. Director, there seems to have been a homicide committed here. In such a case, I have a right to require your cooperation. Take one of my uniformed men and go through this crowd outside. Sort out the people into two groups . . . those whom you or anyone else remembers as being here when you first got on the scene, and those who pushed in later. Let the last bunch get the bum's rush as soon as we have their names and addresses, and take the others into an office somewhere and keep them there. I want to do a little preliminary questioning, though the police stenographer isn't available."

Gwen felt the hand of a policeman on her arm, and leaned her weight against him as they moved back down the hall. Ahead of her she saw Philip similarly escorted, and she realized with a start that already the police knew of her exclamation on seeing the body. She had spoken one short sentence . . . was it going to be a death sentence for somebody? Philip had not spoken since the announcement in Hemingway's office, and he still avoided her eye.

Miss Withers patted her precious hatpin more tightly into her hair and stalked along, saying nothing. The others chat-

tered and exclaimed and complained, even yet—all but Philip.
Gwen still resisted thinking.

If he would only speak to her . . . tell her . . . answer one
of the questions that filled her mind! She was afraid—not for
him, but for herself. She wondered if they were to be taken
back into Hemingway's private office? Yes, they were led
on, past the doors, into the long room, the office lined with
empty glass vessels and odd machinery which bristled with
rubber tubes and metal dials. There were three chairs. One
window looked on the eastern waterfront, where a ship was
pushing out toward the Goddess of Liberty and the Narrows.

Gwen found herself thinking idly of something she had
read somewhere, supposed to have been remarked by a visitor
to our shores when he saw the statue. . . . "Ah, you Ameri-
cans, just as we do at home, erect statues to your illustrious
dead!"

At least, liberty seemed to be dead and gone as far as one
person, perhaps two persons, in that room were concerned.

She prayed for a miracle to come and lift her from this
room onto the deck of the vessel that was rolling out to sea,
towards Rio, Cherbourg, Liverpool . . . anywhere. But the
age of miracles is past.

Piper was at the door. "Stay on guard here," he was
telling one of his men. "Nobody comes out and nobody gets
in, except of course Doc Bloom when he's finished his
examination." And the door slammed.

There were more than a dozen people in the room. Fink,
the guard, had been relieved at the main entrance and now
stood at ease near the window. Miss Withers was standing
with her feet wide apart, waiting. Bertrand B. Hemingway
strode nervously up and down. The others fidgeted, whispered, and moved uneasily. Gwen was too late to get a chair.

Inspector Piper came straight to Philip Seymour. "If you
make a confession now it will save us all a lot of trouble," he
said in a quiet, friendly tone. "It's clear as daylight what
happened, Seymour. You bumped off the husband when he
got inconvenient. We know that. Mrs. Lester gave it all away
when she saw the body in the tank. Come clean. . . ."

Seymour shook his head. "I didn't commit a murder,
Inspector. I'm ready to tell the whole story, just as it happened, to you or to anybody else. It looks bad, but it isn't as

bad as you think. I did have a fight with Gerald Lester, but . . .''

"You not only had a fight with him . . . you killed him by shoving his head into the water and holding it there.'' Piper's voice grew harsher, and more tense. "We know you did it, and we know why you did it! It's the old triangle, Seymour. You're in love with Mrs. Lester, and you killed her husband to make the way clear for yourself. Did you do it alone, or were both of you in it?''

Seymour kept his voice low. "I'm a lawyer, Inspector. I know enough not to lose my temper. It's no use bullying me into anything. I tell you that I don't think I killed Jerry Lester, and that if I did it was an accident. You can't make it more than homicide. . . .''

"I can't, huh? You killed him, and you're going to confess it and save the state the trouble and expense of a jury trial. You killed him, with your bare hands, Seymour. It looks as if the two of you lured him here. If Mrs. Lester was in on it, we'll find that out later, too. Looks like another Snyder-Gray killing to me. Better come clean. . . .''

"I tell you I . . .''

Gwen felt her knees go weak and watery with fear. Fear for her life, fear for her own white body. Fear of walls and bars and a short last walk to an armchair that would not be an easy chair. . . .

Someone offered her a packing box, with a sweep of his hat that might have presented a Louis Quatorze masterpiece. It was Costello, but she could hardly smile her thanks. She sank back weakly.

"I'm a lawyer, Mrs. Lester,'' he whispered. "You need help . . . won't you let me help you?''

A glance from Piper kept her from answering, but her shoulder pressed against Barry's arm. Gwen was desperate. She relaxed herself against her self-appointed protector.

Suddenly a door at the farther end of the room was flung open. There stood a young man, loose yellow hair tousled above thick spectacles, and in one reddish fist he held a small, cringing person by the scruff of the neck, though two officers hurried to separate them.

Everybody spoke at once, until Piper's voice silenced them. "Shut up, everybody!''

He turned to the young Viking in the door. "What do you want, and who are you?"

The stranger smiled a wide smile. "I'm Olaavson. Got to see Mister Hemingway. This man, he's been hiding up in the upper tanks. Maybe he wants to steal my invention. Just now I find him."

"Who are you, and what were you doing behind the tanks yourself?" Piper stared up at the big blond man, and the big man stared down.

Hemingway broke in. "This man is my new assistant, only been on this side a year or so. He's been working behind the tanks for months, perfecting an automatic lung to purify the water for the aquarium fish, and testing it in the circulation system. I forgot to mention him . . . but you can trust him. I forgot to tell you about that door."

"Sure," agreed Olaavson. "I been working on the upper level, up the iron stair and around on the west side. There I set up my machine. All day I work there. I forget to go to lunch. But just now I hear a little noise behind me and there I see this little worm. He has no business back there. When I ask him what he's doing there, he just mock me because of my bad English speaking. He just gobble. I shake him a little, maybe, and then I bring him to Mister Hemingway."

Olaavson dropped his burden, and the little man slumped down disconsolately to the floor. He was sadly battered, no doubt partly from the Viking's little shaking, and he seemed to have little interest in the proceedings.

But there was no mistaking his identity. Miss Withers nodded slowly and thoughtfully, and Fink gasped. Someone else caught his breath suddenly, and expelled it in a sigh.

"It's the man I got with my umbrella," broke in Miss Withers. "It's Chicago Lew!"

The little man opened his eyes, tentatively. Piper leaned over him.

"Hiding behind the tanks, huh? Maybe you got something to tell us? We know you and we know how to treat dips like you. You know something, and you're going to tell it, or we'll find a handy way to make you. Come on, come clean!"

Chicago Lew looked up at the Inspector, and then around the room. His face was strangely bland. His mouth opened as

Piper shook him by the collar . . . the lips moved . . . but only the most horrible medley of vowel sounds came forth.

"Gaw . . . oooooo . . . waw . . ." It was the pitiful mouthing of the speechless. Louder came the mangled sounds. "G-gggggg—awk. . . ."

Then for the second time that day the little man known to the police as Chicago Lew stretched out flat on the tile floor, dead to the world.

In the strained silence that followed, through the half-open door of the long room, a distant cry of the black penguins could be heard, like a raucous and misshapen echo. . . . "G-g-gawk. . . ."

# 3

# I Told You So!

"TAKE him away," Piper said suddenly. "Lock him up. Why, the man's a deaf-mute. Get him out of here."

Two officers led the prisoner through the door. Donovan was one of them. "I've seen Chicago Lew before," he said to no one in particular, "and he could talk as well as anybody before he went back of those tanks!" His voice came gruffly as the door swung shut behind them. ". . . and now the poor devil squawks like those heathen penguins!"

There was another long moment of silence. Piper, however, intended to be master of ceremonies.

"I've got a lot of questions for somebody to answer," he said slowly. "And I want answers, too. Who was the first person to see the body?"

Miss Withers stepped forward. "I was. Go ahead, young man."

It nettled Piper to be called a young man by a woman who could not have been any older than he was. But he ignored it.

"You found the body?" She nodded.

"Alone?"

"No, I was with my class of pupils. One of them discovered it with me, and the rest of them crowded around before I could prevent them. . . ."

"Yeah?" Piper was annoyed. "Where are those pupils of yours? I thought I gave orders for every single person who'd been here at the time of the finding of the body to remain for questioning. What do you mean letting them go home?"

"*Letting* them? You may be a policeman, Inspector, but you don't know children. As long as I tried to keep them away from the gruesome sight, nothing in the world would make them go, but as soon as they heard the officers order everybody to stay, they lit out of here as tight as they could go. Besides it was lunch time. Don't worry, however, for I can produce them for you at Jefferson School any weekday."

"Okay, then. Your full name?"

"Hildegarde Martha Withers."

"Address?"

"One-eleven West Seventy-sixth Street. I share an apartment there with two other teachers."

"Occupation?"

"At present, answering foolish questions. Young man, I told you I was a teacher."

"Why did you come here today?"

"To show a class through the Aquarium. We do it every year."

"Acquainted with the deceased?"

"Saw him for the first time in the tanks, today."

"What time was that?"

"About one o'clock today."

"Tell us what you saw and what you did."

"My attention was called to the tank by one of my pupils, Isidore Marx, who noticed the strange behavior of the penguins. As we watched, we saw the body slip into the tank. Then I called the police." Miss Withers smiled faintly. "They got here in fifteen minutes."

"Then it would have been possible for a man to have slipped out of that door and escaped while you were calling the police?"

"It would not." Miss Withers smiled again. "Because I sent one of my pupils to turn in the alarm, and I stayed right there in front of the tank till you got there, Inspector."

"Hmm, you seem sure enough of that. Notice anything else that might have bearing on this case?"

"Nothing except what the Lester woman here said when she saw the body of her husband. 'What have we done?' and you already know that."

"By any chance, did you notice the expression on Seymour's face here when he came to the tank with the Director and saw the body there?" Piper leaned forward. "Answer this question carefully. Think!"

"Yes, I did notice it. I made it my business to notice things like that. Mr. Seymour . . . well, he looked frightened . . . and . . ."

"And what?"

"And surprised, surprised and hurt is about the only way I can express how he looked." Miss Withers kept on. "Inspector, he didn't look guilty, if that's what you mean."

"Criminals never do except in stories," said Piper coldly. "This is just another mawkish triangle story of the beautiful, idle wife, the busy husband, and the young, handsome friend. . . ."

He walked across the long room, his hands locked behind his back. "That's enough for now, Miss Withers. I may ask you to repeat that before a stenographer." He whirled on Seymour, suddenly.

"You I'll take next," said the detective. The young lawyer was resolute, though slightly pale. He gave his name, and a residence in Tudor City, without hesitation.

"Occupation?"

"Member of the bar, State of New York, since 1926. Junior member of the firm of Billings, Billings, and Seymour."

"Acquainted with the deceased?"

"Very slightly. I attended his wedding to Gwen . . . Mrs. Lester . . . some years ago. Four years this June, to be exact."

"That's the last time you saw him until today? Then you were a friend of only *part* of the Lester family, I take it?"

Philip Seymour looked at the Inspector, and his eyes were hard. "You ought to know better than that, Piper. I can't be angered into anything. I have nothing to conceal. I was in love with Gwen Lester once. She chose another man, which was quite within her rights, and I attended the wedding. That was the last time I saw Gwen Lester until today."

"You expect me to believe that?"

"I don't give a damn whether you believe it or not. It happens to be true."

"And after all these years of true love smoldering and so forth, you made a date with her in this unromantic spot?" Piper waved at the mouldering walls of the Aquarium.

Seymour shook his head. "Let me start at the beginning," he said. "When I reached my office this morning, which is about four blocks from here up Broadway, I found that Mrs. Lester had called me twice. The second time she had left her number, so I called back. Gwen was in trouble, she told me. She had been crying, I could tell. It had been rumored that the Lesters were not happy, but this was the first direct word of it that I had had. She said she wanted to talk to me, for I was one of the few real friends she had. She wanted my advice about . . . about a legal matter."

"Which was?" Piper kept on relentlessly.

"Gerald Lester was a jealous husband, and more than that a beastly cruel one. She wanted my advice about a divorce."

"Are you a divorce lawyer?"

"Our firm does not specialize in divorce, no. We are corporate lawyers."

"Why did she not come to your office in the usual way?"

"I suggested it, but she was deathly afraid of what her husband would do if he found out. Gerald, she said, had been hit heavily in the market crash last month and his disposition was worse than ever. For the same reason she vetoed my suggestion of a hotel lobby. She was afraid that we'd be seen there. Finally I mentioned the Aquarium. I drop down here at noon sometimes to loaf around the tanks where it's cool, and think things out. And it's near the office. So we met here at twelve o'clock. She told me the whole story of her marital trouble."

Piper turned to Gwen, whose soft dark eyes made no appreciable impression on him. "Is this the truth so far, Mrs. Lester?" Gwen hesitated, and then turned to Costello with a wordless question. He nodded.

"Yes, it's true," she said.

Piper frowned. "I don't know who you are, my friend, but I asked that question of Mrs. Lester. In what capacity are you advising her?"

"As her lawyer," said Costello smilingly. "I offered my services a few minutes ago, and was retained."

"Then wait till this case comes to court," said Piper unsympathetically. "In the meantime the counsel for the defense will please get the hell out of the way." Costello with a slight bow moved a few feet away from Gwen.

"We'll go on with you, Seymour. Where were you standing when Mrs. Lester told you her troubles?"

"We moved around, so that we would not seem to be anything but ordinary sightseers. The place was nearly deserted, it being the lunch hour. Then it happened. About half past twelve, I should say, Gerald Lester suddenly confronted us. We were standing then in the little corner under the stair, in front of the penguin tank. We were . . . perhaps a little close together. Lester was at once certain that he had discovered an assignation. I don't know how he found we were there unless he had a detective shadowing his wife. Anyway, he accused me of every crime on the calendar, including breaking up his home and . . ."

"And seducing his wife?"

Philip looked at Gwen, who this time avoided his eye. "Yes, that too."

"Which wasn't, of course, the truth?"

"It wasn't the truth. And I'll thank you to be a gentleman, Inspector."

Piper sighed. "I'd have more time to observe niceties of conduct if you people wouldn't go around drowning each other." It was as near as he had ever come to making an apology. "Go on."

"He was beastly abusive, and threatening. Then, without giving me a chance to say yes or no, he lunged on me. There was nothing for me to do but defend myself. Gerald Lester was a half-back at Princeton, and he kept himself in rather good condition, at least until a year or so ago. I was studying a bit of the manly art, you know, when Lester was plunging the line at school, and by a lucky twist I caught him one on the button just in time. If I'd have got into his clutch he might have broken me in two. He went down and stayed down. It was a knockout. I kept Gwen from screaming. . . ."

"Yes, go on."

"Well, as luck would have it, nobody had seen us. We

were in that little corner under the stair, as I told you. The battle had lasted but a moment, and if you noticed that corner is hidden from most of the rotunda by some cases of stuffed exhibits, swordfish and the like. The guard was near the door, and I could hear the voices of a lot of children asking questions on the upper balcony. Then I noticed that the door beside me was ajar. . . .

"A man thinks quickly in emergencies like that. I had to get Gwen Lester out of the place before there was a hue and cry, and before her husband came to his senses. It would have been a terrible scandal, and killed her father, who is a retired partner in her husband's brokerage firm. So I got the idea of hiding the unconscious man inside the door that led to the tanks . . . though I didn't know where it led, then."

He stopped for breath, and only the scratching of a pencil broke the stillness. Piper glanced around the room. "Who's making that racket?"

Miss Withers showed him a scribbled page of shorthand notes. "I'm taking this stuff down in case you want it, Inspector."

He frowned, and then shrugged his shoulders. "Not a bad idea. Go on, Seymour."

"I told Gwen to hurry away, and to get to the door. She was to wait for me there as if nothing had happened. I knew that her husband would come to his senses in a few minutes, and I hoped that he would be cooled off enough to go away quietly without raising the alarm. Those few minutes would give us time to make plans for Gwen. She couldn't go home, you understand. So I did it."

"You did what?"

"I carried Lester inside the door, while Gwen walked toward the door. After I got him inside I found that there wasn't room to put him down anywhere except up the steps and on the runway. So I laid him there." Seymour's eyes wandered toward Gwen. . . . "Then I . . ."

"Then? I'll tell you what you did, Seymour. You saw that you had the inconvenient husband in your power. You hoped, as fools always hope, that it would be passed off somehow as an accident. Maybe you thought that it would be blamed on drunkenness when they found him dead. Anyway, you shoved him down into the water, you held his head under until it bubbled for the last time . . . and was still. . . ."

Piper's voice was high, staccato. . . . "You murdered an unconscious, defenseless man, Seymour. . . ."

But the young lawyer shook his head. "I *didn't* do it, Inspector. I didn't kill him. If he was in the water he must have fallen there, or someone else pushed him in. I left him unconscious, but already beginning to breathe loudly, and I hurried out. Then I walked up the stair and across the upper balcony to join Mrs. Lester, after a few minutes, at the main entrance. But we were suddenly nabbed by this well-meaning idiot of a Hemingway here, who dragged us into his office . . . and you know the rest."

"Don't give me that line of slush." Piper was insistent. "You killed him, Seymour. You had the opportunity, you had the motive. You held him under the water with your two hands, as cruel a murder as I ever came upon. This has sash-weights beat a mile."

"Beg pardon, young man, but I think he didn't. Anyway, not in the manner you think," Miss Withers was bold enough to cut in. "Because if you remember, I saw the body fall into the water, and there was no one holding it under. Besides, I never left the tank after that, and no one came out the door beside me." Miss Withers pointed her umbrella. "Inspector, this boy here isn't the kind of a person to commit a murder like that!"

"Hooey," said Piper. "He did it all right. He'll confess it before we get through with him. All right for now, Seymour. I'll have some questions to ask you later, when we're alone with a few of the boys." The Inspector turned to Gwen. She had waited for this.

"And as for you, Mrs. Lester! What a story you're going to have to tell in the witness chair! You're an accessory before and after the fact, at the very least. We sent a woman to the electric chair here in New York State only a short time ago. Maybe you saw the pictures in the paper? It's a bad death to die, Mrs. Lester. We'll be easy on you if you come clean. The woman who roasted was another woman who didn't get along with her husband! Your story doesn't wash, Mrs. Lester. You've been seeing Mr. Seymour quite often lately, haven't you?"

Gwen's head whirled. In all this maelstrom only one rock was steady, and that was the encouraging, friendly face of the stranger, Costello, across the room. Even Phil had failed her now. He didn't even look at her. Did he blame her? But she had to answer.

"Yes . . . no . . . how . . . no. . . ." She didn't know what she was answering, nor did she care. It was all a nightmare, every bit a nightmare. Everything that had happened since her marriage to Gerald Lester was a nightmare. . . .

"All right, Mrs. Lester. Just tell the truth, that's all. Just the truth." Piper's voice was suddenly soft, and comforting. "You never got over being in love with Mr. Seymour, did you? Even though you married another man? That's nothing to be ashamed of, Mrs. Lester. And there's no need for denying what we all know. Tell me, aren't you in love with Mr. Seymour?"

Gwen clutched her handbag. "God . . . I . . . I don't know! I can't answer that. I can't answer anything!" Hysterically, she tried to rise.

Piper pressed his advantage. "What do you think a woman ought to do if she is tied to a man she hates, a man who frightens and abuses her?"

"She ought . . . she ought to get rid of him . . . get away from him, so he can never touch her again. . . ." Gwen answered with a voice ringing, before she could catch the warning glance that Costello shot her.

Piper did not smile. "And you feared and hated your husband, didn't you? His death would mean freedom for you, wouldn't it?"

"Look here!" Costello leaped to his feet. "Mrs. Lester doesn't have to answer these questions. If she is under arrest she cannot be forced to testify, and if she isn't she can plead the right to advice of counsel before answering. You can't do this to her, Piper!"

"Sit down," said Piper. "I was just trying to get at the truth of the matter. It will go better with Mrs. Lester if she will come clean. Let me put the question another way. . . ." Gwen cowered.

"Wait a minute," interrupted Philip Seymour. "You win, Piper. There isn't any need to go any further. I'll confess to the murder of Gerald Lester. I feared and hated him too, and I killed him.''

Gwen rose to her feet, and her face showed a battle of emotions. But Costello motioned her to sit down.

"I killed Lester," said the young lawyer again. "Nobody else was mixed up in it but me."

The room seemed filled with an audible sigh that welled from the hearts of the dozen people prisoned there. This was a letdown.

"Okay," said Piper. He was a different Inspector now that he had won his point. "I had a notion that you'd come clean, Seymour. Spill the story. How did you kill him, and why?"

"Well, just like you said. I got his body there on the runway, and I . . . I . . . .''

"You thought how easy it would be to push him into the tank while he was knocked out, is that it?"

"That's it. I pushed him into the water, and held his head under till he stopped breathing. There were a lot of . . . of bubbles for a while, and then they stopped coming and I knew he was dead. I left him there and went to join Mrs. Lester. . . .''

"Buy why did you kill him?"

"Why does anybody kill? Because I hated him. Because he was a beast to his wife, and because he had attacked me, shouting words that I don't let any man call me, that's why. I killed him and I'm glad of it. I dried my hands and . . . slipped out of the door. . . .''

"Did you see anyone there? Miss Withers or anybody?"

Seymour shook his head. "She must be mistaken in what she says about seeing the body slide into the tank. When I came out no one was there. I hurried to the door!"

"Just a minute. Where were the penguins when you killed Lester by holding his head under water?" Miss Withers plunged in before Piper could stop her.

"The penguins? I don't know. They must have got out of their tank. Yes, I remember now. They were up on the runway, squawking to beat the band. Yes, that's it. I slipped away to the door. Gwen wasn't there, but a minute later she joined me from where she'd been hiding behind the exhibits at the western end of the building. Then Hemingway saw us at the door, and recognized her. . . .''

"You didn't know him?" Piper took back the center of the stage.

"I didn't know him, and neither did Mrs. Lester. But he remembered her from somewhere, and insisted that we come in here and see his office. We couldn't refuse, for fear of attracting notice. So we went in."

"But wasn't Mrs. Lester afraid that someone would tie up her being there with the fact that her husband's body would be found in the same building? Hemingway would remember. . . ."

"You forgot that . . . that she didn't know her husband was dead, and I didn't have time to tell her. . . ."

Piper nodded slowly. "Well, that seems to clear the matter up. You'll sign a confession to this effect? If you don't, I've got a dozen witnesses to the oral confession."

"Oh, I'll sign it all right. I killed him, and I'll confess."

"He's confessing all right, but I don't feel so sure that he killed him," put in Miss Withers. "I saw what I saw, young man!"

"It's no use, Miss Withers. The prisoner himself refuses to accept the loophole you offer him. It's nice of you and all that to perjure yourself to save a nice-looking boy from the chair, but under the circumstances. . . ."

"When you know me better, Inspector, you'll realize that I neither lie nor do I go out of my way to help lawbreakers, nice-looking or otherwise. But I've taught school long enough to know when anybody is telling the truth or not, and Philip Seymour is holding something back. He's shielding someone—and I know who it is!"

Everybody looked at Gwen, who turned her head and stared out of the window toward the sky, criss-crossed by the flight of screaming gulls.

Seymour broke the quiet. "Is there any need to continue this seance, Inspector? You've got your confession, now can't we let these people go?"

Piper nodded slowly. "Yes, the case seems to be in the bag," he observed. "And I had hoped for something a bit more sporting, more difficult. But this is just the same old sordid story, after all." He turned to Seymour. "I'll have a typed copy of that confession for you to sign in an hour or two. Take him away, Casey." Piper motioned to the blue-coat at the door. "Take him down to Headquarters and hold him there. I'll be there shortly."

Two blue-clad policemen attached to the Homicide Squad took their places on either side of the prisoner, and handcuffs clicked. They moved toward the door.

"Good-bye, Philip," said Gwen Lester as they led him past. But Philip Seymour did not turn his head, nor did he seem to hear the soft, lovely voice which filled the room with his name. The door slammed behind him.

"And that is that," said Piper. He took off his hat for the first time, and mopped his high forehead. "That's the quickest murder case I ever solved. The rest of you can . . ."

Someone pounded on the door, and called for the Inspector. He stepped out of the room for a moment. When he returned he was biting a cigar. He stood for a moment in the center of the room, his fingers pulling at his lean chin.

"Well, I suppose the rest of us can go now that you've got your man?" put in a warm, deep voice from behind Gwen's chair. "Mrs. Lester here needn't be held, now you've got a confession." Barry Costello offered his arm to the grateful lady who rose to take it.

But Piper took out his cigar and studied it as if the entire problem were centered there. Then he tossed it neatly into an empty fish-globe across the room.

"Shall I type out this confession so you can have it signed?" asked Miss Withers.

Piper shook his head. "You needn't bother, ma'am. That confession isn't quite as good as it sounds. Philip Seymour killed Lester all right, but not the way he told it. Those bits about the bubbles coming up and all that were artistic as the devil. The only trouble is that Doc Bloom, our medical examiner, has just looked over the remains of Gerald Lester and found that however the late lamented did meet his end, it wasn't by drowning!"

"What? How?" The mob pressed suddenly around him. He stilled the hubbub with a glance.

"Only an autopsy will show what killed Gerald Lester," said Piper slowly. "But there wasn't a drop of water in his lungs. He was thoroughly dead before he ever hit the water!"

"I told you so!" announced Miss Withers triumphantly.

Piper stared at her, and his pale eyes narrowed imperceptibly.

# 4
# Friday is Fish-day

GWEN LESTER halted near the door, and her slim fingers slipped from Costello's arm. She had already guessed what Piper's next move would be.

"You'll have to stay, after all," he told her. "I'll try to make it as brief as possible. But we've got to get to the bottom of this business."

She sank back on the packing case again. Miss Withers reached for her pencil. She was glad that she'd picked up shorthand.

"Now Mrs. Lester, suppose you start at the beginning. Start with this morning and describe everything that happened."

"I have nothing to conceal," she said slowly. Miss Withers decided that the young woman was stalling for time. "As a matter of fact . . ."

"Come, come! I know that this is difficult for you, but you must be frank." Piper kept after her.

"I saw Gerald . . . my husband . . . at breakfast. There was a scene. . . ."

"Start at the beginning, I said. Was that the first time you saw him this morning?"

Gwen lowered her head. "We do not . . . we did not occupy the same room, you see. We have not, for more than a month. Our life together has—had become a perfect hell. Gerald was worried about business, even before the market crash. Something he never told me about. But he became very strange, about money and about me. He resented every purchase I made, even necessary ones. He became jealous, terribly jealous. I sometimes thought that his mind couldn't be just as it should have been. I was afraid of him.

"But I didn't know what to do. I couldn't go to daddy. My father is not well, and he retired from the business two years ago, leaving my husband the only active partner. And daddy believed that my marriage was happy. He had arranged it, you see.

"Well, when I came down to breakfast this morning, there was a terrible row. Gerald had found my door locked . . . last night. You understand? And I wouldn't answer him. So this morning he accused me of having gone out. He had been trying to forbid me going out in the evening lately, because of his insane jealousy. He was sure that every man I met was a . . . a lover.

"I refused to deny it or admit it this morning. I refused to discuss the matter at all. And I told him that I was thinking of leaving him. He made a frightful scene in front of the maid and everything. I left the table, in tears, and he went out to his office. That was about nine o'clock, I should say."

"And then what did you do?"

"I put in a long distance call for daddy. He is in Florida, you know."

"Wait a minute. You refer to your father? You said he is a silent partner in the firm your husband headed?"

"Yes. The firm name is White and Lester, and it used to be Charles White and Company years ago. Then when I married Jerry Lester, daddy took him into the firm. His health was going, so he retired. . . ."

"Very good. Did you talk to your father?"

"They couldn't complete the call. Daddy was out at the golf club, on the course. So then I tried to get in touch with Philip Seymour. I . . . ."

"I understand. You called him to ask him to take you away from your husband."

"Nothing of the sort. When I told Philip, four years ago, that I wouldn't marry him, he was very sweet. He asked me to call on him if ever I needed anyone. I suppose that most young men make the same request under those conditions, but somehow I believed Philip. Besides, he was a lawyer. So I called him, but he wasn't at his office yet. I called again, about ten o'clock, and still he wasn't in. I left word for him to call me back. Shortly afterwards he called, and I made him suggest a place to meet. The Aquarium was decided on, and we met here at twelve."

Piper nodded. "Who knew you were coming here?"

"Nobody, of course."

"What kind of a telephone system do you have at home? Extensions?"

Gwen nodded slowly. "You mean, could one of the servants have listened in? It's possible, of course. But I don't think they did. I didn't hear any click on the line to signify a lifted receiver."

"Go on, please."

"Well, then I took a taxi and rode down through town from our place on Central Park West to the Aquarium here. I was a few minutes early . . ."

"Wait a minute. Do you think anyone could have followed you?"

Gwen's eyes widened. "I didn't think of that. It doesn't seem likely. The driver kept up a pretty good pace. He came along the west side waterfront as far as it goes. Indeed, it was his driving so fast that got me here early. It wouldn't seem that anyone could have followed me."

"What one taxi can do, another can beat," said Piper. "I'm trying to find out how your husband knew you were meeting another man at the Aquarium. But go on. You met Seymour. I know his story of what happened then. Is it correct? There was a scene, and Seymour knocked your husband out?"

Gwen nodded. "I didn't look much, I couldn't. Then it was over, and Philip whispered for me to move slowly toward the door and wait for him. I loitered among the cases, and . . ."

"When Seymour at last got to the front entrance of this building, he had to wait for you. How long did it take for you to wander through the exhibits—I think Seymour said you were at the west end of the building—and get to the door?"

Gwen thought. "Say ten minutes."

Piper nodded. "Then if Seymour was telling the truth in his first story, and if he simply knocked out your husband and hid him in the runway to make a getaway, there was time enough while he waited for you at the door for you to slip back to where the unconscious man was lying and to kill him . . ."

He stopped, because for the second time that day Gwen

Lester had fainted. And for the second time that day Barry
Costello caught her before she fell.

The Irishman looked up, and his jaw was set. "I hope
you're satisfied now, you blundering idiot of a dick, you!"

Piper shrugged his shoulders. "It was *touché*, anyway."
He took a glass of water from Hemingway and dampened the
girl's forehead.

"That's all, Mrs. Lester." he said kindly. "You can go
now. I won't hold you yet, but please make no effort to leave
town, because I'll have you dragged off the train inside of
half an hour."

Costello helped the girl to her feet. "You know this is an
outrage, Piper. As Mrs. Lester's legal advisor I warn you. . . ."

"You may be Mrs. Lester's legal advisor," Piper broke in,
"but it doesn't mean a thing to me. It happened pretty
suddenly, didn't it?"

Costello was leading Gwen Lester toward the door, which
Hemingway obligingly held open.

Miss Withers whispered something to Piper, and the detective snapped his fingers. "Just a minute, Costello!"

The Irishman paused at the door. "What do you want
now? Are you going to continue the third degree on my
client?"

Piper shook his head. "She can go. But after all, you're
not here as her lawyer. Not exactly. Maybe I'd like to ask
you a few questions about yourself. You were hanging about
the Aquarium, weren't you? How did you happen to be here,
and why?"

Costello grinned. "It's a public place. And I've always
been interested in fish."

Piper chewed his cigar. "So what?" He crossed over to the
others. "Understand me, my friend. I'm simply doing my
duty. You'll have to account for yourself, just like the rest of
the people who are waiting here."

"All right, Inspector. Go ahead." He turned his head
toward Gwen. "Are you going to let her go home alone that
way?"

"She can wait for you if she wishes," Piper put in. Gwen
waited.

"Okay," said Piper. "Your name and address?"

"Sure, and I thought you knew it. Barry Costello, Attorney at law, at your service. The address is Four Arts Club. . . ."

"Practicing?"

Costello shook his head. "Gentleman of leisure," he said. "I never practiced, being able to get along without. I'm writing a book on the subject of strange and contradictory decisions from the bench, which I hope to have published under the title of *Waivers and Waverings* someday."

"Enough of that. Acquainted with the deceased?"

"Never saw him before in my life."

"Before when?"

"Before I heard people yelling, and crowded through to the penguin tank to see the poor fellow floating there, with his eyes open. . . ."

"Acquainted with Mrs. Lester?"

"Not until I was fortunate enough to catch her when she fainted. But I'm telling you confidentially . . ." Costello dropped his voice so only Miss Withers and the Inspector could hear . . . "I'd like to be."

"All right, all right." Piper showed his distaste for the man. "This is hardly the time and the place . . ." He threw away another cigar. "And you were here in the Aquarium just for pleasure?"

"Sure, officer." Costello grinned again. "Didn't I tell you that I'm very fond of fish? And remember what day this is!"

"Enough . . . take Mrs. Lester out of here. I'll ask more questions if I want answers, later." Piper watched as the big Irishman and the dead man's wife went out through the door. Then he turned to Miss Withers, who was still writing busily beside him, seated on the packing case that had been Gwen's.

"That stage-Irishman would stand a lot of looking into," he pronounced. "But he gets on my nerves. What did he mean about the day of the week this is?"

Miss Withers looked up at the detective. "It's Friday," she told him. "And Friday is fish-day for a good many people. . . ."

"Smart-aleck!" The detective and the school-teacher crossed glances of mingled amusement and exasperation. They were beginning to understand each other.

"He's the type of man who'd have a wonderful time at a wake," pronounced Piper. "I can't stand him."

"Oh, I don't know," said Miss Withers thoughtfully. "He has nice eyes, and a way with him, somehow."

"Even you, huh?" Piper grinned. "Well, anyhow, he doesn't act like a murderer."

"You yourself just said a few minutes ago that they never do," Miss Withers reminded him.

And the investigation went on.

## 5

# Out of the Water

HEMINGWAY was getting restless. "After all, Inspector, this is the Aquarium and it is not police headquarters. I don't mind an investigation, and all the attendant bad publicity for our work. But really, must you take all afternoon?"

Piper glared at him. "Your time is coming, Mr. Bertrand B. Hemingway. And you'll have to wait for it, because I want to get through this list of witnesses first, so they can go. Afterwards you are going to show me through this place. Now stand back and keep still, and we'll get along faster."

There was still seven or eight impatient people at the farther end of the long office. Miss Withers recognized among them the woman who had lost her purse, and had it returned after Chicago Lew was captured for the first time. She turned out to be a Mrs. Douglas of the Bronx, who denied any knowledge of the Lesters, of the crime, or of anything else. She was allowed to go.

Then there was three young men from a Wall Street office, clerks Miss Withers correctly guessed them to be. Their examination brought out only one new fact, that while they were on the upper level they had heard the sounds of scuffling, but had imagined that it was simply workmen making some repairs to the place. They had gone to the edge of the balcony and seen a woman's form disappearing among the exhibit cases . . . evidently Gwen after the fight. But they had not taken much notice. One of them also was of the opinion that he had seen Philip Seymour and Mrs. Lester in close conversation in front of the cat-fish tank earlier.

"That only establishes the less-important parts of the story Seymour and Mrs. Lester tell," decided Piper. "You can go."

The others were even less able to aid. Respectable, unimportant persons they were, sightseers from out of town, one or two loafers from the ranks of the unemployed . . . none of them proved interesting to the Inspector then nor later, with the possible exception of the last stranger to be given the works.

He gave his name as Robert Sproule, address on Chicago's north side, and his business as a buyer of men's wear for a department store in that city.

"I'm in town on business," he said, "but I had a few hours to kill today so I started out to take in the sights. I went up in the new Chanin Building, and then took the subway down here to look at the fish. We're building a new aquarium in Chicago that makes this one look sick. . . ."

"Never mind the civic spirit," said Piper unfeelingly. "Acquainted with the deceased?"

"Not exactly," said Sproule with an air. "But I've met him. Or rather, I should say, he met me . . ."

Piper was suddenly galvanized to attention, and Miss Withers stopped taking notes. "Go on!"

"Well, it was like this. I was standing in the door of the Aquarium about a quarter after twelve this noon, I should say. A man brushed by me so violently that he nearly knocked me down—a big man, with wide shoulders and a red face. I noticed him because he looked mad. He didn't have the usual bored, stolid look that you see on the faces of most New Yorkers. He was wearing a smart raglan topcoat, blue-gray in color, and a derby, and carrying a malacca stick. I always notice such things, being in this business. . . ."

"Wearing a derby?" Piper made a note on an envelope. "Go on. . . ."

"That's all there is. Except that he passed on inside, and I heard the guard arguing with him about checking his stick."

"It's a rule here," put in Hemingway, "that visitors must

check umbrellas and walking sticks, because they're likely to
poke at the glass with them.''

Miss Withers interrupted—''Yes, and if I hadn't come in
with the mob of pupils, the guard would have taken my
umbrella away at the door, too. And then the pickpocket
would have escaped——.''

Piper nodded. ''You can go, Mr. Sproule. But stay in town
for a day or two. You are sure that the man who ran into you
in the doorway was the man whose face you saw afterward in
the tank, when the hue and cry was raised?''

Mr. Sproule was sure. ''That was about ten or fifteen
minutes before the pickpocket chase,'' he put in. Then he
was ushered to the door by Fink.

Piper whirled on the fat guard. ''Did you have an argument
with Lester, the man who was killed just after that, about
checking a stick?''

Fink shook his head. ''That would have been MacDonald,
Inspector. He was on duty at the door until about twelve-
thirty, when he went to lunch leaving me in charge. He ought
to be back now.''

''Bring him here,'' ordered Piper. MacDonald turned out
to be a mild little man in a uniform too large for him.

''Sure I remember the gentleman,'' he announced. ''And a
time I had with him, too. He was bound and determined he
was going to cling to that stick, though I don't know why, for
it was a powerful heavy one. I'd be tired carrying it around.
But when I finally told him he couldn't come in the place
without checking it, he let me take it. It's there in the rack
now.'' He motioned toward the door. ''Shall I bring it?''

Piper nodded. In a moment he was hefting a three-foot
length of malacca, with a silver top. He let it slide through
his fingers and crash to the floor.

''Ten pounds if an ounce,'' he remarked. ''This thing is
more than loaded. It's a weapon that would bash in a man's
head like an eggshell.''

With his pocket-knife he pried at the silver cap, which
came away in his hand. Tilting the stick, which was hollow
for a foot of its length, he let a handful of heavy shot roll out.

''Lester loaded this himself,'' pronounced the Inspector.
''A regular workman would have used molten lead, and

only about half as much. And the silver cap was only jammed loosely back on, not fitted.'' He looked thoughtful.

"Jerry Lester came down to the Aquarium with murder in his heart," the Inspector decided.

"Or else fear for his life," interposed Miss Withers. "That could have been meant for defense, you know."

There still remained Hemingway and his assistant, Olaavson. Piper turned to the big Norseman.

"You were working back of the tanks all morning, until you came down to bring the little man you thought was sneaking your invention?"

Olaavson nodded ponderously. "In the morning I help feed the fish, and then move the little penguins out of the big central pool into the spare tank under the stair," he told the Inspector. "Then about ten o'clock I go up the iron ladder and around to the west side, back of the balcony tanks. There is the main inlet for the water that goes through all the tanks, and there it is that I have my machine set up. I work there, testing my automatic device that keeps the water pure."

"You heard nothing . . . saw no one?"

"Nothing. I was thinking of my work. I even forgot lunch."

"You also forgot to lock the door behind you," put in Piper. "A man's life might have been saved if you had."

Hemingway interrupted again. "That door locks only from the outside, Inspector. That is why we always leave it open when we are working on the inside. The latch works from both sides, but there is no key-hole on the inside."

"Okay," said Piper. "Well, you're last, Hemingway. How long have you known Gerald Lester?"

"As I told you, I knew him for some time, but never intimately. I met Lester at a dinner of the Explorer's Club, a big dinner given in honor of Chasmic, the Frenchman who flew over the Pole. Lester was brought by one of the members, though he himself had never done anything to win membership. We sat together. . . ."

"You're a member?"

Hemingway nodded proudly. "The Directorship of the Aquarium automatically carries that honor with it," he explained. "We have to go collecting tropical fish, you know. Anyway, Lester and I got acquainted while sitting at that dinner, and we met for lunch once or twice, since his office is only a few blocks from here, and we both frequented the same eating places. And then once or twice we went out together in the evening, when he had an extra theatre ticket. He was generous that way, and his wife didn't care to go out with him, I understand. It was that way I met her. She was just coming in one evening when I stopped in at their place after the theatre for a cocktail in Gerald's study."

"You mean Mrs. Lester?"

Hemingway nodded. "She is a very beautiful woman, Inspector. Lester liked to show her off to his friends. But she hardly noticed me. I think she was afraid to show any interest in men before her husband. He was a jealous type, Inspector. We were simply introduced, and we all had a drink together, and then she excused herself."

"That was the only time you met Lester's wife?"

"The only time until I saw her by chance talking to a young man in the door here this noon. Of course I insisted on their coming into the office and having a chat. I wanted to be hospitable, you see. And Mrs. Lester is a very beautiful woman."

"You never had a quarrel with Gerald Lester . . . about his wife, for instance?" Piper smiled as he asked the question. The idea of that gorgeous creature looking at Bertrand B. Hemingway was more than funny.

Hemingway paused for a moment, long enough so that Miss Withers and the Inspector both noticed it. Piper put it down to vanity.

"No," he said reluctantly. "I . . . no, we never quarreled. But we hadn't seen much of each other of late. You know how hard it is in New York to keep track of old friends, much less to cultivate new ones."

"Okay," said Piper. "One thing more. Why was it that when Fink burst in on the three of you, shouting that there was a dead man in the penguin tank, why was it that you led the way out of the door at the far end here, instead of going through this office to the other end and out through the door at the foot of the stairs . . . the door that Olaavson entered by a while ago? That would have been the natural way, wouldn't it?"

Hemingway turned a shade paler. "I . . . well, I guess it didn't occur to me. Oh, I know why. He said a man was in the penguin tank, and naturally I thought of the big central pool where they are usually kept. It wasn't till we got out in the main room that I saw the crowd clustered around the little tank under the stair, and ran there.''

Piper stuck out his lower lip, but made no comment. ''Go on,'' he said.

''That's all there is. I recognized Lester in the tank, and it was the first time I'd seen him in months. Then you know the rest. . . .''

''All right,'' Piper told him. ''Now I want you to lead me through the place, so I can get an idea just how it is laid out.'' He lit his fourth cigar for the afternoon. ''Miss Withers, you don't need to stay if you want to get home. It's been good of you to stand by me with those notes, because I might have forgotten a point or two. . . .''

''Nonsense,'' said Miss Withers. She had filled page after page of her little notebook. ''I've had the time of my life. That's why I came to New York ten years ago, instead of keeping on teaching school out in Iowa. I wanted a little excitement, though it's little enough I've got at Jefferson School. This is great fun, and better than any detective story I ever read. Will you let me stay?''

''Why not?'' said Piper. And the strangely assorted pair followed Hemingway out of the office.

The big rotunda was dark in the early winter twilight, though a few dim electric bulbs high above them cast a sickly glow. Hemingway's nervous, squeaky voice echoed through the empty place as he led the party on a tour of inspection. It was the third that day for Miss Withers. She was getting sick and tired of the Aquarium.

Fink and MacDonald were discussing the exciting events of the day in their little cubby to the left of the main entrance, where the check room was. Olaavson took a noisy leave of the entire affair, disgusted with the interruption to his labors.

Miss Withers wanted to know if there was some sort of a guard at the main entrance, which of course had been closed to visitors since the tragedy. Piper shook his head.

''Not necessary,'' he told her. ''I had them put it on a night latch, so that nobody can get in but any of us can get out. And I've got two uniformed men at the penguin tank.''

As they went, Miss Withers filled one page of her notebook with a scribbled sketch of the important end of the building, which centered now in the little glass-enclosed tank at the end of the line, under the stair.

This was the sketch she made:

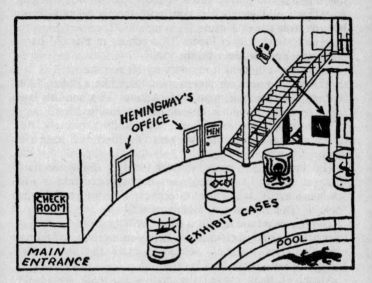

At last Piper had the place clearly in his mind, he said. "Except for the runway behind the tank. Let's have a look in there."

Hemingway hung back.

"Don't worry," Piper told him. "The body has been removed, and by this time Doc Bloom is making the complete autopsy. We'll just have a look-see back there. . . ."

The two stalwart policemen moved aside to let the Inspector pass. He stopped suddenly.

"Casey, I want you to do something for me." He drew one of the men aside, and gave him swift instructions. ". . . bribe her or make love to her or chloroform her, but get me those stockings tonight!" Miss Withers caught only the last phrases. Casey left with ill-concealed elation.

"Shall I stick here?" asked the other cop. Piper looked at him.

"Those were your orders, weren't they? What's the matter, are you afraid of ghosts or something?"

The policeman shook his head. "It's only that . . . well, I've got a strange feeling that there's somebody here who doesn't belong here. Me and Casey, we both felt it, sir. Just a rustling and whispering and soft footsteps that don't belong anywhere. And then when you look, there's nobody there, but you hear a door closing."

"Fiddlesticks," said Piper. "It's echoes in this old barn, that's all. You stay here on the job."

"Yes, sir. I thought it my duty to tell you, sir. . . ."

"There's no need for you to stand there like a statue," put in Piper. "Get a chair, man, and sit down. This must be your first job on the Homicide Squad, isn't it, Rollins?"

"It's my last one, too, I hope," said Rollins sincerely. But he brought a chair from the guard's office and leaned it against the wall.

The three of them passed through the door and up the short flight of steps. "I wish we knew what happened here five or six hours ago," said Piper reflectively. "Can't you give us some light on the subject, Hemingway?"

The Director fumbled for a cord that hung from the ceiling twenty feet above their heads. There was a click, and then a ghostlike glow that only served to make the place more strange and unearthly than ever.

Ahead of them curved the narrow cat-walk, above the shimmering squares of the fish-filled tanks. The curved and jointed lines of pipe cast weird shadows on the water and on the faces of the three who stood there above the penguin tank where a few hours before Gerald Lester had lain.

"Well, now you see it," said Hemingway. "Suppose we go back?"

"Why all the fuss? A person would think that you didn't want me poking around back here!" Piper stared at the Director, who tried to laugh it off.

"It's just that it's a bit creepy. . . ."

"Tosh, man. Don't tell me that you, who're used to this place, feel that way. Come along, now. We'll have a look at the upper level."

Miss Withers lingered above the murder tank, staring down into the murky obscurity of the water as if the secret of the murderer were hidden there. Suddenly she ran dizzily along the cat-walk, and caught at Piper's sleeve.

"I'm trying not to scream," she said softly. "But a . . . a hand just clutched at me from the murder tank! A hand that rose up out of the water!"

6

# One Hat and Seven Cigarette Butts

THERE was a silence during which one might have counted ten. Piper looked at the woman in ill-concealed disgust.

"You, too? And I took you for a steady one. I didn't think you'd go to pieces like that silly flirt of a Lester woman. I'm disappointed in you."

Then it came again, and Miss Withers clung to the Inspector's arm instead of answering. But it wasn't a hand. It was nothing human, nor superhuman either.

There was a swirling of the waters, and the sleek black head of a penguin rose inquiringly into the air, to subside again with a plop. Miss Withers could laugh now, along with the Inspector.

"Nox and Erebus just wanted to see what was going on here, what with the lights and the excitement and all the people," explained Hemingway. He leaned over the narrow square of water and extended his fingers for the two friendly birds to nip.

Miss Withers was perturbed. "You mean that you didn't take the penguins away? They're still in the tank where Lester died? I thought of course that you'd drain it."

"I didn't insist on it," said Piper. "But maybe it would be a good idea."

"Draining the tank is a big job," explained Hemingway. "And besides, we haven't any other place to put the penguins. So after the police had taken the body away, I suppose Olaavson came back and put the penguins where they belong. The water keeps fresh, you see, through circulation. . . ."

"Well, first thing tomorrow I'll have a couple of men here,

and you can drain that tank,'' ordered Piper. "There might be a clue of some sort. I wish murderers would always leave an initialled cuff-link about the scene of the crime, but they usually don't. It would make things much easier for us. Well, let's be getting along. Careful of your head, Miss Withers, these pipes are everywhere. I'm lucky if I don't knock my hat off.''

The three of them walked along the runway to the iron ladder, and then climbed to the top level. "Here," said Hemingway, "is Olaavson's precious invention. It's a device for purifying the Aquarium water so that we have to get new sea water only once or twice a year. There's an automatic business that dumps the right percentage of the right chemical combination, whenever the place needs it, into the stream at the source. I don't understand it, but it works. He's thinking of nothing else, Olaavson isn't.''

"Interesting," said Piper, "but hardly productive of any results in this business of who exterminated Gerald Lester. Let's be moving back. We can't do anything here in pitch darkness.''

"There's a flashlight in my office," offered Hemingway. "Shall I get it?''

Piper nodded. "A good idea. Then we can look-see. Run on ahead. . . .''

And Hemingway was gone. "I wanted a chance to talk with you anyway," said Piper to Miss Withers. "Did you notice the splotch on Hemingway's coat? It's nearly dry now, but it showed fairly plain when I first arrived. I'd give anything to analyze that.''

Miss Withers nodded. "I saw it, all right. You think it might be`. . . ?''

"I think it's water from the penguin tank," Piper told her. "I can't be sure without analysis. And it wouldn't necessarily prove anything." He paused above the iron ladder that led downwards. "I forgot that the cop at the door doesn't have orders to let Hemingway through without me. He may be held up there.''

"Wait a minute," said Miss Withers. "Why do you go to all this trouble if you know that the Seymour boy killed Lester?''

"My dear woman, I don't know that he did. Anybody

might have killed Gerald Lester. Maybe you did it yourself,
you had time enough while your pupils were hunting for your
hatpin. You could have slipped in there and done him in.
Only we don't know yet how he was bumped. It might be
heart failure caused by the crack on the chin that Seymour
gave him."

Piper saw the look of alarm on Miss Withers' face. "Mind,
I don't say that I really believe that you did bump the man,"
he told her. "You haven't got motive, for one thing. And it's
motive, and not opportunity, that makes crimes. Everybody
had an opportunity to kill Lester. The pickpocket, Chicago
Lew, might have done it. But why? He was hiding in the
runway to escape pursuit, and would hardly stop to murder a
man. Maybe Olaavson did it, because he thought his invention was endangered . . . though it's not likely. Hemingway
could have slipped out of the farther door of his office, done
the job, and still had time to be cordially boring to Mrs.
Lester and Seymour at the main exit."

Miss Withers grasped his shoulder. "Then you believe that
Seymour didn't kill Lester? You agree with me that his
confession was a fake, to save Mrs. Lester?"

"Possibly, but I doubt it. No, I still think that Seymour
was giving us a phoney confession to a crime he did commit.
Maybe Mrs. Lester was mixed up in the actual killing. Maybe
she did it, and he was just an accomplice. There was time for
her to slip into the runway and pull the job while he waited
for her at the door." Piper shrugged his shoulders. "But both
Mrs. Lester and Philip Seymour had a good old-fashioned
motive for the killilng, and I'm holding Seymour for trial.
But that shouldn't keep me from digging deeper and deeper
into the thing, and it won't."

"Then you haven't really got any definite idea about the
murderer at all?" Miss Withers was surprised.

"My dear lady, if I did I'd have him in a chair at Police
Headquarters with seven detectives and the Commissioner
himself asking questions till tomorrow night . . . and later if
need be. All I know is that a man has been killed, and a mess
of threads lead off into nowheres. I've got to satisfy the
papers, I've got to have an arrest. The logical arrest is
Seymour."

"It's tough on him if he's innocent," Miss Withers pronounced.

"It's tougher on him if he's guilty," Piper told her. "Let's be going." Suddenly he caught her arm, and they listened in the semi-darkness. From far below there came the sound of a splash.

"The penguins again, or a fish jumping," Miss Withers decided aloud. But Pipr motioned her to hush.

Then for a moment the pencil streak of a flashlight played over the tanks below them, flying off at a tangent on the beams overhead . . . and was gone. They heard the runway door close softly. Then all was still.

"Hemingway!" Piper called. "What are you doing? Bring the flash up here."

But there was no answer. Swiftly the two of them slid down the ladder and ran along the runway to the pool of the penguins.

There was a dark puddle on the top step. It was water Miss Withers found, and not blood. The penguins were agitated, and one of them was trying to get out of the pool again.

Piper swiftly led the way down the steps. There were drops of water here, scattered. He flung the door open and called aloud, "Rollins!"

No one answered. "Rollins, why did you leave your post? I say, Rollins!"

The Inspector's voice made the echoes ring, but no answer came. "Has the fellow bolted?" asked Miss Withers.

Then the office door opened and Hemingway stuck his head out. "I say, Inspector, I've looked everywhere for that flashlight, and it's gone. I know it was there this afternoon."

"Never mind that flash now," ordered Piper. "Quick! Was Rollins, the officer, here when you came down after the flash?"

Hemingway hesitated. "Why . . . no! He wasn't here at all. I remember wondering if he'd gone to join Fink and MacDonald in the cubby. But I didn't think anything of it."

"You didn't think anything of it! When you hear me put a man on duty, and then in ten minutes he's disappeared, you don't think anything of it! You're a fool, Hemingway!"

Piper bent over the floor, just outside the door. There were more dark spots, and these were not drops of water. His fingers came up dark at the tips.

"Blood!" he said softly, whistling through his teeth. "Poor Rollins."

"But a man can't disappear, chair and all, in thin air," insisted Miss Withers. "He *must* be somewhere."

Piper motioned to a door at their backs, between the stair and the door to Hemingway's office. "What's that?"

"The . . . the Men's Room. . . ." said Hemingway. "You can see the sign if you go up closer. I know our homemade lighting plant is weak, but we never open the place after six in the evening."

"Bother the sign," Piper told him. He thrust open the door and found what he had expected to find. Rollins, with a gash in his forehead, sprawled in his chair. He was bound and gagged, and he was still out cold. But he was alive.

"And you scolded him for imagining that he heard footsteps and noises," Miss Withers remarked accusingly.

"In the line of duty," said Piper. "I see he's gagged and tied with strips of denim, Hemingway. Ever see it before?"

"It's one of Olaavson's old work jackets," decided the Director. "It always hangs here in the doorway. I'll get some water for the poor fellow."

Miss Withers and Piper looked at each other. Then they ran to the main entrance. The door was still closed, but opened easily from the interior. From the outside it was impossible of access.

"Any other entrance?" Piper demanded of Fink and Mac-Donald, who poked their heads out of the cubby. They denied it.

"And you two dumb oxes didn't hear a sound or see anybody go by?" They shook their heads in unison.

"We were playing pinochle," Fink announced. "We always play pinochle here at night, till MacDonald goes home at midnight. Why?"

Piper walked back to where Rollins was already coming to. "He won't remember anything but a step behind him and then a blackout," prophesied Piper.

"I heard a noise in the Men's Room," was Rollins' story. "I saw the door move, or thought I did. So I decided to investigate. I went over there and I went in. There was nobody there, and I was fumbling for the light switch when wham . . . somebody got me."

"It's back to pounding a pavement for you after a dumb thing like that," Piper told him. "You have a flash, haven't you? Why didn't you use it? Afraid you'd see something, huh?"

He left his aide to the merciful ministrations of Hemingway and Miss Withers. "Unless the guy that slugged Rollins was Hemingway or one of the guards, then he stayed in this place since this afternoon, because there was no way for a man to get in since then." Piper told himself. "I gave orders for them to turn everybody out . . . but I wonder if those dumb guards . . . hey, Fink!"

The fat guard came on the run. "Yes, sir!"

"When you turned out the crowd this afternoon, did you look in the Men's Room? Couldn't a man have hidden away in there?"

"I always look there at closing time," Fink declared. "Nobody hid there, unless he made himself mighty small. Yes, siree, that was the first place I looked."

"Then a man could have slipped back in there after you searched the place, and while you were shooing the mob out the other side?"

Fink admitted that it was possible. Inspector Piper led the way into the Men's Room, and found the light button.

There were a few drops of blood where Rollins' chair had stood. And behind the door, which swung inward, was a little cluster of cigarette butts and ash. Seven of them, Piper counted. Seven butts . . . all Camels . . . all smoked to the same length, and not one of them really wetted at the tip.

"A man stood here for well over an hour, waiting," said Piper. "A man who was so sure of himself that he dared to smoke . . . and a man who lured Rollins in here and slugged him without changing his position. See how easy it was? He must have had a weapon. . . ."

Pipers fingers naturally fell to the doorknob, and he drew them sharply away. There was a glaze of something sticky on it. Blood . . . in a thin film. The knob unscrewed easily. . . .

"And a ready-made weapon," said Piper. "Cupped in a man's hand, or a woman's either, this would knock a man down like a base-ball bat." Carefully he wrapped the thing in his handkerchief. . . . "Though I've probably ruined any prints there might be on it, anyway,'' as he told Miss Withers a moment later.

"But aren't you going to collect the cigarette butts, and study them?''

Piper grinned. "Why should I? You've been reading too many fiction stories. The murderer leaves a rare cigarette, with his own monogram, on the scene of the crime. Bah! Those are the commonest brand of fags. What would they prove that I don't know now? If the person who smoked them had only chewed on his butts, then I'd have teeth prints, but this smoker was polite and dainty.''

Ten minutes later, with Rollins back on duty and weak and willing, Piper once more tackled the runway.

"I'd give a lot to know why the person who slugged Rollins came back here to the tank, and what he wanted,'' Inspector Piper observed to Miss Withers, who stuck with him.

"I'd give more to know what it was that dropped this pool of water on the top step, and on through the door,'' Miss Withers replied. "If only we'd been quicker to get down here . . .''

"Maybe we're lucky we didn't,'' Piper told her. "I'm a detective, not a strong-arm squad. I'll mix with a crook if I have to, but I'd rather not mix with a killer.''

He paused above the pool of the penguins. "I'd give a lot to know how that murder was committed, if it was a murder. Doc Bloom said there were no wounds on the body except for bruises on the chin and back of the head, neither one big enough to cause death. Let me see . . . Seymour would stand here to lay the body along the catwalk . . .''

Piper knelt, while Miss Withers watched. "And the murderer, supposing that it *wasn't* Seymour, would come up on him this way. Hello . . .''

The Inspector's gray Stetson had knocked against a low-hanging water pipe and dropped lightly into the water beneath, where the inquisitive penguins nibbled at it. He fished it out gingerly. "Damn. Beg your pardon, Miss Withers, but I love that hat. I've worn it for five years.''

"Wait a minute, young man.'' She looked at him intently. Then she turned, but Hemingway had given up and gone into his office. "Inspector, do you remember the hat that was

floating in this same pool when Costello and that silly Donovan were trying to give artificial respiration to the corpse?
What kind of a hat was it. Think!''

Piper thought. ''I didn't see a hat there! But Donovan
mentioned one—''

Miss Withers nodded slowly. ''I saw it! A gray fedora.
And what kind of a hat was it that the Sproule person from
Chicago was sure Lester wore when he came in? Remember
his testimony? I have the notes right here. . . .''

Piper jumped to his feet, nearly losing his own hat again in
the process. ''Good God! A derby! I remember! Then the hat
that was here in the tank when the body was discovered
didn't belong to Lester, as we thought! Unless Sproule is
mistaken, it must be the hat of the murderer, then! And he
came back tonight to fish for it in the penguin tank. Therefore
the water . . . on the step!''

''Maybe it wasn't the murderer who lost it here,'' Miss
Withers reminded him. ''And we don't know that he got it if
he did. Can you find out if they took away a hat with the
body?''

''I sure can and I will,'' Piper told her. In a moment they
were in Hemingway's office. Piper paused for a moment
beside the Director, who was waiting impatiently to go.

''What kind of headgear do you wear, Director?''

''A derby, winter and summer. There it is over on the wall
. . . why?''

''Never mind why,'' said Piper. ''And . . . oh, by the
way. Do you happen to have a cigarette about you?''

Hemingway proffered a package of Luckies, and the Inspector took one. ''You don't happen to smoke Camels,
then?''

Hemingway looked puzzled. ''No, I don't.'' He saw Piper
hunting for an ashtray and handed him one from the desk. It
was a massive glass basin. The Inspector stared at it absent-
mindedly, and then butted the Lucky there. ''Well, Director,
we won't keep you any longer. I've got a few more questions, but they'll wait until another day. Thanks for the help
you've been able to give us.''

The Director left them to take the uptown subway, and
Inspector Piper hailed a taxi. ''You've been a wonder,'' he
told the school-teacher as she settled beside him.

"It's the ambition of my life to play detective," she confessed. "But you said you had another question to ask Hemingway, one that could wait. What was it?"

"The first one was what happened to the trayful of Camel butts that I saw in that glass ashtray on his desk this afternoon," said Inspector Piper.

"It's possible that the man empties his ashtrays," Miss Withers reminded him.

## 7

## The Passenger in the Empty Taxi

MISS WITHERS was early astir that next morning. It was earlier when she reached yawningly toward her tin alarm clock than was her wont to rise, even on a weekday. And this was Saturday, with no wide-mouthed fledglings waiting to be crammed with knowledge. Besides, Miss Withers had spent half the night at her clattery little portable typewriter, deciphering her shorthand notes of the previous day, in spite of the sleepy and bewildered protests of the two ladies who shared an apartment with her. Sleep or no sleep, Miss Hildegarde Withers was determined that the notes of the inquiry must be ready for Piper's call.

But she did not expect the call to come at seven o'clock in the morning. It was some seconds before she realized that her sleep was being shattered by the telephone bell, and not by the usual alarm. She lifted the receiver, and at the crisp voice which greeted her she came awake as if under a chill shower bath.

"Miss Withers?" It was Piper, and the Inspector's voice tingled with eagerness. "I've got something to discuss with you. Can you have breakfast with me? Fine. Pick you up in fifteen minutes."

Miss Withers realized that she must have said yes, for he hung up at once with a cheerful good-bye. She was dressed in her decent best and downstairs within the fifteen minutes, her notes in her hand.

"Never mind them now," the Inspector told her. They were perched on stools at the nearest drug store counter, honey buns and coffee before them. He paused a moment. "I found out about the hat!"

"Well, was I right?"

He bent his head. "You were right. Donovan, by the way, bears out your story. He saw a dark gray or black fedora in the pool when they were taking the body out. But the men from the Coroner's office who took the body away are dead certain there was no hat around, and none was taken to Headquarters along with the rest of the property. Therefore, if Sproule, the Chicago men's wear buyer, is telling the truth, and there's no reason to suppose otherwise, then the hat that was floating in the penguin pool belonged to the murderer! He knocked it off when he was bending over the corpse, just as I knocked mine off when going through the motions."

"That doesn't make sense to me," said Miss Withers. "He wouldn't leave it there to convict him, would he? He'd take it, and besides, he'd have to wear a hat if he was to mix with the crowd and get out without attracting attention."

"My dear lady," said Piper heavily. "A hat that falls into the water is apt to be damp. The murderer, if it was the murderer, couldn't risk having a dripping hat brim. That would be enough to mark him. He had no time to waste, because he didn't know when somebody would be coming by. So, being a smart person, he took the hat from the dead man in place of his own!"

Miss Withers put down her coffee cup. "Then the murderer wore a derby away from the Aquarium! Provided he didn't get away before the hue and cry started, then he was there at the inquiry. All we have to do is to remember which men wore derbies. . . ."

"I remember, all right," Piper told her. "It's going to be a big help. Take Seymour first. He's the murderer, I'm still pretty sure. He wore a derby."

"Well?"

"All right, Seymour wore a derby. Hemingway showed us *his* derby, hanging on the hall-tree in his office. Sproule himself wore one. Costello, the big hearts and flowers man, carried a tin hat, as did two of those Wall Street clerks. I'll bet you ten to one that even Olaavson went out of there wearing a derby. So what? Tin hats are as common in New York in the autumn as sneezes in the spring."

"But one of those men wore a derby that wasn't his," Miss Withers insisted. "It probably didn't fit!"

"Tell me which one and we're in the bag," Piper announced. "But you can be sure he's got one of his own now, one that does fit. No, we're right back where we started. Except that we've got some idea why some person or persons unknown came back to the Aquarium last night while we were on the upper level. All the same, I'd like to know where was that felt hat from the time you saw it in the pool until somebody came searching for it with a flashlight."

"Maybe the thing sunk," Miss Withers suggested. "The pool is kept fairly dimly lighted, and there are a lot of rocks and so forth in the bottom. A hat might be able to lie there unseen. Anybody that saw it would mistake it for another stone, perhaps. You should have drained the tank, Inspector."

"I know it. It will be done this morning, but the horse is stolen. Well, we've definitely established one thing, anyway."

"What one thing is that?" Miss Withers wanted to know. They left the drug store.

"That the murder was committed by a man . . . if it *was* murder. Remember, we don't know yet how Lester was bumped off. They may find it was heart failure, caused by the blow on the chin that Seymour admits he gave him. But I doubt it. This smells too much like murder, somehow. Anyway, it was a man's hat."

Miss Withers looked at him. "You don't suppose that it was meant to be?"

"Meant to be what?"

"Meant to be a man's hat, and meant to be found in the tank? So that a woman wouldn't be suspected?"

Piper shook his head. "It doesn't fit. And why should the woman come back for it, if it was a plant? No, that's too complicated. Real crimes are simple, if you can only get the right slant on them."

"But suppose the woman didn't come back? Suppose the man to whom the hat belonged came after it, for fear it would pin the murder on him?"

Piper nodded slowly. "Possible," he told her. "A red-herring across the trail, what? You know, you have the makings of a sleuth, my dear lady. You've been more help to me since yesterday noon than the whole Homicide Squad. I wish I . . ."

"Well," interrupted Miss Withers. "I suppose that just the same you'll take these notes, thank me very kindly, and tell me to go back to my school children, won't you?"

Piper hailed a taxi. "But my dear Miss Withers, a detective would look funny dragging around a woman with him. Things aren't done that way. Besides, you do have your school, you know."

"I can get a substitute for a few weeks," suggested Miss Withers eagerly. "I'm having the time of my life. And I tell you for your own good that some person like me, who doesn't look at all like a detective, could find out more in ten minutes from most people than any three of your operatives. And besides, after the way you were fooled by that man Seymour's fake confession yesterday, you *need* a nurse!"

"All right, all right." A taxi whirled up beside them and Piper started to get in. "Miss Withers, you've been a big help and all that, and you've given me some good slants on the situation. But these things are done in a certain way, you see? Well, good-bye. . . ." He turned to the driver. "Fleming Trust Building, 138 Wall Street . . . and drive down the west-side waterfront, it's quicker. . . ."

Miss Withers shrugged her shoulders and watched the taxi go down the street toward the Hudson River . . . she saw another, a rusty Checker taxi, nose out half a block behind . . . and she put two and two together.

Then she ran for the subway entrance. She took a down-town Seventh Avenue express, changed to a local at Fourteenth, and got off at Canal. Then she walked leisurely toward the river for two blocks and took her stand near the corner.

In ten minutes along came a certain taxi. She hailed it, and the driver first shook his head and pointed to his clicking meter, then slowed to a stop as Piper rapped on the glass. He opened the door. "Miss Withers, what in the hell?"

"Shut up and listen," she told him as she determinedly climbed into the taxi.

The driver shifted gears and the taxi sped on. Miss Withers glanced out of the rear window, and then leaned back comfortably.

"I suppose it didn't occur to you that it must have been down these same streets that Gwen Lester came yesterday morning, a few hours later than this?"

Piper shook his head impatiently. "But . . ."

"Never mind. The Lesters' apartment is only a block south of mine, though it's over on the Park and I'm near Broadway. Anyway, Gwen Lester rode down these streets yesterday to meet Seymour. You mentioned yesterday the possibility that someone might have shadowed her in another taxi?"

"Yes, but . . ."

"Well, somebody is shadowing you today in a rusty Checker taxi! If you look around carefully you'll see them about a block behind. I thought you might like to know, so I took a subway and got here ahead of you. I heard your directions to the driver. . . ."

"Yes, yes." Piper was silent. "But who got into the taxi you saw follow me? Man or woman? Recognize him?"

She shook her head. "I just saw the taxi move out from the curb and follow," she said. "I watched as it slowed down in the middle of a block, so as not to come up too close behind you when you stopped for traffic. That's how I knew."

Piper was looking back. "The Checker, you say? But who'd want to shadow me? Anyhow, thanks. I'll show you a little trick we use in cases of this kind, just as soon as we reach a line of stop-lights again." Piper caught the handle of the door and turned it.

"Driver," he said sharply. "I want you to beat the next red light just as it goes on." He showed his badge. "Then pull up about half way down the block." He was tensed to spring, and Miss Withers waited as the cab rolled on several blocks more, and then suddenly sprang past the stop-light and swirled to the curb. In a second Piper was out and running back through the crowd of office-bound humanity.

Miss Withers fished a crumpled dollar bill and three quarters from her purse to pay the exact fare, and then ran after the Inspector. The rusty Checker taxi was jammed in with a cluster of other assorted vehicles, caught by the red light.

The light changed as they neared the corner, but Piper flashed his badge and yelled at the Checker.

His hand went to his coatpocket, and he jerked the taxi door open. There was nobody inside.

"Where's your fare?" he demanded of the blankfaced driver. "Describe him, quick!"

"I didn't have anybody in my bus, mister. You must be crazy. I'm just cruising around. . . ."

Piper leaned into the taxi and gave the rear seat a careful scrutiny. Then he tried the far door. It was swinging, unlatched. He stared at the meter, but the flag was up. Then the detective shrugged his shoulders and motioned the man to drive on.

Miss Withers arrived, breathless, just as he reached the sidewalk. "False alarm," Piper told her.

"A man could have slipped out of the far door and lost himself among the cars and trucks that were there," she pointed out. "He could have made the other curb before you got there."

Piper shook his head. "Doesn't sound plausible to me. I think you were suspicious of an innocently cruising cab. There's more than one battered Checker left in this town. Probably just coincidence that you found this one on my tail when . . ."

Miss Withers was walking along the sidewalk, staring into the gutter. Suddenly she pounced on a little yellow slip of paper that fluttered from under the flying tires of traffic.

She showed it to Piper. He read the following, peering to make out the fine type. "Meter receipt, Checker Cab Company—$1.75— pay no more. . . ."

"I just paid your taxi bill down from the drug store where we had breakfast," Miss Withers told him. "It was a dollar seventy-five . . . the same distance!"

# 8

# Lambs to the Slaughter

MISS WITHERS and the Inspector looked at each other. "It's deeper than we understand, this business," Piper told her. "Maybe you'd better come along with me, for today at least. I'm going down to have a look at the murdered man's office before the clerks get down." They hailed another taxi, and this time no shadow hovered behind them.

It was well after eight-thirty when they arrived at last before the door of the Fleming Trust Company on upper Wall Street. Already a few early clerks and bookkeepers, the vanguard of the vast financial army, were moving deviously through the short street that starts in a graveyard and ends in a river. This was before the advent of the hundreds of "unemployed" apple salesmen, but already hawkers were offering the latest novelty on the corner.

It was a perfect reproduction of a check bearing the name and insignia of the ill-fated Bank of the United States, printed on an oblong of thin rubber!

But Miss Withers and the Inspector did not pause to wonder at the type of mind which could find humor in such a philosophic view of a fair-sized catastrophe. They were hunting bigger game than bank officials.

There was a brass plate beside the door of the Fleming Trust Building, which bore in worn but polished letters the legend "White and Lester—members of N. Y. Stock Exchange—first floor."

The brokerage offices founded by Gwen's father, and continued by her husband until noon yesterday, were up one flight of narrow stairs. Piper did not wait for the elevator, and Miss Withers followed him up. It was hard to realize that twenty-four hours ago an ordinary, everyday business man climbed this stair for the last time.

"I've got a search warrant to show if I need it," the Inspector told her. But he didn't need it. There was only an office boy in the place, and he stepped back in awe at Piper's badge.

"Here is where we get a line on Jerry Lester," the Inspector announced. Miss Withers surveyed the deserted place, the empty desks for clerks, the empty benches for messengers, and the silent tickers under their glass domes. The entire scene made her realize for the first time, with a slight catch of her breath, that Gerald Lester had once been something more than a case, a problem to be solved. He had been alive yesterday at this time. He had been a living man, breathing, loving, hating, working . . . and now he lay on an autopsy table somewhere.

Piper gave the office boy instructions to make himself scarce. On the bench was a morning paper he had been reading. Miss Withers caught sight of the headline. "Broker A Suicide in Fish-tank?" it blared forth. Then Piper hadn't give Philip Seymour's confession to the press.

Miss Withers followed the Inspector into the largest private office, through a door marked "Private—Mr. Lester" . . .

She remarked to Piper that it seemed somehow fitting for this vast place to be deserted and quiet now that its head was gone. Piper stopped his casual survey of the office.

"More likely the place is deserted because it's an early Saturday morning," he informed her. "The Exchange is closed today, you know. It's a good thing, it gives the tickers a chance to catch up with the market. Since the crash last month there's been hell to pay."

He walked over to the big desk, and sat down in the cushioned armchair behind it. Then he lifted one of the four black and gold fountain pens that slanted up from a massive slab of malachite and scribbled on the desk calendar. "I thought Lester would be the type to use a stub pen," he remarked. Then he poked through the drawers. Miss Withers leaned over to watch as he came to the top one on the left side. It contained a .45 Savage automatic pistol.

It was brand-new and showed no signs of having been fired, though it was fully loaded. Piper put it in his pocket and felt for a cigar. Somewhere there was the sound of a door closing, and he put away the cigar swiftly. Then he pulled

Miss Withers into the lee of a rank of file cases that stood to the left of the door, and gripped her wrist.

In a moment a young woman came into the room. She did not stop to close the door behind her, and she was still wearing her hat. She went directly to the top lefthand drawer of the desk and fumbled there.

"If you are looking for Mr. Lester's gun, I have it here," said the Inspector gently. The young woman whirled like a flash, her gray eyes wide with terror. Then a cool mask of self-possession came over her.

"You have no business in this office," she said in a low voice. "I am Mr. Lester's private secretary. I . . ."

"And your name is . . .?" Inspector Piper showed the silver shield once more.

"I am Miss Templeton, Marian Templeton." The girl, not more than twenty-three or four, drew herself up rigidly as Piper motioned her to a chair.

"I'll stand, thank you," she said. Miss Withers scrutinized her carefully. Blue turban, not the latest style but very becoming. Smart gray coat trimmed with fox, over a fitted blue suit which did not conceal lines more womanly than businesslike. Sheer gunmetal hose, and kid shoes a trifle rundown at the heel. Miss Withers always noticed shoes.

Marian Templeton slipped off the turban, exposing a short, smooth bob and a high forehead. Inspector Piper slid comfortably into a chair and lit his cigar.

"Just a few, a very few questions, Miss Templeton. You will naturally wish to help us in the investigation of the death of your employer? I knew I could count on your help. But to begin, why did you come for the gun, first thing this morning?"

Miss Templeton shrugged her shoulders. "Because I was afraid that the police would be snooping around, and I knew that Mr. Lester hadn't had a permit. I was afraid there would be trouble. . . ."

"I see. Been with Mr. Lester long?"

"I've been his secretary for five years," she told him. "Mr. Lester brought me with him from his old office when he came here as a junior partner. Mr. White was here then. And now . . . now this terrible thing has happened! I didn't sleep any last night. To think that he would kill himself!"

"Don't you worry, Miss Templeton. Your employer didn't

kill himself. He was murdered!'' Piper brought out the last
word with a crash, but the girl kept her face set. "I gave the
suicide story to the newspapers because as yet there was no
definite proof of murder, but we know it was done,'' he
went on. "All we need to find out is who did it. Can you
help us?''

"*I* help? I don't see how.'' Marian Templeton suddenly
leaned forward. "But why don't you ask his charming little
wife? I'm sure *she* would know more than I. *I'm* just the
secretary!''

Piper nodded. "You were here yesterday morning when
Mr. Lester came in? Suppose you start at the beginning and
tell it your own way. Everything . . . all he did and said.''

"It was just as usual,'' the girl began. "I got here at
nine-fifteen as I always do, and Mr. Lester came in about half
an hour later.''

"Did he seemed troubled, or upset in any way?''

"No more than usual,'' said Marian Templeton. "He's
always been troubled since the crash last month. It hurt Mr.
Lester's business terribly. It hurt every brokerage house on
the Street. You see, he was interested in the moving picture
leaders, and he lost heavily. And then the trouble with his
wife . . . I shouldn't mention that, but everybody knows it.
They didn't get along.''

"And why was that?''

Marian Templeton shrugged her shoulders. "Really, I don't
know. . . .''

"Bother that,'' said Piper. "A good private secretary, who
has been with her employer for five years, knows more about
him than his wife, more about him than he knows himself.
Now be frank with us.''

"His wife is a silly little fool that only cared about spending
money,'' said the secretary after a moment. "And when there
wasn't so much money to spend . . . she had no patience, no
sympathy for him. I don't think she ever cared much for him.
Her father, old Mr. White, arranged the marriage, they say.
That was how Mr. Lester got to be junior partner. I know that
Mr. Lester didn't marry Gwen White for love. . . .''

"How do you know that?'' said Piper very softly. For a
moment Marian Templeton's mouth hardened, and the line of
her red lips grew straight. Then she smiled sweetly. "Be-

cause, as you say, a good private secretary knows more about her employer than he knows about himself.''

"Very good. And after Mr. Lester came in the office yesterday . . . ?''

"He said good-morning to me and I took his hat, coat and stick, as he passed my desk, which is just outside this door here. In a moment he rang for me, and I brought him his mail. Then he dictated some letters.''

"Wait a moment. Anything in the mail that might upset him? Anything at all?''

The girl shook her head. "I'll dig the letters out of the file if you want them. Also the carbons of the ones he gave me. They were all pertaining to business, though.''

"Never mind. Go on.''

"Then he asked me to call Mr. Fairchild into his office. Mr. Fairchild is the chief customer's man.''

"Any other callers during the morning? Anybody at all?''

Miss Templeton paused to think. "No, there wasn't anybody else at all. No customers came in during the morning. Business has been very slack, you know, and lately Mr. Lester has been letting Mr. Fairchild and the other customer's men take over most of the outside work. He . . .''

"How long was this Mr. Fairchild in Mr. Lester's office?''

"Nearly an hour. Then he came out, and a few minutes later—I should say about noon—Mr. Lester hurried out of his office. He seemed in a hurry, and he didn't leave word with me as to when he would return, as he usually does . . . I mean did. He took his hat.''

"What kind of a hat was that?'' put in Miss Withers. The girl looked at her in surprise, but Piper nodded for her to answer.

"It was a derby,'' said Marian Templeton. "Mr. Lester usually wore a derby.''

"And his coat and stick? What kind of a stick did he usually carry?''

The secretary thought again. "It was his heavy malacca one that he carried yesterday. But usually he carries a curved whangee.''

"This is very important, Miss Templeton,'' said Piper. "Just when did Lester stop carrying the bamboo whangee and change to a heavy malacca—a loaded malacca, was it not?''

"I didn't know it was loaded," the girl said. "But he's been carrying it for a week or more, no longer. I noticed it about that long ago. But why?"

"You've been very helpful," said Piper. "One thing more. Do you know what it is that Mr. Lester and Mr. Fairchild were discussing during that hour yesterday?"

"No, I do not," said Miss Templeton.

"Your chair is just outside this partition," Piper pointed out. "You didn't hear anything?"

"I don't listen to my employer's conversations."

"Of course you don't. But I had hoped that maybe you had a suspicion what it was all about. You haven't?"

"No-o, I haven't." But there was a shade of hesitation in the girl's voice. Piper leaped to the breach.

"Come, be frank, Miss Templeton. You can't obstruct justice, you know. We don't want to be unpleasant, but . . ."

"Well," admitted the girl, "I do know what some of it was about. Because after Mr. Fairchild went out, Mr. Lester gave me this memo to type out and hold for his signature." She disappeared into the outer office, and returned shortly with a neatly typed notice on a yellow sheet marked "Inter-office."

Piper read it aloud. "To Mr. Lathrop, from G. L., copy to——blank—— In view of Mr. Fairchild's resignation on this date, November 18th, please make out an immediate account of his commissions due, and send me the check for my signature."

Piper handed it back to the girl. "Mr. Lathrop is the treasurer of the firm, I suppose?"

She nodded. "It didn't go to him, because Mr. Lester didn't come back to sign it," she said evenly.

"Do you think Mr. Fairchild resigned in actuality, or is that a form?"

She shook her head. "Of course I don't know. Why don't you ask him? But I don't mind telling you that Mr. Lester has had to let several high-salaried employees go on account of the crash. Mr. Fairchild had a drawing account of eight hundred dollars a month against his commissions."

"I see," said Piper. "By the way, where did you have lunch yesterday, Miss Templeton?"

"In the Exchange Grill, where I usually eat. Why?"

"Alone, or with some other member of the office force, or a friend?"

"I was alone," said Marian Templeton. There was a sound of bustling in the outer office, and she moved restlessly. "Anything more to ask me, Mr. Inspector?"

Piper relit his cigar. "I don't know that there is," he said slowly. "You might bring me the file on a customer . . . Mr. Sproule of Chicago?"

The secretary frowned. "We never had a customer by that name," she announced.

Piper nodded. "Then let me have the file on Mr. Costello!"

He was watching her face like a hawk, but it retained its bland innocence. "I'm afraid we never had a customer by that name, either. . . ."

Piper nodded. "Then bring me what records you have on the account of Mr. Bertrand B. Hemingway, please." Miss Withers knew he was aiming blindly.

"Mr. Hemingway? Why, we sold out Mr. Hemingway's account about three weeks ago, because he couldn't put up any more margin!"

# 9

# Again the Garnet Pin

"BEFORE you go," said Inspector Piper to the secretary, Marian Templeton, "please tell me one more thing. Did Mr. Lester have a phone call, by any chance, just before he went out yesterday?"

The girl shook her head. "Not as far as I know. His calls all come to my desk, and then if I recognize the person calling, or the name, I ask Mr. Lester if he wants to talk to them."

"Pretty complicated system," Piper observed. "Why did Lester surround himself with so much red tape?"

"He had to do it," flashed Miss Templeton. "You see, a

lot of our customers lost their shirts—I mean, they lost everything in the market crash. Of course a broker has no choice in such cases, when the customer is buying on margin. If the stock drops, the customer has to put up more margin or lose everything he's got. Like every other brokerage house, we had to sell out a lot of our customers, and some of them didn't realize how serious it was. They blamed Mr. Lester, or the firm, rather. And a lot of them used to call him and there was some unpleasantness, so he evolved the system of having me take his calls. But no, there wasn't even one call yesterday morning.''

''All the same, will you send in the telephone girl who was on duty at the switchboard yesterday forenoon?''

Miss Templeton nodded, and withdrew with not-too-well concealed haste. In a moment there was a knock on the office door, and at Piper's ''Come in'' there entered a plump, red-haired young lady with a great many freckles and a good deal of chewing gum.

''I'm Maggie Colton,'' she announced. ''Switchboard op. You want to quiz me?''

Piper shook his head. ''Just one question, Miss Colton. Why did you put through a phone call to Mr. Lester yesterday morning about twelve o'clock without buzzing it on Miss Templeton's wire?''

The girl clicked her gum. ''Yesterday morning about noon? Yeah, I remember. Well, the man said it was very important. He said that Mr. Lester was in trouble, or something. I don't just remember what. So I put it right on Mr. Lester's wire. That's all I know.''

Piper looked at Miss Withers. Then he turned to Miss Colton again. ''What kind of a voice was it? You said a man's voice, didn't you? Was it deep and low?''

The girl shook her head. ''It was just . . . just a voice.''

''It wasn't high and nervous, like this?'' Piper gave a passable imitation of a Hemingway tenor. The operator shook her head, doubtfully.

''It wasn't a bit of an Irish brogue to it, the like of this?''

This time she shook her head emphatically. ''No, it wasn't one of those accents. It sounded sort of far away, because I thought it was long distance at first. The way a voice sounds when it comes over the hook-ups from Los Angeles. Only it was a local call.''

"It couldn't have been a woman, could it? A woman disguising her voice?''

Once more Miss Maggie Colton was positive. It couldn't have been a woman. Piper told her she could get back to her switchboard. "And get Spring 3100 for me while you're at it," he told her. "On this phone. And you don't need to put the call through Miss Templeton.''

A few minutes later he was in connection with Police Headquarters. Miss Withers listened as he asked impatiently for a report from Doctor Bloom.

"Well, call him back and tell him that I want to know if he thinks this is a murder case or a Tammany Hall investigation? I want some service, see? An autopsy doesn't need to take more than a week, as a rule!'' said Piper to the invisible copper at the other end of the line.

"And something more. Tell Lieutenant Keller to send down a couple of his operatives who know something about Wall Street offices and accounting to go through the books and files of White and Lester, here in the Fleming Trust Building. Yeah, this morning. Yeah. And I want another operative, I'd prefer Taylor but any man will do, to get a search warrant blank and come down here. Okay. If Bloom reports, shoot his call here to me. Yeah. Yeah. G'bye.'' He turned to Miss Withers. "At last we're getting somewhere.''

"Are we?'' She was poking about the file cases. "It looks more and more complicated to me.'' Then . . . "What's this?''

She was reaching down behind the file, groping in the dark. Then her fingers touched the bit of bright metal which had caught her eye. It was a silver vase, of the type which holds a single rose.

Piper came over to look at it. "Well, you don't think Lester was killed with that, do you?''

Miss Withers shook her head. "All the same, as a rule people don't throw silver vases behind filing cabinets. And I've heard you say several times that if we could only notice all the things around us that were unusual, we'd stumble on the mystery. Well, here's something unusual.''

"More likely it simply fell down there, and was forgotten,'' said Piper. But he placed the vase on Lester's desk and stared at it reflectively. "Looks like it belonged there," he observed. "Matches the ashtrays and the rest of it." He dropped into the chair again.

"We've got to wait here for a while," he told Miss Withers. "We might as well check through those notes you took in the inquiry yesterday, and refresh our memories."

They were still at it when a knock came on the door, and the three plain-clothes operatives were shown in by Miss Templeton. Piper did not introduce them to Miss Withers. He waited until Miss Templeton was well out of the room, and then spoke shortly to the biggest of the three, a man who looked like a truck-driver, except for his mobile hands and fingers. "Taylor, did you see the little girl who let you in?" He spoke in a low voice. "Name's Marian Templeton. Lives in a Greenwich Village apartment on Morton Street, number 19. I want you to give her place a look-see sometime today before she leaves the office here. Then I want you to tail her, unless you find out something worth reporting to me by phone at the office. She's private secretary to Gerald Lester."

"Okay," said Taylor. He was gone.

Piper lifted the phone. "Will you ask Mr. Fairchild to step into this office, if you please?"

In a few minutes there came a timid knock on the door, and a young man entered. Frederick Fairchild was a tall, somewhat gangling young dandy with a carefully waxed moustache and what was meant to be an ingratiating smile. He wore a double-breasted blue suit, light pearl-gray spats, and a bosomed shirt that matched his tie.

"I didn't know you'd be down today," observed Piper slowly, "after your talk with Lester yesterday morning. You know what I'm here for, of course. These people with me are my assistants. Can you help us any?"

Fairchild twisted his eastern moustache tip vigorously. "Don't know that I can," he said. "Fact is, I didn't intend to come back today, after Gerald gave me the works yesterday morning. But he didn't come back to sign my check, so here I am waiting for the dough. If I can tell you anything to help you in this business . . ."

"Have a sort of brawl with Lester when he gave you the sack?"

Fairchild looked up quickly. "Good Lord, you don't think

I had anything to do with it, do you? They're whispering that he was killed, and that it wasn't suicide at all. But I didn't have a brawl with him. Nothing like it. He just told me that the company wouldn't keep me any longer. I knew it was coming. I'm the only customer's man here who gets any dough; the others draw fifty a week against their commissions. I draw four times that, but then, I've been with the outfit for three years, and I had the clientele. Up until the October crash, there wasn't a week when I didn't have a check coming to me in advance of what I'd drawn on the drawing account. But since then all my customers, like everybody else, took a rap on the chin and don't trade. No trade, no commissions. No commissions, no use for a big drawing account like mine. Lester asked me if I wanted to drop down to fifty a week with the rest of the boys just a year out of Yale and I said no. So that's all."

"And you didn't have a fuss with Lester yesterday?"

Fairchild shook his head. "Of course not. I knew it was coming. It was strictly business, nothing personal at all." Miss Withers noticed that he was twisting the fingers of his left hand, the hand away from Piper. They fingered invisible objects, nervously.

"All right," said the Inspector finally. "By the way, these gentlemen are from my office. I want them to go through the books and the files of the company. Here is a search warrant if you insist. All I want from them is a list of the biggest losers in the late unpleasantness of October among your customers. I'll appreciate it, Fairchild, if you'll introduce them to the treasurer and so forth."

"Gladly," said Fairchild. He had almost reached the door when Piper's voice halted him.

"Oh, by the way, Fairchild! Where did you have lunch yesterday, and with whom? Just for our records?"

Fairchild hesitated. "The-the truth of the matter is that I didn't eat lunch yesterday. It was sort of a shock, finding out that I was tossed out on my ear. I walked by myself in Battery Park. . . ."

Piper looked at Miss Withers, wonderingly. "You know that Battery Park is at the steps of the building in which your employer was killed yesterday?"

Fairchild nodded. "I know it. But I didn't go in."

"All right," said Piper casually. "And one thing more. Ever see this before?" He pointed to the silver rose vase that stood now on Lester's desk.

The customer's man stared at it, and then nodded. "Sure I have. That's what we used to call Lester's burnt offering. The little girl, Miss Templeton, you know . . . she used to keep a fresh rosebud in that vase, on the boss's desk. They used to kid her about it, because she bought them out of her own salary. Lately I haven't seen her coming in with the rosebud wrapped in green tissue paper as she used to do. I guess she got over her crush on the boss."

Piper nodded, sticking out his lower lip. "Sort of an office-wife, huh?"

"Yeah, something like that. The little girl's been with him a long time, you know. He wouldn't have another secretary, not even when . . . not at all."

"Not even when Mrs. Lester objected to Miss Templeton?" Piper hazarded.

"Not even then. I didn't know you knew about that. Yeah, Mrs. Lester had an idea that her husband ought to have one of these plain, efficient ladies around. But nothing doing. Gerald Lester knew his women. Why, he even had Miss Templeton sewing buttons on his overcoat one day, I remember. She was sewing them on with the thread she keeps to mend silk stockings with. And they certainly did kid her about it!"

"All right, Fairchild. That's all I need to know now. I may want to talk to you again one of these days. Now you can show these two gentlemen around a bit."

The two detectives who had stood motionless beside the door all the time moved obediently after the customer's man. Even to Miss Withers they looked more like baseball players than either accountants or detectives. But detectives usually did look like that, she knew now.

"That's that," said Piper to her. "Well, how do you figure this case now?"

"I don't figure it," confessed Miss Withers. "But I'm just a woman. You're the master-mind. And suppose you tell me just what track you're on?"

Piper burst out in hearty laughter. Miss Withers had never seen him laugh before, and it was pleasant. "Good Lord, woman. I'm not on any track. I'm like the man in Leacock's

book who jumped on his horse and rode off in all directions.
This is a real case, not a puzzle out of a story magazine. I'm
a detective, not a super-sleuth. Sherlock Holmes would know
all about this case in no time, what with a magnifying glass and
his knowledge of the bone structure of Polynesian aborigines.
Philo Vance would solve it between puffs of a Regie cigarette, from simple deductions based on the squawks of those
penguins we met up with yesterday. But not me. I don't
know any more than you do. Maybe less, only I know how to
act wise. I'm just blundering ahead, trying not to miss any of
the more apparent lines of approach. Sooner or later the
murderer will leave something open, and I'll stumble in. It
works, lady, where the gum-shoes and the shag-tobacco and
violin combination don't. Remember this one thing, the sleuth
has one tremendous advantage always. It's that sooner or
later the criminal will get either scared or reckless, and show
his hand thinking that we know as much as we pretend to
know. Then we nab him."

"I see," said Miss Withers. Piper lifted the phone again.
"I'm making one phone call, and then we'll get under way,"
he told her.

Into the phone—"Spring 3100 again, baby." He waited a
moment, and then asked for his office.

"Hello, lieutenant? Well, what do you hear from Doc
Bloom? Is that sawbones still trying to find out what killed
Lester, or did he give it up and call in a chiropractor? Oh, he
did, did he? Well, tell him . . . no, I'll have them get him on
the phone for me. Hello? Sure I'll talk to Casey. Hello,
Mike? Did you get to first base with the maid? Yeah. You got
the socks? Well, send 'em down for analysis. Particularly the
left leg, about half way up, on the outside. Sure. Sure. Save
the rest of it till you see me, or make a written report. Sure.
Now have them transfer this call to Doc Bloom, will you?"

There was a long pause, and much clicking over the line.
Piper put his hand over the mouthpiece. "Remember my
sending Casey last night to snoop around the Lester apartment? Well, he got to be pals with Mrs. Lester's second
maid, and he got the stockings the dame wore yesterday. I
noticed a stain on them. Interesting if they show traces of
blood that she might have washed off in a hurry, huh?" Then
he suddenly burst forth into the mouthpiece. "Hello, Bloom?

Yeah, this is Inspector Piper, Doctor. Yeah. How you coming? I can't go ahead until you give me some more dope on the stiff. Yeah."

He listened for a few minutes. "Well, that's your end, Doctor. But you know and I know that heart failure is the cause of every death. It's the question of what *makes* the heart stop. And I don't believe that a big husky like Lester would pass out cold from a crack on the chin. Sure, go ahead. If a cranial autopsy will show anything more, try that. Yeah, call me back. Headquarters will let you know where to find me. Sure. And hurry, will you?"

He crashed the receiver and lit another cigar. Lester's silver tray now held four, each practically intact except for a quarter inch of ash on one end and two inches of chewed pulp on the other.

"Can you beat that?" He looked up at Miss Withers, and his face was contorted with a puzzled frown. "Bloom, the smartest medical examiner that the department ever had, can't find anything wrong with the corpse. No water in the lungs, no poison in the intestinal tract, no wound . . . what do you make of that?"

"Perfectly clear to me," said Miss Hildegarde Withers. "Gerald Lester was frightened to death by seeing his own face in the glass of the penguin tank. Or maybe somebody was giving him an absent reverse-action treatment in Christian Science. Possibly somebody shot him with an icicle from a cross-bow, so that the weapon melted and left no trace. Oh, I can think of a dozen causes of death. And judging by the number of people you figure might have been in that runway with him, maybe he was trampled to death in the traffic!"

"Well, anyway we've done all we can hope to do here," Piper told her. "We might as well run down and confront Hemingway with the news that we know he got taken for plenty in the recent market crash. Funny he wouldn't tell us about that, wasn't it? Claiming that his friendship with Gerald Lester was so casual and all that. . . ."

Miss Withers took a last look around the room. "Just about twenty-four hours ago Jerry Lester hurried out of this room bound for the Aquarium, and a destination a lot farther than that, if he'd known. I wonder if that phone call that the girl put right through to him as so important regarding Mrs. Lester had anything to do with his going?''

"Nothing else but," Piper told her. "Somebody called him up and told him where to find his wife and another man in *tête à tête*. And I'm going to know who did that calling before I get through. Maybe the call could be traced. I hadn't thought of that." Again he picked up the instrument.

"Hello, baby. Give me the chief operator, will you? What exchange? I don't know what exchange. I want to trace that call that came in to your boss yesterday morning. They keep a record of calls somewhere, don't they, so they can bill 'em? Why do you have to know the exchange the call came from? Oh, yeah? Well, give me the supervisor, then."

He waited for some time, and then succeeded in explaining what he wanted. "Listen, madam. This isn't fooling. I'm Inspector Piper of the Homicide Squad and I've got to have that number traced. I don't care if it takes fifty clerks all night to dig it out. Somewhere you must have a record of that call to this number. Yeah, twelve o'clock noon, yesterday. Yeah. No, it was a local call, somewhere on Manhattan Island. Yeah. Well, when you find it, call me at Headquarters. Yeah. Yeah."

He put down the phone. "That's that," he observed to Miss Withers, who was beginning to think that detective work wasn't as interesting as she had hoped. "Somebody warned Jerry Lester about his wife, maybe one of the servants at his house, maybe not. If that call came from . . ."

"Br-r-r-ring. . . ." The phone jangled under Piper's hand. He snatched it. "Yes, this is Inspector Piper. Yes. Who, Bloom? Get him back for me, for God's sake. Yes, I'll hold on. Yes . . . hello, Doctor. What's up now?"

There was a long silence, and then Piper said good-bye. His voice was at once relieved and constrained as he spoke to Miss Withers, who waited for him beside the door.

"That was the medical examiner, Dr. Bloom," he told her. "He knows how Lester was killed. He . . . ."

"Then it *was* murder! Go on!"

Piper seemed reluctant to spill it. He fished for another cigar, and then finding his own vest pocket empty, took one from the mahogany humidor on Lester's desk, and bit off the end appreciatively.

"Until he started the cranial autopsy he couldn't find a

thing wrong," Piper went on. "But as soon as he started to work on the brain, he found . . ."

"Don't be so dramatic," Miss Withers insisted tensely. She was holding her breath. "Out with it . . . I won't faint."

"All right," said Piper. "I'm telling you. Gerald Lester was killed by some sort of a devil's skewer forced through his right ear, eardrum, skull, and into the brain for at least two inches. Death must have been instantaneous, for he didn't struggle and there was practically no flow of blood. The weapon was removed without leaving an apparent trace of its entry, and if I hadn't insisted on a cranial autopsy Lester would have been put down as heart failure. Doc Bloom says that the weapon was smaller than a stiletto, since it made a hole less than one-sixteenth of an inch in diameter in the bone of the skull. It takes good steel to break through like that, without snapping or turning on itself, even though the ear is a vulnerable spot."

"I've got an idea," said Miss Withers after a moment. "Is there any regulation that you have to give full and correct details about this business to the press and to the public?"

"I don't get you," Piper admitted.

"Well, the medical examiner makes his report to you and to nobody else, doesn't he?"

"Quite right. Of course, he appears as a witness in the trial, at which time he is under oath and has to tell the whole truth."

"Splendid." Miss Withers was aglow with enthusiasm. "I've got a wonderful idea. Then there are only three people who know that Lester met his death just that way . . . the medical examiner, you, and myself?"

"One other person knows," said Piper softly. "Have you forgotten the murderer?"

"Exactly," said Miss Withers. She explained what her grand idea was.

Piper whistled. "Can't do it, ma'm. It would be bound to get out. I have to report everything to the Prosecutor, Tom Roche. He'd skin me alive if I did what you suggest."

"Not if it caught the murderer, or the murderers," Miss Withers reminded him. "And something might happen before the case comes to trial. Will you do it?"

Piper reached for the phone. "You just bet I'll give the

story out that way, Miss Withers.'' Then he hesitated, staring at the blue beaded hat which the school-teacher was wearing again today.

She became very thoughtful. "A skewer, you say . . . or a stiletto? Why then, Lester might have been killed with my hatpin!''

Piper looked at her, and the friendliness was gone from his face. His lower lip came further out, and he tossed his cigar out of the open window.

"That occurred to me just now,'' he said softly.

10

# The Rift in the Lute

MISS WITHERS slowly drew the garnet hatpin from her bonnet and extended it toward the Inspector. To her eyes it did not seem as glittering as usual.

"I suppose this will be Exhibit A?'' she asked.

Piper did not move.

"Snap out of it, Inspector,'' she said acidly. "If you are going to be stupid enough to think that I committed the Lester murder, why don't you put the handcuffs on me now?''

He shook his head. "Shut up a minute, please, will you? I'm just trying to think. You say that you lost your hatpin yesterday, and that you had your whole natural history class looking for it all through the Aquarium?''

Miss Withers nodded. "And my little black Abraham—a fine boy, Abraham—found it on the lower step of the stair above the penguin tank. Heavens, man, I've got fifteen witnesses to prove where I was every minute of the time down in the Aquarium. That class of mine sticks to me closer than the proverbial leech. I wasn't out of their sight for a second until we started to leave the place and I found that my hatpin was missing.''

"How about afterward?'' Piper wanted to know. His usually smooth voice was thin and tense.

"Afterward?" Miss Withers stopped short as Piper took the hatpin from her hand. "No chance of prints on it now, anyway," he observed. "But as a matter of form I suppose that we ought to see if it fits the hole in Lester's skull. And the analyst ought to find traces of blood on it somewhere." He wrapped it carefully.

"Tell me again," he said to Miss Withers. "You say that you weren't out of sight of your class until you started to leave the place and found the pin missing? That was after the pickpocket episode, I gather. And then you started your class after the hatpin?"

"That's right. And I followed along behind."

"No doubt at all," said Piper genially. "But a district attorney could make a jury believe that while your little demons were hunting the hatpin, you had time to slip in and puncture Jerry Lester with it, while he lay unconscious. Then you might have dropped it on the stair where one of the kids would find it."

"You don't believe that, do you?"

Piper shook his head. "My dear Miss Withers, a detective has no beliefs. He either suspects or he knows. I have to suspect everybody and everything. But I don't mind telling you that I suspect your hatpin had more to do with the killing of Gerald Lester than you did. There's a certain lack of motive for your killing him."

Suddenly he stopped, and his green-gray eyes clouded. "Wait a minute. Didn't you tell me that you'd stopped teaching school somewhere in Iowa to come to New York?"

"Of course. Why?"

Piper said nothing, but crossed swiftly to the desk and fumbled through one of the dead man's drawers. He found what he was looking for, underneath several folders of a "Summer Cruise Through Norway's Fjords" and other assorted literature. His eyes had rested upon this bit of card for only a second, yet they had noted it well.

It was an old postcard addressed to Gerald Lester, and the message typed on the reverse began "Dear old alumnus—just a 'line' to let you know of the 'big doings' at dear old Boggs Memorial High School on October 15th, with a Homecoming football game and a general 'feed' afterwards. Let us know how many of the 'folks' you are bringing with you. Here's for a big time,— signed—Horace Fleetwit, Pres. Boggs High School Alumnae Association.''

The postmark of the card was "Cedar Rapids, Iowa."

"Where was your home in Iowa, Miss Withers?"

"I was born in Dubuque. Christened and schooled and graduated and taught in Dubuque. Why?"

"Just idle curiosity on my part," the Inspector told her.

Miss Withers marched over to the desk drawer and dragged it out. Before Piper could stop her she was reading the postcard.

"Hmmp! So I did do it after all, huh? Because we both happen to come from the same midwestern state, the murdered man and I! People have to come from somewhere, don't they? I've been in New York for years, and never yet have I met anyone who was born in this town. Figure it out for yourself. Gerald Lester left Cedar Rapids, which is in the center of the state, to come east to college some years ago. It must have been long after I was given my first-grade certificate at the end of five years of teaching in Dubuque, which is so close to the Iowa state line that it is practically in Wisconsin. The two towns are farther apart than New York and Philadelphia!"

She paused for breath, and then plunged on. "I must be anyhow ten years older than Gerald Lester was. So how can you make me out as the deserted little hometown sweetheart in a gingham apron, waiting patiently among the lilacs?"

"I guess I can't," said Piper. "Nobody's arguing with you, ma'm."

"I started this business because it thrilled me," said Miss Withers slowly. "But now that I'm in it, I'm going to stay in it till we know who did kill him."

"Listen," said Piper. "You're going to stick with this investigation whether you like it or not . . ." He almost added the word "now" on the end of the sentence. "Well, I must be getting along."

They came out of the offices marked "White and Lester," pausing in the downstairs lobby to look out at a swirl of sooty rain. "I've got to take this hatpin up to HQ," Piper announced. "Want to wait somewhere for me, and then in about half an hour we'll go to the Aquarium and ask Hemingway why he didn't tell us he had had business dealings with Lester?"

"I'll tell you what I'd rather do," Miss Withers offered. "I'd like to have a chat with that Seymour boy. There's something he hasn't told, and maybe I could get it where you couldn't."

"Talk to him all you like," Piper told her. "If you get another confession out of him, one that will hold water this time, I'll make you a deputy."

"That's not a fair test," Miss Withers protested. "Because I told you that the boy was no murderer, and I still believe it. What man would kill anybody with a hatpin? That's more like a . . ." She paused.

"More like a woman, eh?" Piper nodded. "I was thinking that, too. Well, let's get on with it. I'll drop you at the Tombs, and then pick you up when I get through with the routine stuff in my own office."

There was a good deal of red tape to be brushed aside, and then at last Miss Withers was shown down a long corridor, from which opened cells on either side, most of them empty and all of them dark, even at noon. Here and there a face leered at her from between half inch bars of steel. At the farthest end of the passage stood a wooden chair. "Here's where I usually sit, ma'm," the guard explained. His name was Schmaltz, and he was fat and cheerful. "That is, if my work doesn't call me somewhere else. Not much need for a guard over these boys in here, because if they did get out they couldn't get through the cell block and into the main hall. I'll just give you my chair inside the cell, so you'll have a place to sit, and run along while you talk to your son. . . ."

"He's not my son," snapped Miss Withers.

"Beg pardon, ma'm." apologized the guard. "I need some new glasses pretty bad, I do. Well, I'm supposed to search you, but as long as the Inspector sent you in I won't. You can stay twenty minutes, according to rule. . . ."

He turned an old-fashioned key in the big lock of a cell in the middle of the row, and then shoved Miss Withers and the wooden chair through into the dimness of the interior. Then the door clanged.

Philip Seymour was sleeping, sprawled out on the canvas cot which hung by two chains from the wall. His hair was tumbled, and he had not shaved.

He moved restlessly, and then opened his eyes. "You've come from Gwen? You've brought me a message? She sent you?"

Miss Withers killed the appeal in his eyes with a shake of her head. "No, Mrs. Lester didn't send me," she said. "I'm meddling on my own."

He sank back listlessly. "I know you," he told her. "You're the school-teacher who didn't think I looked like a murderer. Still feel the same way about me?"

"Yes, I do," lied Miss Withers. He certainly did look more like a murderer now. "But whether you look like a murderer or not, tell me, are you one?"

Seymour was instantly on the defensive, Miss Withers could see. "Didn't you hear my confession yesterday?" He motioned at the stone walls. "Why do you think they put me here, in durance vile?"

"I know why you're here," Miss Withers told him. "So do you, but it isn't for killing Gerald Lester. At least, not the way you confessed to it. Because he didn't die from a crack on the head and he didn't drown." Miss Withers searched Philip's face for a sign, but he kept it passive.

"No?"

"No! Gerald Lester died from having a hatpin jammed through his ear and into his brain, while he lay in the runway, unconscious."

She paused, for a dramatic effect. This time Seymour started for an instant. "And so they found that out, eh?"

She nodded. "Just this morning they found it out. The weapon was my own hatpin, which I lost for a time in the Aquarium. Now you see why I'm involved."

Seymour nodded. "Now what do you think of that?" His voice was heavy with irony.

Miss Withers looked at him. "Have you heard from Mrs. Lester since you've been in the Tombs here?"

"No, I haven't. But why should I? Tell me, how is she?"

"She's standing your incarceration beautifully," Miss Withers assured him. "I just thought you might agree to have the same lawyer or something. It's usual in cases of this kind, I believe. Inspector Piper expects that the grand jury will find against both of you, as co-defendants."

Philip Seymour caught Miss Withers' arm. "Tell me, is Gwen under arrest? Have they . . ."

Before he could finish his question the cell-door swung open again, and the gray-clad form of Inspector Piper was silhouetted in the doorway.

"More third degree, Inspector?" Seymour inquired.

Piper stuck out his lower lip. "Not exactly," he murmered. His voice was so soft, so unassuming and calm, that Miss Withers knew he was up to something. "I just got a message from the District Attorney, Mr. Tom Roche," said Piper. "He had such interesting news that I thought I'd step right across the Bridge and let you folks in on it. You see, Seymour, he just got a phone call from Costello, Gwen Lester's lawyer. And Costello wanted the D. A. to promise Gwen a suspended sentence. In exchange he offered her testimony against you, as state's evidence!"

"Against . . . me?"

"You heard it right. The lawyer promised that Mrs. Lester would unburden herself of the whole story of the killing, in which she is supposed to have been only an unwilling accessory, by the way, in return for the promise of clemency."

Philip's face was white. "Is the . . . is the District Attorney going to go through with it?"

Piper shrugged his shoulders. "He asked my advice on the matter. You know, Seymour, it's about time you told us the truth about you and Gwen Lester. Don't you see, that woman is pinning the rap on you, just like Ruth Snyder tried to do on Judd Gray? She wants you to suffer while she goes scot-free . . . to marry Costello, most likely."

Piper drew closer to the cot. "Come on, Seymour. What did you do after you had laid the unconscious body of Gerald Lester on the runway? Where was Mrs. Lester?"

Philip shuddered. "Where was Gwen? Just where she always has been, taking care of Gwen. So this is the second time that beautiful devil has made a fool out of me. The second time . . ."

"Tell us, Seymour." Piper's voice was honeyed.

"I'll tell you. What difference does it make? She'd like to see me go to the chair. No, she wouldn't. I'll bet she'd be moderately unhappy that night, and unable to sleep until after she knew the session up at Sing Sing was over. Unless she forgot which night it was. She's always been like that, Gwen has. And I've always loved her!

"You see, a long time ago, Gwen White and I were engaged. I was in law-school then. We were sweethearts, more than sweethearts. But Gwen's father was an old tyrant, and she insisted on our keeping it a secret. He had other plans for her, and she always said that she'd have to win him over."

Philip Seymour paused, and then plunged on. "She was always going to get his consent, always going to win him over. But she never did.

"Well, we waited, and waited. Gwen loved me, as much as she is capable of loving anyone. But she ran around with a lot of other fellows, telling me that it was to keep her father from suspecting us. You see, in those days I was even poorer than I am now. And her father made money, and lived for money.

"Then it happened. One day, without a bit of warning, Gwen wrote me a sweet little note saying that she was going to marry Jerry Lester on the twenty-first of June and that she hoped we'd always be the best of friends, and she wanted me to come to the wedding."

"Yes?"

"I went to that wedding. With a gun in my pocket. And when I saw her standing there, so radiant and happy, next to big, handsome Jerry Lester, who had just been taken into her father's firm as partner . . . I couldn't do it. I couldn't shoot that beautiful, white picture-book girl . . . though I knew her to be a traitorous little tramp. I just sat there and watched her marry the greatest catch on Long Island, and pretty soon I got sick and walked out and nobody noticed me. And I never saw Gwen Lester again until yesterday morning when she called me up out of a clear sky and begged for my help. Hearing her husky little voice over the phone made me forget everything I'd ever sworn."

"I understand," said Piper casually. "But weren't you pretty violent about losing her when she married? Unless there was a reason why you belonged to each other?"

Philip looked up, startled. "There was. It was one of those things. Nothing vulgar about it, at the time. We were in love, and we couldn't marry, and so we ran away one week-end and pledged our lives to one another above the Hudson River, in the moonlight. It was very beautiful, then. We lived together. There were other week-ends. It was only to be until her father could be won over, Gwen insisted. Well, he won her over."

Seymour drew a crumpled pack of cigarettes from under his pillow, and took one between fingers that were none too steady. "I don't know why I'm telling you this," he said with his face to the wall. "Nobody else ever heard it. But I'm through being a fool. I confessed to that murder yesterday to save Gwen Lester. It seemed the thing to do. It was a grand gesture to make, heaping coals of fire on her head and all that sort of rot. But all last night in this dark hole I was remembering things I'd read about the electric chair, and then to have Gwen offer to sell me to insure her own freedom . . ."

"Will you help us, then," said Piper slowly, "to pin her husband's murder on her? If she did it alone, then she must pay for it alone. Suppose I could promise you clemency . . . ?"

"Then I'd be playing Judas, too, wouldn't I?" Seymour shook his head. "Besides, you know the truth, if you want to believe it. I left Lester unconscious. I think his wife slipped back to kill him, but I didn't see her. We met outside Hemingway's office, just as I said. She was agitated. So was I. That's all I know."

"Is it, now?" Piper didn't wait for an answer. "Well, young man, it would be better for you if you'd help us. Chivalry is very fine, but not when you face the blackout. Maybe you'll be changing your mind, and if you do, just send for me."

Miss Withers and the Inspector left the young lawyer lying there on his narrow bunk, with his face to the wall.

"Still think he didn't do it?" Piper wanted to know as Schmaltz let them out of the cell block.

Miss Withers shook her head doubtfully. "I don't know. But somehow, I wish he hadn't said that Gwen did it. That wasn't like him, not a bit. . . ."

"Men change their ideas when the Chair stares them in the face," Piper told her. "Then it's everyone for himself and the devil take the hindmost. Well, we've got to step back to my office for a minute, and then we're off for the Aquarium. I'd still like a bit of a chat with Hemingway."

They passed quickly over the enclosed bridge, the famous Bridge of Sighs, that connects the Tombs with the Criminal Courts Building and offices. A few minutes later they were in Piper's office, its walls lined with glass cases containing exhibits which Miss Withers found gruesome yet fascinating. She noted dozens of revolvers, of varying makes, a knife or two rusty with brownish stains, a coil of silk rope, a hatchet . . . and a sash-weight.

"Those are murder instruments I've collected in fifteen years on the Homicide Squad," said Piper. "Your hatpin will be an added feature, won't it?" He rang a bell on his desk as Miss Withers shivered.

"Send in Casey," ordered the Inspector. In a moment a ruddy officer appeared in the door, and saluted before Piper's desk. He nodded politely at Miss Withers and she recognized the uniformed man who had been on guard at the door of the Aquarium tanks with Rollins, and who had been sent on some mysterious errand involving stockings.

"Well, Casey, so you came through? Tell us about it, and make it quick."

Casey reached for a well-thumbed notebook, but the Inspector waved it aside. "Just the outline, Casey."

"Very good, sir. I went, as you ordered, and made the acquaintance of Mrs. Lester's maid, sir. It was the upstairs maid, a Belle Gayly, sir. Before she knew I was an officer, she had talked to me about her mistress. Telling me all about the quarrels Mr. and Mrs. Lester used to have, sir, and about the woman Mr. Lester was supposed to be keeping in the Village somewhere, and . . ."

"Re-enter Marian Templeton," hazarded Piper. "Go on. . . ."

"And then I told her that she'd be arrested as a witness unless she helped the police, and she consented to bring me the stockings her mistress had worn home yesterday afternoon. They'd been changed right away, as soon as Mrs. Lester got in, but they were in the laundress' bag. . . ."

"Did Miss Gayly mention seeing her mistress come in yesterday?"

"She did. Mrs. Lester was crying, said the maid. She came home about five o'clock, alone in a taxi. The extras were already out on the street, and that's why the servants were noticing, sir.''

"Very good, Casey. If you remember to give your testimony accurately and fully in court I'll try to have you put on my squad permanently, and in plain clothes. That's all.''

The big cop swung proudly out of the door. Piper pressed the button again. "Is Von Donnen out to lunch? Fine, will you ask him to step in here at once?''

Piper turned to Miss Withers. "Max Van Donnen is the finest laboratory expert that any criminal bureau ever had,'' he assured her. There was a rap at the door, and a little weazened man crept in, peering from behind thick lenses at the Inspector. He looked rather more like a push-cart peddler than a laboratory chemist. But his speech was low, resonant, and richly guttural.

"I haf the stockings analyzed,'' he announced when introductions had been completed.

"Great,'' shouted Piper. "And you found traces of blood on the left one? People are always trying to wash away blood with warm water, and it never takes it all out. . . .''

"Nein . . . there wass no blood on this stockings,''-corrected Herr Von Donnen. "No sign of blood. But something more stranger. That spot was stiff with dried water . . . water faintly tainted with the excreta of fish!''

Piper lit a cigar to hide his honest astonishment. "Tell me, then, Herr Von Donnen, was this substance similar to that which might reasonably be expected to accumulate in an Aquarium tank?''

The little man nodded so hard that his glasses slid along his nose. "To tell you the truth, Inspector, an Aquarium tank is the only place in the wide, wide world where such an accumulation could occur.''

"Very good,'' said Piper slowly, throwing away his cigar. "You'll be called upon, I fancy, to testify to that in court. Turn the stockings over to the Property Clerk downstairs again, and thank you very much. Good day. . . .''

When the little man had gone the Inspector turned to Miss Withers. His lower lip protruded, as it always did when he was excited.

"I guess that busts up Mrs. Gwen Lester's story that she didn't go inside the door of the tanks,'' he announced triumphantly. "Why, that report is twice as good as one of bloodstains!"

Miss Withers saw his point. "Maybe . . . then maybe Philip Seymour is right in saying Gwen did it," she said thoughtfully. "Unless . . ."

"Unless nothing," Piper told her. "This case is ripe for the grand jury already."

11

## The Tumbler in the Booth

IN the long silence that followed the Inspector's words, the telephone buzzed like an angry snake. Miss Withers jumped nervously as Piper lifted the receiver. "Hello," he shouted.

"Is this Inspector Piper?" came a sweet voice from over the wire.

"You must have asked for me in order to get put on this line, so you already know that this is Inspector Piper," said the detective testily. "What do you want?"

"Are you the gentleman that asked us to trace a phone call that was made yesterday noon to White and Lester at Worth 4438? This is the supervisor of central telephone office speaking. . . ."

"Yes, yes . . . of course, madam. You got the number?"

"Excuse it please, but I was not allowed to give out the number until the manager had made sure who you were. You see, so many unauthorized persons attempt to have numbers traced . . ."

"My God, madam, I don't want a history of your life. Have you got that number?"

". . . that we have to be very, very careful," continued the serene young voice at the distant end of the wire. "Please excuse it, Inspector Piper. The call you referred to came from Hanover 0200, which is a pay station . . ."

"A pay station *where*?" pleaded the Inspector.

"A pay station located in a booth in the New York Aquarium in Battery Park," cooed the voice. "Thank you, please."

"Glug," said Piper incoherently as he replaced the instrument. He told Miss Withers what he had just heard, and they looked at each other for a moment.

"I think we'd better go down to the Aquarium anyway," said Miss Withers.

"I think we better had, too," said Inspector Piper.

Half an hour later they stood before the single public phone booth of the Aquarium. It was of stained oak, of the general shape and size of an upended coffin, with a glass door behind with a young man was at the moment attempting to convince an unseen young woman of something or other. Then he grew restless under the unwavering gaze of the Inspector, and shortly afterward hung up the receiver and left.

The Inspector waved the door back and forth a few times, and after the air had cleared he stepped inside. For the sake of anyone who might be passing he lifted the receiver from the hook, but all time with a pocket flash he was scrutinizing the walls of the little cell.

Then he opened the door. "I was hoping to find a scribble on the wall above the phone," he told Miss Withers, "possibly of the Lester office number, or something. You can learn a lot from scribbles sometimes, but there weren't any here. They've tacked oilcloth over the wall, to keep people from writing there."

He saw Miss Withers' eyes glisten, and smiled. "No, it's not new oilcloth, either. It's been there for years. But there is one thing of interest there. Take the flash and see if you notice it."

Miss Withers took the flash, and entered the booth. A moment later she came out. "Nothing there unless you count this as something," she said, and she showed Piper an ordinary tumbler, a water glass. "It was down behind the door. . . ."

Piper's face was dark. "And so you had to handle it and get your prints all over it, yes?" He took it gingerly from her, and wrapped it in a handkerchief. "I don't know what it may mean, but it means something. People don't need a glass in a phone booth. Unless they plan on a long chat in the stuffy place, and take a glass of ice water along, which seems doubtful to me. Of course, it may be nothing . . ."

"Anyway," Miss Withers announced as they went in search of Hemingway, "we've seen the spot where the phone call originated. Somebody stood there and called Lester to warn him that his wife was in the building, meeting another man. Now if we knew who that somebody was . . ."

"If wishes were fishes we'd have some fried," scoffed the Inspector. "We've got to find out who made that phone call. And we will, or my name isn't Oscar Piper. At least, we know it was a man. . . ."

He stopped short. "Let's have another look at Hemingway, for luck."

Bertrand B. Hemingway, they were informed by a chastened looking Fink, was not in.

"Very well," said Piper politely. "We'll just wait for him." And he shouldered his way through the door marked "Bertrand B. Hemingway, Director." Miss Withers followed, and they came face to face with the Director. He was picking up bits of glass from the floor.

"Just a broken fish bowl," he explained quickly. "I was afraid I'd get the soles of my shoes cut. And what can I do for you today? I'd hoped that we were through with all this awful publicity. If it hadn't been for your men at the door of this place today the reporters would have run me ragged. . . ."

Miss Withers understood why the few visitors in the Aquarium were posed so nonchalantly against the pillars.

"You can help the course of justice," said Piper in his sweetest voice, "by answering just one question."

"Gladly, gladly," said Bertrand B. Hemingway. "Have a chair first, won't you? Sorry that I haven't a Camel to offer, you . . wasn't that what you asked for last night? Would a Lucky do? Now, what's the question?"

The little man had struck an attitude. Miss Withers glanced around the long room. She could never feel at ease here, she knew.

"The question? Oh, yes." Piper smiled as if in amusement at its unimportance. "The question? Yes, I wanted to ask you, Mr. Hemingway, to ask you . . . just why you concealed your stock deals with Gerald Lester, yesterday? Why it was necessary, or why you thought it necessary, to claim you hadn't seen him in months when he sold out your account three weeks ago and ruined you?''

Bertrand B. Hemingway collapsed like a pricked balloon. He gasped like one of his own fish out of water.

"Come clean, Mr. Hemingway. Why was it?''

The little man puffed vigorously on a dead cigarette. "I was afraid," he finally admitted. But his strength and self-possession had returned.

"Afraid of what? Afraid of suffering the consequences for what you did to . . .''

"No, not that. I didn't kill him, and you shan't trick me into confessing. You shan't! I was afraid that you would question me and drag me to jail and to court, and dig into my life and stir up all sorts of trouble. I hoped that if I didn't mention the stock deals that you wouldn't find out about them . . .''

"We find out about everything," Piper told him. "Go on.''

"And most of all I was afraid of losing my Directorate here. Not for this murder investigation. That is considered an unfortunate accident. But if the Board of Trustees should learn I'd been gambling on the Stock Exchange, they'd oust me in two seconds. You don't know my Board of Trustees, Inspector.''

"I have no desire to know them," Piper told him. "We'll talk about this another time, Mr. Director. I advise, however, that you rack your brain and try to remember any more details affecting this case which you haven't told us.''

Hemingway showed astonishment. "But I thought the case was settled? With the Seymour fellow pleading guilty, and so forth. The late papers said so!''

"The papers say what they guess or what I tell them," said Piper. "I'm not so satisfied that Gwen and Seymour did the job. Tell me . . .'' he was very casual . . . "tell me, can you remember any details about how they looked when you glad-handed them into your office yesterday noon? Any little detail that might help the investigation? Did they look guilty? Any marks of a struggle on either of them?''

Hemingway paused, but he did not fall into the trap. "No, I can't say that they showed any signs of a struggle, or looked particularly guilty. They were both upset, I realize now, but not panicky. They seemed polite, and interested . . .''

"Yes, of course." Piper rose from his chair. "Please don't leave town, Hemingway. You'll testify at the grand jury hearing shortly, and at the trial if there is one. Good day."

But instead of leaving the gloomy and almost deserted place, Piper led Miss Withers to the little tank under the stair. It was empty now, and the penguins swam merrily in their own rightful pool in the center of the big hall. Before the door that led to the tanks lounged a plain-clothes man. Miss Withers realized that she was getting to be an insider, for she could recognize a plain-clothes man a block away. Whenever one sees a man who looks as if he had a trade, but weren't working at it, and a man who hangs about as if he had a place to go if he only wanted to, that man is a detective, she told herself.

The plain-clothes man did not salute, but simply strolled on. Piper and Miss Withers stared for a few minutes into the empty tank. With the water drained away, and the circulating current shut off, it was just a square tank, lined on the back and both sides with cunningly painted plaster and rock to simulate the natural habitat of some fish or other. There was an inlet pipe at the bottom and an outlet at the top. Now that the water was gone they could look through and see the cat-walk, and the tangle of pipes above, faintly in the dim light of the runway.

"They went over the bottom with a fine-tooth comb this morning," Piper told Miss Withers. "But my boys found only fish slime."

They went through the door, up the fatal steps, and stared at the curving runway. "And if only we'd searched the place instantly on finding the body," Piper said ruefully, "we'd have caught the murderer somewhere back here. . . ."

"All you'd have caught would have been the big Swede ichthyologist and the pickpocket," Miss Withers told him. "And neither of them did it."

"But what dumped the body of Lester down into the tank, while you watched just outside?" Piper wanted to know.

"Ten to one it was the meddlesome penguins," she told him. "Anyway, it wasn't the murderer, because he was outside and far away by then."

"Perhaps he was *outside*," Piper hazarded, "but I doubt if he was far away. That's the devil of this case. The murderer is right here, among us, so to speak. And I can't lay my hand on him, or her. Everything points at Gwen and Seymour. They had motive and opportunity. Everybody else, it seems, had opportunity, and a lot of them had motive. I'm not satisfied . . .''

He went on, leaning against the door. "In most murder cases, we have definite things to work with. A murder is premeditated. The victim is lured to a certain place, murder is committed with tools which can be traced, and a good clue or two is left. The whole thing is a matter of finding out who had a reason to bump the victim, who had an opportunity, and how he did it. But here . . .''

He shruged his shoulders. "No premeditation, because nobody could have known that Gerald Lester would be lying unconscious in this little hideaway. Not even Philip Seymour, supposing that Philip did make that phone call to lure his girl's husband down to the Aquarium, which seems impossible. Nobody would plan to commit a murder here. It was a case of seizing an unusual opportunity . . . and of seizing a god-sent weapon which you had provided, Miss Withers. That hatpin made things a thousand times easier for the killer. He had only to drop it, and everything was clear for him but the getaway. He could never be traced through it.''

"How do you know for sure that Gerald Lester was killed while unconscious?" Miss Withers wanted to know.

"First, because it would be practically impossible to stab a man in the ear if he were conscious. The victim would struggle and break away. No, it would take a swift, sure blow. After the pin had been punched in by some heartless devil, and then driven home with a whack from the flat of the hand, it was drawn out, dipped in the penguin pool to cleanse it . . . accounting for the few traces of blood there . . . and then returned to the stair where it had been found. Somebody was doing all that while you hunted for the hatpin. You haven't a vague memory of anyone at the foot of the stair?''

"Let me think," Miss Withers said quietly. "I believe I've got something. Not just what you hoped for. It's the opposite, in fact. But I know this fact. We were up on the balcony, the children and I, hunting the pin for at least twenty minutes before we got to the foot of the stair where it turned out to be. The stair is visible from any part of the balcony, you know.

And during all that time I kept my eyes open, for the pick-pocket episode had made me restless, and I was afraid that someone would find the hatpin and take it away before we found it.

"And I know this one thing, that all during that time, up to and including the moment when little black Abraham found it, there wasn't another person on these stairs above us, nor near the foot of them, though of course there were visitors among the tanks and cases downstairs . . . is that any help?"

"I don't know," Piper admitted. "That would go to show that the murder was committed earlier than I thought . . . long before the body was pushed into the tank, if you saw it fall. The murder must have been committed during the pick-pocket chase, or even before!"

They were leaving the murder scene. Miss Withers started to follow Piper down the three high steps and then suddenly she vented a gentle scream.

Her eyes had accidently turned upward at the rough, unfinished bottom of the stairs above. And they had been caught and held by a ribbon of light. . . .

As Piper whirled in the doorway she searched her purse for a pencil. She found a colored automatic one, and poked it upward at the thin crack in the wood through which blazed illumination. . . .

"Go around to the stair and see which step this comes out on," she whispered. Piper left her, and she poked the pencil up through the narrow crack and then let it fall from her fingers. She was soon at the Inspector's side, at the foot of the stair.

He was staring down at her red and black eversharp, which lay on the bottom step. The crack was hidden by an overhang.

"How big was the garnet on your hatpin?" He wanted to know.

"No bigger than the eraser on this pencil." She picked up the little writing instrument and replaced it in her bag.

"It was on this step, the bottom one, that little black Abraham found my hatpin," Miss Withers remarked soberly.

"I thought of that," said Inspector Piper. He fumbled for another of his everlasting cigars, but he did not light it.

"Then the murderer needn't have come out on the stair at all, or even approached the foot of the stair," Miss Withers reasoned. "He might possibly have been in behind the tanks, or perhaps in the doorway where Olaavson hung his denim overalls, when I saw the body fall into the tank."

"I also thought of that," Piper said.

There was a long silence. "Do you think that the murderer could have hidden behind those overalls, or just stood back under the steps in the darkness, while we all pushed in behind Donovan to look at the corpse . . . and then walked out innocently with the rest of us when you got here?"

Piper shrugged his shoulders. "I think we ought to have a couple of cups of coffee," he said at last. And they left the Aquarium.

12

# The Patch in the Lute

NEITHER Miss Withers nor the Inspector was to have much solid comfort from the steaming coffee and sandwiches which soon appeared before the two weary sleuths. For on the heels of the coffee there arrived in the little waterfront café—an indistinguishable wailing, which shortly resolved itself into "Extry paper . . . read all about it . . . Lester murder solved. . . ."

Then a grubby-faced urchin poked his head in the door, brandishing a sheaf of poisonous-looking green tabloids. "Paper, mister?"

The Inspector bought two of them, handing one to Miss Withers. "I know what this is," he told her wearily. "Leave it to the D.A.'s office to mangle things all up."

The headline was plain enough. "TWO WOMEN BATTLED FOR LESTER'S LOVE" it announced in three inch letters. Beneath it were three pictures, one showing Gwen Lester at Palm Beach in a bathing suit that bared most of her back, one showing Gwen in her wedding veil and gown, and one spread all across the bottom of the page showing a girl sitting on a stone balustrade outside some city building with her legs disposed to their best advantage, and captioned "Marian Templeton, office-wife, admits love nest with dead man, shown here after questioning by Prosecuting Attorney. . . ."

Piper turned over a page angrily. "So the Lester case is solved by our bright light of Tammany Hall, Mr. Tom Roche, huh?" He glowered, and then read aloud . . . "At a late hour this afternoon, announcement was made from official sources that Miss Marian Templeton, secretary of Gerald Lester, had admitted illicit relations with the deceased over a period of five years, and has told of Lester's breaking off relations recently because of threats from his wife, Gwen Lester."

He cleared his throat and went on. "This recent development in the case comes as a result of a clever investigation after the Sherlock Holmes method of operatives of the Prosecuting Attorney, Mr. Thomas M. Roche, under the personal direction of Mr. Roche." Piper grunted derisively. "Got his name in twice in one sentence, so Roche will be happy now." Then he read on.

"As soon as it was definitely established that Gerald Lester, Wall Street broker and playboy, had met his end by a stiletto thrust through the left ear into his brain, agents of Mr. Roche's office took up the case in earnest, supplementing the efforts of the regular police forces. Search of Miss Templeton's apartment in the art colony of Greenwich Village disclosed wearing apparel belonging to Gerald Lester in the closets and bureau drawers, including a hat marked with his initials. (Get that, Miss Withers, a hat marked with his initials) . . ."

"I got it," she said.

"When confronted by this evidence, Marian Templeton confessed to her relations with her employer and after questioning divulged further information concerning incidents in the domestic life of the blue-blood Lesters upon which the Prosecutor is acting at the present moment. An early and startling arrest is promised by Mr. Roche, details of which for obvious reasons may not be announced, although Mr. Roche intimated that it will be in a direction hitherto ignored by the regular police investigation."

"Which is us?" asked Miss Withers.

"Which is us," Piper told her savagely. "I'll bet that the

root of the whole thing is that Taylor, the operative I put on the Templeton girl, talked to somebody in the D.A.'s office. That means back to a beat in the suburbs for him. And it means that Gwen Lester is going to be arrested by that bungling idiot!''

"But suppose she is guilty?" Miss Withers wanted to know.

"If she's guilty there's all the more reason for letting her go free until she incriminates herself. We'll never get a jury to convict her, or Philip Seymour either, on such flimsy circumstantial evidence. Seymour knows that. That is why he confessed. He knew that he could repudiate his confession at the last moment, particularly since he confessed to a mode of killing that wasn't used. He's a lawyer. He knows that if he stands trial and is acquitted he can never be arrested for that murder again, not even if he confesses to it, and not even if we produce non-shatterable evidence. He knows he's safer in jail than anywhere else, and it builds public sympathy, too."

Miss Withers felt that matters were rapidly getting too deep for her to follow. She suddenly realized that she was very very weary, and that somehow the day had slipped by. She folded up her copy of the green tabloid and put it under her arm. "I might as well go home," she suggested. "I've got some notes on the day's questioning, and I suppose you'll want them typed out. . . ."

Piper nodded. "You know, Miss Withers, it's been a good thing that the regular police secretary is having his tonsils removed at St. Luke's this week, because you've been twice as much help. You have a certain flair for this, you know? And a good many times an outsider like you will notice a thing or two that we miss in the course of regular routine investigation. It's been a big help. . . ."

He was paying their checks. Miss Withers stopped short. "You mean that it's all over as far as I'm concerned?"

"It's all over as far as anybody is concerned," the Inspector told her. "All that remains is to dig up a few more proofs that Tom Roche can put before a jury. And that won't be long. Philip Seymour and the Lester woman are already starting to blame it on each other. That's the beginning of the end in all these triangle cases. Gwen will incriminate Philip and Philip will incriminate Gwen, and they'll both face a trip up the river and maybe worse. I was stalling along trying to get complete evidence on them before making public announcements, but as long as the D.A. has spilled the beans, I'm turning over what evidence I have for the grand jury, and we wash our hands of the whole thing. See?"

"I see," Miss Withers said bitterly. "I see that you are taking the easy way out, and choosing the most obvious suspects. You are bound to treat this case as if it were just another triangle case, as you call it. And deep down in your heart, if a detective has any heart, you suspect that Gwen and Philip didn't do it. Don't tell me any different. You know that there is more to the murder of Jerry Lester than meets the eye. And now, just because the Prosecutor announces that his case is complete, you are going to drop the case just where it begins to get interesting, and let two people suffer for a crime you aren't sure they committed. Isn't that true?"

Inspector Piper shrugged his shoulders. "You don't differentiate between belief and evidence, and between duty and individual ideas. As soon as I get to my office, or get in touch with it by telephone, I'll be officially notified by the Commissioner that the case is closed and that I am to turn in my evidence to the D.A. In other words, I'll be told to quit."

"I won't be ordered to quit, though," Miss Withers pointed out acidly. "And I'm not going to see a miscarriage of justice if I can help it. So there!"

And she stalked down the street toward the subway, rode northward for twenty minutes on a Broadway-Seventh Avenue Express, and got off at Seventy-second.

•   •   •   •   •

At that same moment Gwen Lester was sitting in the depths of an enormous easy chair in her own drawing-room, with the colored sheets of a late tabloid newspaper scattered around her slim feet. The tall windows which looked out on Central Park to the east were mantled with heavy drapes, to shut out the crying of "Extry" which rose at varying intervals.

Across the long room a man moved restlessly, his hands locked behind his back.

Gwen broke the silence. "Anyway . . . anyway they haven't come yet, and here it is seven o'clock!"

Barry Costello shot her a glance of sympathy. "They'll come, all right. Tom Roche will want to make this arrest in time for the Sunday papers. You saw his announcement in the extra, didn't you?"

Gwen nodded her shapely head. "If I could only get money enough I'd run away," she announced. "With funds I could get to Mineola and hire a plane . . . but I haven't a cent. Jerry's money is tied up, what there is of it. There's only his insurance, and the Stock Exchange seat, which ought to be worth a lot. But . . ."

"By the way," asked Costello softly, "did your husband have a lot of insurance?"

Gwen paused. "I think it was seventy-five thousand. I got him to double it last year, because he was approaching his thirty-first birthday when the rate jumps. Why?"

"That's bad," the Irishman told her. "They won't pay the premium, now, without a fight. You see, it's a bad combination, your urging your husband to take more insurance and then your being held for his murder. Insurance companies are . . ."

Gwen looked at him from beneath eyelids darkened by weeping. "You think I did it, don't you? Just like everybody else. And you aren't trying to figure out how to prove I'm innocent, you're just trying to save my life because you're my lawyer!"

"I'm a lawyer, yes. Because I happened to be on the spot and was lucky enough to be of service to you, Mrs. Lester. But I'd rather be your friend." He crossed swiftly to her side. "I'm *going* to be your friend, Gwen. Because you need one. And I'll tell you this much, I'll believe anything you say." Costello caught at her cigarette, which was burning merrily into the varnish of a side-table, and dropped it neatly into a tray. "Tell me, not as a client to a lawyer but as . . . as one friend to another. Did you kill your husband?"

Gwen gave him a long, straight look. Her heavy lids raised, and her lips parted tremulously. Her filmy green lounging pajamas fell away from her throat.

"As God is my judge, I didn't," she said solemnly. "I never did Gerald Lester any wrong except by marrying him in the first place. But I don't expect you or anyone else to believe that. The detectives won't believe it. The judge and

the jury won't believe it. They'll send me to the chair. . . ."
She was breaking, and Costello knew it.

He took her slim hand between both of his. "I believe
you," he told her earnestly. "Nobody in the world is believ-
ing in you any stronger than I am, darlin' . . . for I feel in my
heart of hearts that your little hands are innocent of blood.
And I'm the one that's going to keep you from going to the
chair. Believe me."

"I . . . I'll try," said Gwen Lester. "God knows I haven't
got anyone else. Even the servants have left, after all the
questions and fussing around of the detectives here this afternoon. And now the police are coming back for me . . ."

Barry Costello took both her hands in his. "You know I'd
gladly go with them to the Tombs in your place, if I could!"

Gwen nodded blindly, her eyes wet. Sympathy, honest
sympathy, was the one thing hardest to bear, the one thing
that made her break. Suddenly she turned and buried her face
in Costello's shoulder, clinging with her fingers to the lapels
of his coat. He smelled comfortingly of a faint scent of
perfumed soap, and a strong scent of tobacco.

Costello leaned back, letting her weight come on his chest.
Gwen felt the astonishing strength of the man as he held her
there. "Don't cry darlin', don't be doing that at all . . . come
now! Barry will see you through. Trust him."

With a sort of numbed surprise, Gwen felt him searching
for her lips. Limply she yielded them, with a mental reserva-
tion. She felt like a chip, tossed upon waters turbulent and
swift, toward a hidden goal. They clung there, the beautiful
young widow and her self-appointed lawyer, until the screaming clatter of the doorbell came between them. Gwen went
rigid with fear, and Costello with a comforting grip of her
hand moved toward the door.

"May you never be sorry for that kiss," he said tenderly.
Then his face hardened as he turned toward the door. "Remember, darlin', you must refuse to talk except when I'm
present, as your lawyer. Remember!"

"I'll remember," Gwen promised voicelessly. Her eyes
were on the opening door, on the blue-clad policeman she
expected.

But Miss Hildegarde Withers marched in, with a nod to

Costello. She came over to Gwen, who sat up stiffly in her chair.

"Do you know who I am?"

Gwen nodded. "You're the school-teacher who told the Inspector what I said when I looked in the tank yesterday. . . ."

Miss Withers nodded. "I did so! Because it was my duty, and besides, there were twenty people who heard you cry out 'What have we done?' But that isn't why I came here. . . ."

Gwen nodded. "That's right. Just why did you come here?"

Miss Withers glared at Barry Costello. "Young man, there are likely to be detectives in this apartment in a few minutes. Why don't you wipe that lipstick off your cheek?" Then she turned to Gwen.

"I came here because I happen to live three blocks away, and because I heard that they are going to arrest you tonight for your husband's murder. I thought maybe a word of warning would be a good idea, but I see that you have an advisor, and that you've already seen the paper."

Gwen was wondering. "But still I don't see why you should come to warn me. . . ."

"Because, young woman, whatever you've done I don't think you killed your husband. Not even if Philip Seymour says so before detectives. . . ."

Gwen shook her head slowly. "Phil didn't say that. You must be lying . . . Phil couldn't say that. He's not . . . it's not the kind of a thing Phil would do to me. And it isn't true, besides . . ."

"He did say it," Miss Withers told her shortly. "I heard him. And I thought it would be a good thing for you to know before they took you to the Tombs. And what's more, I don't know that I exactly blame Seymour for saying it. Doesn't that work both ways? Maybe Philip was surprised to hear that *you* had bargained for clemency. . . ."

Gwen's eyebrows shot up. "I? . . . ." And then the doorbell once more shrilled through the long room. There was a long moment of hesitation, and then Costello moved toward it.

"You let me go," Miss Withers ordered. "Stay with Gwen a minute. . . ."

She swung the hall door open, and there stood Oscar Piper, Inspector of Detectives. He brushed swiftly past her.

"You here, Miss Withers? What in blazes for? Anyway, don't tell me now. Where's Mrs. Lester?"

He dashed into the drawing-room. "Excuse this haste, ma'm. But you don't know what's down in the lobby. There are twenty newspaper reporters, twice as many photographers, and even a sound newsreel truck, preparing for the big event. Even the Commissioner is there, though he tipped me a wink when he saw me slip by, and I know that he isn't happy at being a party to this dodge of Tom Roche's.

"Don't you see? They're waiting for Tom Roche to drive up in his limousine, and then march up at the head of a lot of the D.A.'s detectives to arrest you, amid a blaze of flashlights, fireworks, speeches, and so forth. Can't you see the headlines over photos of you being dragged in chains to a police car . . . 'TIGER WOMAN NABBED BY VIGILANT DISTRICT ATTORNEY'?"

He paused for a second. "You know what that'll mean. It'll build public feeling against you, maybe swing a jury. That publicity may send you to the chair. . . ."

"What do you care?" Gwen Lester wanted to know.

"I don't," said the Inspector calmly. "But I don't like fireworks and speeches. I don't like statements to the press about how the D.A.'s office steps in and solves a crime over the heads of the regular police force. Therefore, I arrest you, Gwen Lester, for the murder of your husband, Gerald Lester!

"The front lobby is blocked, and I couldn't take you out that way without being over-ruled by the Commissioner himself or one of his deputies. They're waiting now for the big shot to get here."

He came closer. "But if there's a service elevator that goes to the basement, or any other way for us to sneak out of here, I promise to take you down to Headquarters with no publicity at all, and to give you a square break, which is more than you can count on from the big guys. How about it?"

Gwen looked at Costello, who nodded eagerly. But she shook her head.

"It's no use, Inspector. I'd go with you. But there's no dumbwaiter, no rear stair, and the service elevators are operated only in the daytime, and that by one of the regular boys. Besides, they run right into the main lobby, too. There's only one way out of here, and that's the regular entrance."

Piper chewed his cigar savagely, and then threw it across the room in the general direction of the fireplace. "Then we're stuck, and you'll have to face the music," he told Gwen.

Miss Withers took off her hat. "I've got an idea," she offered.

• • • • •

Ten minutes later a nervous Irish lawyer and a woman in green lounging pajamas heard the doorbell ring for the third time that night. Costello waited until the second signal, which was followed by a gruff order to open the door before it was broken in.

He swung it wide, and was immediately seized by two stalwart plain-clothes men. The corridor outside was jammed with people, but a lane opened——

Then a little man in complete evening dress, from silk hat to patent leather pumps, strolled into the apartment. He was followed by half a dozen more detectives, by two photographers, and by a little group of sheepish reporters.

He stalked into the drawing-room, and struck a pose before the woman who waited in the big easy chair, holding an unsmoked cigarette in her hand.

"Gwen Lester," announced Tom Roche in ringing tones, "as part of my duty toward the people of the City of New York, I order these officers to arrest you for the wilful murder of your husband, Gerald Lester." He was ready to duck at a sign of trouble.

There were two hollow explosions, followed by blinding, glaring flashes of white light, and the photographers leaped back through the doorway, clutching their precious cameras.

"Put the handcuffs on her, men," ordered Tom Roche. "And be careful, for she's dangerous. . . ." He turned to a thin, tallish gentleman who sported a gardenia in his buttonhole, and who now put in a bored appearance in the doorway. "Commissioner, here's your prisoner! Gwen Lester, the Tiger Woman. . . ."

There was a long pause. Then from the street outside came three long blasts of a taxi siren, and the roar of a motor.

"What are you waiting for?" demanded the District Attorney. "Go on, officers!"

"Wait a minute, chief," said the foremost plain-clothes man. "That don't look like the Lester woman to me. It don't look a bit like the picture in the papers . . . and it ain't the woman who was here this afternoon when we searched the place!"

A titter went up from the cohorts of the Fourth Estate. But Tom Roche was raging. He blazed at the woman in the chair. "Are you Gwen Lester? Don't trifle with the law, my good woman."

"Trifling with the law is the last thing I'd think of doing," Miss Withers answered him politely. "No, I'm not Gwen Lester. I never said I was. But she lent me those green lounging pajamas, though I think they're a little loose around the hips. . . ."

"Answer me! Where is Mrs. Lester?" He waved his hand, and detectives ran like frightened deer to search the far corners of the apartment. Roche was positively vibrating. . . .

Miss Withers smiled, faintly. Again she was having the time of her life. "I don't know where Gwen Lester is at the present moment," she said softly, "but when she went out of her ten minutes ago in my hat and overcoat, she was under arrest and in custody of Inspector Piper of the Homicide Squad. Why don't you look for her down at Police Headquarters?"

There was a long silence, broken only by sounds from the hitherto bored Commissioner suggesting that he had just laid the egg . . . a large egg, of which he was very proud.

"Arrest this woman," screamed Tom Roche. "Arrest her for resisting an officer, aiding and abetting a criminal, accessory after the fact . . ."

The Commissioner came slowly forward, still trying to keep a straight face. He put his hand gently on the District Attorney's shoulder. "My private opinion would be, Tom, that you've sufficiently established your asininity already tonight. Think of the newspaper boys you insisted on bringing!"

They both turned toward the hallway, but already the squad

of reporters had disappeared in the direction of the nearest telephone booth.

The Prosecuting Attorney made a gesture with his well-manicured fingers indicative of chagrin. "I suppose you're right," he admitted, "but darn it all to hell, anyway!"

## 13

# A White Knight Goes Riding

"I SUPPOSE you know what you're up to, Piper." It was ten o'clock of the next morning, a bright Sabbath. "I *hope* you know, anyway. For your sake and the sake of the department." There was no answer.

The Commissioner rose from behind his barricade of telephone and onyx desk pens and moved over to stare out of the long window into the vacant downtown streets. "Don't think I'm sore, Piper, because I'm not. I didn't want to be in on Tom Roche's publicity hunt, and I was tickled at the way it came out. The arrest was made from this office, just as it should have been. That was a smart sneak you made with your prisoner, dressing her up like the school-teacher."

Oscar Piper, Inspector of Detectives, sat on the edge of his Commissioner's desk, also looking out of the window.

"Yeah, I guess I know what I'm up to," he told his superior.

"Because if you don't, you're in a tough spot," the Commissioner finished. "You've made Tom Roche the maddest man in this city. He's a hound for publicity, but it wasn't this left-handed kind that he wanted. Be sure you've got evidence enough to justify your arrests, that's all. There's motives enough in the Lester murder sure enough . . . fear, passion, and cupidity. You've got your case built up, and you've got your prisoners both under arrest. All you've got left to do is to lay your evidence before Roche so that he can get a conviction. He's sore as a boil now. Make certain your end of the job is beyond any chance of being torn apart."

"I *am* certain," said the Inspector. "There's a cast-iron case against Gwen Lester and Philip Seymour. Only it's completely circumstantial. There wasn't an eye-witness to the murder. There hardly ever is, you know. But I've got a chain of evidence that will send Gwen and her boy friend to the chair just as sure as God made little apples. Only——"

"Only what?"

"Only suppose, just for the sake of argument, that the little lady and the lawyer didn't happen to do it? Bump her husband, I mean."

The Commissioner looked annoyed. "What do you mean they didn't do it? It's open and shut, like this. Didn't the husband catch them in an assignation? Didn't they have opportunity? Didn't they have both an immediate motive and a built-up one? Remember, not only the woman's freedom, but her husband's big life insurance and the value of the seat on the Stock Exchange . . . there's motives for you. Isn't that enough, if you bring it out in the right way?"

"Sure," said Oscar Piper. "It convinces me plenty. It's too good. I've got a sort of a picture of the crime in my mind, and everything doesn't jibe perfectly. Maybe if I smoke a couple of cigars over the idea I can get it set in my mind. You see, it isn't enough for us to believe that they committed the murder, it isn't enough for us to *know* that they committed the murder. I got to know exactly how they did it, so we can prove it on 'em. Even with a confession nowadays you can't get a conviction in first-degree murder without proof and plenty of it."

Inspector Piper tipped his hat over his eyes. "Well, I'll be seeing you, chief. I'll give your love to Tom Roche if I meet him."

"Better keep from seeing him, or being seen by him, for a while," advised the Commissioner. "Don't answer your phone."

Piper grinned, and slammed the office door behind him. Ten minutes later he was in his own office. He dismissed the plain-clothes man on guard at the door, and after getting a cigar well under way, he tackled the heap of material on his desk.

It all related to the Lester case. Everything else had been sidetracked for that since the story had broken in the newspapers.

The first item was a report from the two operatives who had at his request made a complete survey of the books and papers of the Wall Street firm of White and Lester.

They found the firm solvent but not exactly prosperous, and as Piper had requested, they appended a list of the seven or eight customers who had suffered worst from the recent market crash of "bloody" October.

Five of these, Inspector Piper saw, were of the usual type, all of them men listed in the telephone directory and most of them in the credit rating books. They were quite evidently men who could afford their losses, or at least to whom the crash had not come as a terrible and final financial shock.

But the sixth, instead of appearing in the Inspector's worn copy of Dun and Bradstreet, was listed only in *Who's Who*. It was Bertrand B. Hemingway.

Piper noted that Hemingway had been taken for a toboggan ride on a certain famous radio stock which opened at ninety-four dollars a share on a Wednesday morning, and closed the next afternoon at something under thirty. As margin for his speculation in the radio stock, Hemingway had put up what stocks he owned outright, some five thousand dollars worth of them.

According to the records of White and Lester, this margin, together with some seventeen thousand dollars worth of paper profits, had vanished into thin air during those two days of trading.

Guessing is apt to be more successful in a bull market than during a crash, the Inspector decided. Hemingway had guessed that Radiozome would weather the storm, and Radiozome hadn't.

"And this is what the Director called investing a little money, huh?" mused Piper. He laid aside the papers for further perusal, and read on.

The last name on the list of heavy losers among the White and Lester clients was that of a Mr. Parson, no initial given. It had been listed in the files of White and Lester as "Mr. Lester's client—special."

The Inspector wished that he knew more about the routine of Wall Street. Maybe there was something out of the ordinary about this special account. Only he couldn't see what it was. He read on, doggedly.

Neither the telephone book, Dun and Bradstreet, nor the Social Register gave any information regarding a Mr. Parson. He had however, according to the sales slip and transaction records, been a customer of White and Lester for more than a year.

During that time on or about the fifteenth of every month he had deposited additional margin, either to bolster his account or extend his trading scope, in actual cash. There was no record that he had ever given orders for a stock to be bought outright, but had used his margin to speculate among the stocks known as "active erratics." Several times a sudden drop had wiped out his paper profits, and even encroached upon his capital, but Mr. Parson, like a good sport, had plunged back into the melee to recoup, somehow raising more capital. Most of the time, the records showed, Parson had been a good guesser. He had made substantial winnings for a while, which as a rule he applied as additional margin against the purchase of larger blocks.

There was a note from one of the police auditors to the effect that there was no record in the Lester books of any check payment at any time to Mr. Parson. He had taken, as he had paid, actual hard cash. That was an unusual thing nowadays.

But this was establishing no motive for the unknown Mr. Parson to have cherished a resentment against his broker amounting to homicidal mania. And that was what Piper had to search for.

Then he came to the records for the fatal October days when the bottom dropped out of the bull market and left the Republican party in the spot. On October 17th, Piper read, Mr. Parson had "owned" a large block, some thousand shares, of Wagner Brothers Preferred, with a cash margin against them of about fifteen thousand dollars and a potential profit of several times that much.

The statement also showed that on October 18th the firm of White and Lester had sold out the account of Mr. Parson to protect itself, but as such a loss that the original margin and paper profits were both quite thoroughly gone.

The file also contained a scribbled memorandum on a telephone pad "Mr. Parson called while you were out and left message . . . he says sell out and save what you can." The slip was dated October 18th, at nine-thirty in the morning.

Anyway, nothing had been saved. There was the carbon of a final statement to Mr. Parson, showing in clear figures why his stocks had tobogganed, without any offers, until almost the end of the trading for the day, when it had been cleared out in time to save the broker from suffering, but not the client.

There were newspaper clippings showing sales on the New York Stock Exchange for October 17th and 18th. On the first day, a blue pencil check drew attention to the fact that 1250 shares of Wagner Brothers had changed hands, at a closing price of thirty dollars asked and twenty bid. On the following day twelve shares changed hands at a closing price of fifteen dollars a share.

Piper tossed this paper on top of the others. There was hardly a chance that Mr. Parson, whoever he was, could have blamed his broker for his own bad judgment, at least to the point of seriously threatening his life. Besides, the account had been closed out twice before for the same reason, though for smaller amounts, and Parson had taken it like a man.

So much for the customers' records. Piper resolved to discuss them with Miss Withers; maybe the school-teacher would know about such things.

Next Piper turned to what he had long ago learned to be a most fertile source of information . . . the dead man's cancelled checks.

He noted in passing that the amounts of Lester's checks for the running expenses of the household, to Mrs. Lester, etc., were cut from one half to a quarter after the crash. The broker had been hurt, and badly hurt, by the slump.

But he had not been badly enough hurt to prevent his making out a check for one thousand dollars to Miss Marian Templeton, his private secretary . . . ten days before his death.

One thousand dollars must have been a large sum to a man who was pinching and saving to pull through, to a man who was making his pretty, luxury-loving wife get along on less than half her usual allowance. But the check had been signed, and cashed.

There was only one other bit of meat along the hash of Lester's personal checking account.

On the 19th of October, in the midst of the terror-week in the Street, he had signed a check for one hundred dollars made out to a Mr. Ralph Hodge, which was endorsed "Ralph Hodge, Pres. Hodge Private Detective Bureau."

Piper knew of the organization, given for the large part to the shadowing of suspected wives or husbands, the search for lost heirs, and the fabrication of divorce evidence.

In five minutes he had Mr. Hodge on the telephone. That worthy gentleman apologized for not coming forward before, and explained that he had accepted the hundred dollars as a retaining fee from Gerald Lester.

"He was afraid that something would happen to him," said Hodge. "He wanted a guard on himself, so we fixed one for him. The charge for that sort of thing is ten dollars a day, and he didn't renew the order, so the man was taken off at the end of the ten days. Lester wouldn't tell us any more than that, so all our man could do was to stick around. Too bad now that Lester didn't retain us permanently, eh Inspector?"

"Yeh," said Piper. "What was the name of your operative who was put on the job?"

"MacFee's his name, Inspector. Want to talk to him?"

The Inspector told Mr. Hodge that he most emphatically did want to talk with Mr. MacFee, and that immediately.

An hour later a sad-faced individual walked into the Inspector's office, laid his hat in his lap, and waited. He was gaunt, rugged, and had shaved too closely.

"You McFee?"

The private detective nodded.

"You were on the job of guarding Gerald Lester?"

"I was."

"For ten days only?"

"For ten days. That was all he paid for. He told me at the end of the time that he didn't think it was necessary to be on his guard any longer. He admitted that he'd probably been panicky without reason in the beginning. But he was afraid that somebody was after him, and that's a cinch."

"And somebody was?" Piper leaned forward.

"Not to my knowledge. I had no idea that he was . . . you know, funny. He was upset and nervous enough, but he wasn't willing to tell us anything more than that he was afraid of his life."

"Anything suspicious while you were trailing him?"

"Not a thing."

"You were with him day and night?"

"Just in the daytime. I saw him to his door at night . . . whichever door it was."

"You mean . . . ?"

"He had a girlfriend in the Village," McFee admitted. "Sometimes he stayed there, but never for long. For a while I thought that maybe he was afraid of her, because he usually came away looking pretty upset. But then I figured him out to be just a scarey sort of a guy."

Piper nodded thoughtfully, and chewed his cigar. "That's the only job you ever did for Lester?"

"Sure it is, why?"

"You didn't accept the job of shadowing his wife, Gwen Lester?"

"I did not. I can prove where I was working since . . ."

"Never mind." Piper came closer. "You weren't shadowing Gwen Lester on the morning when she left their apartment and went down to the Aquarium in a taxi to meet Philip Seymour?"

"No, Inspector, I tell you . . ."

"You didn't see her meet Seymour inside the Aquarium and then run to a phone booth and call up her husband, did you?"

For a third time McFee gave indignant denial. Piper leaned back and threw away the remains of his cigar.

"You'd better have some pretty good proof where you were last Friday afternoon," he said slowly. "Because somebody tipped off Gerald Lester to what his wife was doing, and it looks just like you . . . or some dick . . ."

"It wasn't me," said McFee complacently. "Because last Friday all day I was in court, testifying in a divorce case where we had to bust down a hotel door up on Forty-eighth Street. I guess that's a pretty good alibi."

Inspector Piper guessed that it was, too. "But we'll want to hear more from you later," he told the man.

Then Piper turned absent-mindedly to the heap of material which still lay on his desk. For a moment he had seen an answer to the one big difficulty which lay in the path of the conviction of Gwen and Philip . . . the question of whe phoned Lester from the Aquarium? If it had been a private detective hired by Lester, the whole case against them would have been bullet-proof. But now——

These were his thoughts as he shuffled the litter on his desk, and then suddenly he forgot telephone calls entirely.

He picked up an enlarged and glossy print of one of the photographs taken by a headquarters photographer of the "scene of the crime." Piper had glanced at this as it was drying in the dark room, but here it was in all its detail.

And the first thing that met his eye was a darker blotch among the dark water-blurred rocks of the penguin tank, a blotch which might have been part of the "naturalistic" scenic background . . . and wasn't!

For the photograph, taken hurriedly on the afternoon of the crime, while he himself was locked in Hemingway's office and questioning suspects, showed when enlarged that this darker "rock" was loosely blocked and dented in the shape of a man's hat! No doubt about it, it *was* a man's hat!

And now Inspector Piper knew for sure what it was that someone had come back for, across the prostrate body of the policeman on guard. It was this hat, left by the murderer on the scene of the crime! or left by someone——

And did this eliminate Philip Seymour? He had been safely in the Tombs at the time. Unless there had been an accomplice . . . unless perhaps Gwen Lester had slipped back to take away the incriminating evidence? Only, would a woman have been able to strike down a husky cop . . . and would a woman have hidden herself in the men's wash-room? That was unlikely . . .

Piper studied the print again. Was this his imagination, after all? Mightn't that be a real rock, and look like a sunken hat to him only because of an irregularity, and because Miss Withers had suggested the idea to him?

He laid it aside, and took up the remaining memoranda. These were from the fingerprint department, which announced, as he had suspected, that no readable prints had been taken from the handle of the door, from the edge of the tank, from the nearby steam-pipes, nor from the hatpin of Miss Withers which by now was accepted as the cause of Lester's death).

Indeed, the print experts declared, it would seem that everything had conspired to remove or smudge every trace of

possible print. The mob which had rushed through into the
runway on the heels of Donovan had helped to do this, of
course.

A dozen fingers had touched the handle of the door, and at
least several pairs of hands had gripped the metal edge of the
tank top. Donovan hadn't simplified matters any by mistaking
the case for one of simple drowning, and bringing in that
lawyer fellow Costello to help mess things up.

Anyway, whatever fingerprints the murderer might have
left were effectively wiped away before the fingerprint men
had a chance to get them. Inspector Piper expected that this
would show up, and he was not particularly disappointed,
knowing the difficulty even in this late day of getting fingerprint evidence before a jury.

Suddenly the telephone on his desk vibrated dully. Inspector Piper leaned toward it, and then thought better of the
matter. He went to the door.

"Taylor!"

The big detective came slowly up the stair. "Yes, Inspector?"

"Taylor, hop on that phone. If it's the D.A. I'm out of
town on a case. Get me?"

"Hello, Inspector Piper's office," said Taylor into the
mouthpiece. Then he looked up quickly.

"It's Warden Hyde of the Tombs," Taylor told his superior officer. "Wants to talk to you. Okay?"

"Okay," said Inspector Piper. "But stick around, I may
need you." He lifted the receiver and spoke crisply. "Yeah?
What is it, Warden?"

"Just wanted to tell you that we discovered a watch on that
dummy pickpocket that you turned in to us Friday," said the
Warden. "It had slipped down into the lining of his pocket
or else he'd hidden it there. It's a swell timepiece, a solid
white-gold Gruen. Twenty-four jewel . . ."

"That's no news," Piper told him. "Why Donovan, the
cop on the beat down there, took four or five tickers away
from the dip when some lady snagged him with her bumber-
shoot. What if one did slip into the lining of his coat?"

"You're handling the case, and not me," said the Warden
stiffly. "But if I was trying to solve a murder case, and if
some obliging friend of mine told me that he'd discovered the
murdered man's watch in a pickpocket's coat . . . well . . ."

"That would alter the case," Piper admitted gravely. "Did you?"

"I did," said the Warden. "Initials, I mean monogram on the case. G-M-L . . . there they are. Gerald Maurice Lester. And besides, I took the initiative and sent it up to Mrs. Lester, who is also a guest of ours as you know, and she identified it willingly. I'm sending it down to the Property Clerk unless you want it. Do you?"

"I do not," said Piper. "But that opens up a new train of thought. Do you know, I wish we knew of some way to make that dummy speak. I suppose we could try pencil and paper, but it would be pretty hard to give a guy the third degree that way. All the same, there's a chance that that dip knows more than we do about who killed Gerald Lester . . ."

"That's just what this lawyer fellow, Costello, was hinting at half an hour ago," said the Warden. "He came, of course, officially to see his client—Gwen Lester. But he also spent half an hour in the men's wing, talking to Seymour. I believe that he is going to handle the case for both of them. But what I started to say was . . . Costello is a real smart lawyer, and he says he believes that the pickpocket could tell us plenty if he wanted to."

Piper was thoughtful. "Say, Warden—when did Costello leave?"

"Why, he hasn't gone yet. He's locked in the cell block, talking to Seymour, or else trying to get something out of the dummy, Chicago Lew or whatever his name is."

"Hold him there," shouted the Inspector as he reached for his hat. "That Mick lawyer hasn't got any business fooling around with material witnesses that way! Why, he might find out something ahead of us!"

It was only ten minutes later when Piper hurried into the Warden's office at the Tombs. He almost ran headlong into Barry Costello, who was just entering the office from the cell-block side. At a sign from Piper, the Warden withdrew.

Costello extended his hand with a wide smile. "Well, if it isn't the Inspector! I've got news for you, what I think is big news!"

It was thus that he forestalled what Piper was about to say. "I've been having a chat with the pickpocket. That is, a one-sided chat. I was just beginning to get somewhere when the Warden here comes up and tells me that you object to my asking questions, even when I can't get any answers.''

"You know what your rights are, as a defense attorney," the Inspector told him shortly. "I don't know how you talked the Warden into letting you see the pickpocket anyhow.''

"Because I'm Gwen Lester's attorney," said Costello coolly. "I'm fighting to save that wonderful young woman from the electric chair. She didn't kill her husband, and yet the net of circumstantial evidence is tight around her. I don't expect you to believe, Inspector, that I would give anything short of my life itself to save so lovely a girl from an unjust end!" His voice boomed eloquently.

Costello's eyes shone with a glint of sincerity, but Piper was tempted to write this, too, off as an example of the dramatic tendency of the lawyer's Celtic blood.

"I don't particularly," said Piper. "But what has the pickpocket got to do with saving Gwen Lester, anyway?''

"That pickpocket knows something," insisted Costello. "Perhaps he has lost his speech through fear, or through injury, or perhaps he's really voiceless. Maybe it is shock which makes him unwilling or unable to communicate with us in the means left to him. But I have just made an attempt to gain his confidence. I have evidence that he can hear what is said to him, anyway. And I'll stake my life on that man's knowledge of the facts of Gerald Lester's murder which will save Gwen Lester from the chair! He was behind the tanks when the murder was committed, and besides the murderer he was the only man, excepting that more than idiotic dolt of a Swedish scientist, that *was* there! Now do you admit that there is justification in my interviewing him? Can't we work together to find out the truth on this tangle?''

Piper gave the Irish lawyer a long stare, and then extended his hand. After all, there was something genuine in this blustering fellow.

"The truth is what we're after," said the Inspector. "Remember that if Gwen Lester has clean hands, I don't want to see her stand the rap any more than you do. If this dummy of a pickpocket has anything to say that will clear Gwen Lester, I want to hear it. But tell me, first. What actually were you able to get out of the fellow?''

Costello drew back, holding up his hand. "Nothing tangible, and yet a whole lot. He'll nod yes and no to my questions, sometimes. And I want to try him with a pencil and paper tomorrow. I'm winning his confidence, Inspector, where you hard-boiled coppers scare him into a blue funk. Let me have a day or two more, Inspector, and I'll get something out of the fellow that will solve your whole murder mystery, I know. I'm guessing what it'll be, but I don't want to say until I can lay the whole business before you, in a form that can go into court. Okay?''

"Sure it's okay,'' said Piper calmly. "You seem plenty interested in this business, for a lawyer . . . suppose you do free Gwen Lester, what then?''

"Of course I'm interested. Anybody but a blind detective could see that I'm interested, and why. Suppose you were a young man of parts, heart-whole and fancy-free, whose best girl had given him the mitten a few weeks ago . . . just suppose. And then imagine that when you gather with a crowd at the cry of 'murder' you find yourself in a position to give first-aid to the most beautiful girl you've ever seen in all your born days . . . and not only first-aid, either, but a chance to use the legal powers that you have never had a real chance to exercise, in her behalf? A white knight, riding out to save a maiden, Inspector. It wouldn't appeal to you, I'm afraid. You wouldn't understand. But if I save Gwen Lester—you ask—what then?''

"Yeah,'' said Piper, not unfriendly. "What then?''

"I'll kiss her hand,'' said Costello dreamily. "And then I'll ask her to marry me, if she'll have me. And if she won't, I'll give her my blessing and get out of the way.'' Suddenly he smiled wide. "But don't you breathe a word of this, Inspector. We've sworn to be allies, you know . . .''

"Sure,'' said Piper. "I'll never breathe a word of it. But I'm afraid you will. I've got to be getting busy, though. . . .''

"Righto!'' Costello picked up his hat, which Piper idly noticed was a derby. Every man in this town was wearing a tin hat these days. But for that fact the Lester murder might be solved now. Anyway, this derby fitted the Irishman as if it had been built for him, so this wasn't the missing hat.

"Okay,'' said the lawyer. "I'll be on my way. There's much to be done before the case goes to the grand jury, you know. Money to be raised, a lot of money. Gwen Lester hasn't got a thing, you know, except her husband's estate which she won't touch until her name is cleared. Her father was about cleaned out in the crash, I find. But we'll find some way out of it. . . ."

He paused at the door. "I don't suppose you'll object to my having a little chat with the pickpocket tomorrow when I come down to visit my client?"

"I'll leave word with the Warden that you're okay," Piper promised. Against his will he was beginning to approve of the big Irishman. The fellow was sincere about trying to save Gwen Lester, anyway. Witness his interest in the pickpocket. . . .

Suddenly the Inspector got an idea. Suppose . . . suppose that Costello were going to extreme lengths in his attempt to save Gwen? Suppose he were engaged in planting evidence, in suggesting things to the pickpocket, perhaps even bribing him?

Swiftly he strode to the door, and called for the Warden. Five minutes later they both hurried past the cell where Philip Seymour lay staring at the ceiling, and stopped before the iron box at the end of the long corridor where Chicago Lew muttered and mumbled.

"You can go free," suggested the Warden in a voice that concealed his eagerness. "You can go free if you're willing to write out for us what you know. If you keep on this way you'll stay here the rest of your life. Will you come clean?"

The man stared at them with lifeless, dull eyes, and then shook his head slightly.

"Playing deaf as well as dumb, huh?" Piper was impatient. "Well, if you're spilling stuff to the lawyer you can spill it to us, see? Or else we'll fix it so that you go up the river for the rest of your days. Picking sisal isn't such a pleasant lifetime, you know. You've been up there a couple of times, so come clean."

The guard unlocked the iron door for them, and in a moment they were inside the dimly-lit cell. The pickpocket cowered away from them as if he feared attack. Piper felt like using a nightstick on the fellow, and resisted the temptation with difficulty.

"Will you come clean?"

The fellow mouthed meaningless sounds, pitiful sounds.

"Do you understand us? Can you hear what we say? Look, man, we promise you your freedom if you help us. Will you talk . . . I mean, will you write, or even nod yes or no?"

There was a pause, and then Chicago Lew buried his face in his arms, shaking with either sobs or delirious laughter, the Inspector was not sure which.

"Costello is nuts if he thinks this looney can bring out any evidence to save Gwen Lester," Piper decided as he moved toward the door.

"It's a clear case for Mattewan," agreed the Warden, and the turnkey clanged the door noisily. Their footsteps died away down the corridor.

Behind them, in the dim little cell at the end of the passage, Chicago Lew heaved a sigh of relief, and drew the acrid smoke of a cigarette into his lungs.

14

# Follow the Swallow

"THAT'S how it stands," said Inspector Piper to his guest. Miss Withers sat somewhat primly on the edge of her chair, and tried to keep her eyes from falling on the gruesome exhibits which lined the walls of his office. "My dear lady, the case is complete against Gwen Lester and Philip Seymour. I've turned over all the evidence to the District Attorney, from Gwen's first exclamation at the sight of the corpse to the attempts of each of the defendants to bargain for a suspended sentence by pinning the rap on the other."

"But do you believe that?"

"Of course I believe that! The case is ripe for the grand jury already. I know that to the mind of the layman, there are a thousand possibilities, a thousand ingenious twists that present themselves as to the possibility of these people's being innocent. But I've had enough experience to know that things have a way of happening just as they've always happened, ninety-nine times out of a hundred.''

"And how about the hundredth?" Miss Withers was very serious.

"Nonsense." Oscar Piper fumbled with the papers on his desk. "I've done everything that can be done in this investigation. The fact that you have a private opinion, a hunch, that Gwen and Philip are too nice a pair to commit a murder has no weight. My dear lady, you're a romantic. You've been reading too many magazine stories where a loving couple are reunited in the last chapter. In this story, there's going to be no reunited couple, no tinkle of wedding chimes.''

"I'm romantic, huh?" Miss Hildegarde Withers was on her feet. "You men! Anything that you don't have plain common sense enough to understand in a woman, you have to call names! You have eyes, why don't you look beyond your nose?''

With her anger, the air of stern aloofness fell away from Miss Withers, and her blue eyes flashed. "And you're a detective! A fine detective you are! I could be a better sleuth with my eyes bandaged and both arms tied behind me. My children in third grade at Jefferson School would make better detectives than you! You're not digging for the truth, you're just trying to find evidence enough to send somebody to the chair. You don't care who!

"Now I warn you, Oscar Piper, I warn you fair and square. I've got my dander up, and I'm going to show you a few things. You've got the law and all its facilities, but I'm going ahead on my own and find out who did kill Gerald Lester! So there!"

She slammed the door of the Inspector's office so hard that the pistols rattled on their shelves.

He sat at his desk, tapping his teeth lightly with a pencil. After a moment he spoke softly to the photograph of the Commissioner which hung on the wall beside the window.

"Whee! What a woman!" Then he tapped his teeth again, more thoughtfully. "And now I wonder if she could be right, even one tenth of one per cent?"

Miss Withers paused for a moment as she came out into the busy street, and then suddenly hailed a taxicab. She was not used to taxicabs, and her salary did not warrant such expenditure, but she had taken a large bite, and she was going to chew it or bust. And all she had at her disposal was energy.

Halfway home she rapped on the glass and changed the directions which she had given to the driver. "The Four Arts Club, on East Eightieth Street," she ordered. Then she leaned back in the cab.

The cab at last roared down a quiet street in which here and there still lingered a pair of box trees and a hedge or two, relics of the days when these sober brownstones had been private houses. Now they exhibited, most of them, signs in the front windows bearing the word "Vacancy."

There was nothing about the house at the end of the street to justify the word "club" except an unpolished brass plate above the door. The storm door stood ajar, and Miss Withers entered to survey a line of push-buttons opposite names. "Hennesy, De Pauw"—There it was . . . "Captain Barry Costello. . . ."

She pressed the button with her thumb, and lifted the telephone receiver which hung from a hook above the buttons, but without a word from above the door suddenly burst into clacking activity, and she caught the knob. Up three flights, and then she signalled upon a door in the rear by a painted bit of metal knocker in the shape of an up-side-down parrot tapping on a tree.

The door opened. Barry Costello held the knob. He was wearing a purple silk dressing gown, and smoking a black pipe which Miss Withers eyed distastefully. A fat spaniel peered between his legs.

The handsome face broke into a smile of genuine surprise. "Miss Withers! Come in, come in! I was just wishing that I could talk with you, and wondering if I dared to telephone you. And like a bolt from the blue . . ."

He showed her into soft tapestry chair at the farther end of a room whose walls were lined with books, many of them heavy legal tomes, Miss Withers noticed. The curtains were drawn as if to shut out the gray November day, and the air of the room was heavy with tobacco smoke and the odor of dog.

There was a large desk near the door, with a vast heap of correspondence, papers, and pamphlets pushed up in the center of it. Here was where Barry Costello had been working when Miss Withers arrived. He seated himself on the edge of the desk, and offered cigarettes, which were refused none too graciously.

"Excuse my being dressed this way," said Costello, "but I was plowing through some of my law books in an endeavor to brush up. If I'm going to handle Gwen Lester's case I've got to be a whale of·a good lawyer, you know. Innocent or guilty, she needs the very best that a man can do, and it's an honor that I'm to be the man. . . ."

"That's why I came up here to see you," explained Miss Withers. She eyed the fat spaniel distrustfully as it approached her, sniffed at her low oxfords, and then moved pompously off toward a corner. The dog was gray with age, and it wheezed unpleasantly.

"Good old Rags," said Costello. "He's pretty old now, but I can't make up my mind to have him put away. I'm that way about animals. . . ."

"I was saying that I came up here because I have my own theory of the Lester murder," said Miss Withers crisply. "I believe that Gwen Lester is innocent of that murder, if not morally, at least actually. I don't believe that she was mixed up with the business in any way, and I doubt very much if Philip Seymour was, either."

"And where do I come in?" Costello wanted to know. He lit his black pipe carefully.

"You can save Gwen Lester, if you really want to," said Miss Withers. "It's too much for me to do alone. But listen to my theory. . . ."

She paused for breath, and wished that the windows could be opened. Costello, reading her thoughts, explained "Rags can't stand the air, the poor old fellow has rheumatism. . . ." But the lawyer was watching her intently, hanging on her words.

"Anyway," she began, "here is how I think Lester was killed. First of all, the motive. I believe that a man killed Gerald Lester, a man actuated by desire for revenge! A man who had a motive, a man who had been wronged, or thought he had been wronged, by Lester in business."

Costello did not move, but he blinked his eyes, and jammed his pipe into the pocket of his dressing gown. Miss Withers plunged on. "This person saw Lester's wife go to the Aquarium with another man, and his desire for revenge caused him to telephone the broker, taunting him with the facts. Then he lingered to enjoy his handiwork, and saw the fight between Lester and Seymour. He saw Seymour carry Lester back of the tanks, and leave him there. Then the murderer chanced upon my hatpin, snatched it up on an unholy impulse, and drove it into the left ear of his unconscious victim, replacing it and escaping all in a minute or two. . . ."

Costello was leaning forward. "You know, it sounds dashed convincing, Miss Withers. You're a real sleuth. And the murderer?"

She paused a moment. "Who could it be? Who was the man who had been sold out on the Stock Exchange market by Lester, his broker? Who was the man who had an opportunity to commit the crime after Gwen and Philip had mingled with the other visitors in the place and were working their way toward the main entrance, knowing that no matter what he did, they would be blamed for it?"

"All right . . . quick, who was it? You mean . . ." The lawyer was burning with eagerness. Miss Withers realized that he must care a lot about Gwen Lester, after all.

"The murderer, as I figure it, was . . . it was Bertrand B. Hemingway," she said softly. There was a long silence. The lawyer exhaled a deep breath.

"By the Lord Harry, I think you've got it!" Costello was striding back and forth across the room. "Why didn't I think of it before? I was sure that Philip Seymour had done it, which would implicate Gwen somehow even though she weren't actually an accomplice. But now . . ." He was bubbling with happiness. . . .

"Now all we have to do is to get together and prove it, not only to our satisfaction, but to Piper's and the District Attorney's," he was reminded. "We'll have to work together, and it isn't going to be easy . . ."

"You're right it isn't! But the man must have left some trail behind him! There must be something that the Inspector overlooked, some bit of evidence, some discrepancy . . . suppose we go down to the Aquarium, right now, and look around? There are a few things that I don't get straight in my mind yet. One thing is how the body ended up in the pool when from the time it went in until the cops came you, and for that matter I myself, were right outside the tank, Miss

Withers. I came running from the doorway, just like every other casual visitor, when you called out. And the body was still settling in the tank when I got there. . . ."

"I've got a theory about that," said Miss Withers. "I'll tell you about it later."

"I know it now," Costello guessed. "You think the pick-pocket did it."

"I do not," said Miss Withers shortly. "Not even though I hear from the Inspector that they found Lester's watch on the little man called Chicago Lew. I believe that there wasn't a human being closer than I, outside the tank with little Isidore, when the body went into the tank!"

Costello looked puzzled. "You'll have to show me," he said.

"I will show you, if you'll come down to the Aquarium with me." Miss Withers rose from the brocaded chair.

"That I will," Costello said. "Though Lord knows I'm weary enough. I've spent the day trying to raise money for Gwen's defense, you know. She won't and can't touch her husband's estate, of course. Until she's cleared she won't have a dime, and investigations cost a great deal of money." He motioned toward the farther wall, where two glaring white squares showed on the time-darkened plaster.

"My two family portraits, Greatuncle Denis, Lord O'Doyle, and his wife Deirdre, went to the dealers this morning," he confessed. "Lucky for Gwen Lester that they were in Tyk Eel's best style. Believe me, they were a last resource, those pictures. But I had to have the money, and they promise me a check tomorrow. . . ."

Miss Withers was touched, in spite of herself. "You seem to care a great deal for Gwen Lester, considering the fact that you only met her a few days ago," she pointed out. "Isn't this a bit unusual?"

"Is it?" Barry Costello rose to his feet. "I'm a romantic, certainly. And I've known a lot of women, but never one as beautiful and as troubled as Gwen Lester. I thought I got over falling for women a few weeks ago when a girl I was engaged to threw me over for a wealthier fellow, but when I saw Gwen Lester I knew . . . well, it was like that. I suppose it sounds odd to you?"

At that moment Miss Withers loved the man. "No, it

doesn't sound so odd to me," she said softly. "It sounds just like something out of a story. It sounds like romance!" For a moment her tone softened.

Costello smiled. "I believe in loving at first sight," he said. "I believe in living with a gesture, living like something out of a story. That's how I'm made. But you . . . why are you so interested in saving Gwen Lester from the chair?"

Miss Withers was sober again. "You wouldn't understand, I'm afraid. It's nothing as simple as love, though perhaps I know more about young love than you think. I was not always a school-teacher, you know. I had an unfortunate . . . well, never mind. Since you've asked me, Mr. Barry Costello, and since we've agreed to go ahead on this together, I'll tell you why I'm interested in solving this case.

"It's not because I'm getting such a big thrill out of playing detective, though you may imagine it's the most exciting thing that ever happened to me in all my born days. It's not just human sympathy for a nice girl and a nice young man who are caught in the net of the law. It's more than that. It's the fact that I was born and brought up to an old-fashioned ideal of justice . . . blindfolded, uncompromising justice.

"I believe there is something holier about the truth, about justice and right, than there is in cleanliness and even some godliness, young man. Justice is bigger than human hates and loves and sympathies, not only legal justice, but abstract justice. The kind of justice that lets the letter of the law go sometimes to follow the spirit instead!" Miss Withers was aflame. "I want to solve this murder because I'm a good citizen, the kind of citizen who in another generation rode as a Vigilante. Understand?"

"Lady, lady, what a perfectly marvelous witness you're going to make on the stand when this case comes to court!" said Barry Costello. "Positively, you make shivers run down my spine, ma'm. I'm sure tickled that you're not on my trail."

"I'd turn you, or Gwen Lester, or myself over to the police in a second if I thought you or she or myself had done the job," Miss Withers told him. "Now let's waste no more time, but be off for the Aquarium. I only hope we can get in after we get there. . . ."

"Don't you worry, we'll get in all right." Costello glanced apologetically at his apparel. "Will you be excusing me a moment while I change? Just a moment. ..."

He strode toward the door of the bedroom. "There's an afternoon paper there on the table, with all the latest guesses of the newspaper boys on the Lester case," he told his guest. "You may be interested. ..."

But Miss Withers did not pause to inspect the newspaper. She knew it would be full of the unusual thin-drawn rehash of the case, which was already beginning to shrink in public interest for lack of new developments. Well, maybe she could rectify that.

She moved idly toward the long bookcase that lined one wall, letting her eyes run along the volumes. The law books did not interest her . . . "Quincy on Torts . . . Blackstone . . . Laws of the State of New York. ..."

But many years of forcing the young idea how to shoot, particularly to shoot forward into literacy, had taught her to evaluate her fellow men through their tastes in books.

She noted volume after volume of Sabatini, Rex Beach, Conan Doyle (the adventure and historical novels, not the detective works) and Walter Scott. Here was a man who turned to light fiction for his recreation . . . a man of action. She knew that many lawyers have similar tastes, although the reading was not what she would have prescribed.

At the end of the shelf was a familiar looking volume, its gilt lettering worn away from use. She drew it forth idly . . . it was "Butterworth on Moths and Butterflies", a required text book in practically every biology class since her own girlhood.

Costello came out, neatly dressed in topcoat and hat above morning clothes, and saw her replace the volume.

"I see you have a hobby," Miss Withers remarked as she moved toward the door.

"I used to have a hobby, rather," said Costello. "It's been years since I had the urge to collect the little winged creatures of the night. But I used to have the place filled with cork cases, and I tell you I had some fine specimens. But my ideas have changed since my student days. Every boy goes through the stage of collecting, whether it's bird's eggs or butterflies or postage stamps."

Miss Withers knew that well enough, having been confronted with problems of such nature in her classes now and then . . . particularly did she remember the time when little Abraham brought his collection of white mice to school one afternoon.

"I sometimes wonder," Costello said as they got into a cab, "if our friend Hemingway hasn't got the collector's mania in a big way? They say that every man's life work comes as a result of something that happens in boyhood. Maybe Hemingway is just a boy collector of fishes grown into a Director with a paunch?"

"Maybe," Miss Withers agreed. She was thinking.

It was well after closing time when the taxi finished its long trek through the downtown thoroughfares and paused at the entrance to Battery Park. That was as close as the driver could come to the ancient pill-box of a building that had been constructed as a fortress, first used as a concert hall and freak show, and at last turned into the greatest home of caged fish in the world.

Miss Hildegarde Withers was surprised to notice in herself a certain shrinking, a feeling of dread, as she followed the lawyer toward the grim stone pile that loomed gray in the reflected light of the city behind them. There it stood, the last outpost of Manhattan, its old stones stained with the wash of the Harbor. Somehow, she felt that the Aquarium did not belong in hearty, blustering, sky-scraping New York. Nor did that twisted deed, that dark murderous thrust of a long steel needle, belong in this age of progress, waste, and energy. It was not the way for a man to die.

As they approached the old building, Costello motioned toward a light that glowed from the one high window of Hemingway's office, to the left of the entrance. "He's in, the old fox," said Costello. "And now the question is, will he let us in?"

"I have my doubts," Miss Withers admitted. No light showed beneath the heavy door, but as Costello raised his fist to knock, she touched his arm. She pressed experimentally against the door, and turned the knob. It opened inward, noiselessly.

After a pause of a second, they stepped into the thick darkness. Not even the high ceiling lights were on, as Miss

Withers remembered them from the other night. Costello closed the door behind them with a little click, and Miss Withers knew that she was afraid.

This was no ordinary building, and she was in no ordinary company. Perhaps a murderer was within these walls, moving through the darkness toward her. . . .

She touched Costello's sturdy arm, and was reassured. They moved forward, slowly. As their eyes became accustomed to the darkness, Miss Withers could make out a faint phosphorescent glow from the rows of tanks. Her hypersensitive ears caught a continuous sound of soft, hidden movement all around them. Life was here, even in the lingering presence of death. But it was cold life, chill-blooded life, life that moved swiftly through a forbidden element and builded itself constantly by feeding on other life, by the bringing of death. Miss Withers knew that she hated fish, hated their filmy eyes and their sleek, snakelike bodies.

The blackness was so thick that for a moment Miss Withers felt that it was a solid element, the depths of great waters perhaps. She shuddered to realize that if this were so, if the thousands of fish which moved about her were free to come toward her, they would come with gaping mouths, with serried lines of teeth more fierce than ever a tiger wore, to tear at her flesh. Big and small they would come, the mammoth jew-fish, the little sand-sharks, the terrible morays . . . to hunt Man as they would have hunted each other, for food.

Suddenly Costello's hand stopped her. They had been moving forward toward a ray of light that showed from beneath the door marked "Bertrand B. Hemingway, Director." . . .

"I thought I heard something," he confessed. His voice was a shade less steady than it had been at the door.

The sound came again, but louder now, horribly louder. It began as a whisper, a choking whisper, rising into a hoarse shriek. It chilled the blood, even to the last quavering note that died gasping away. Miss Withers knew with a sudden intuition that this was no human voice.

"Holy Mary! Defend us. . . ." The words were torn from the throat of the man who stood beside her, gripping her arm with fingers of steel. Miss Withers guessed that the young Celt, with all his inheritance of belief in the supernatural, was

expecting to see the pallid face of Gerald Lester floating
lividly through the darkness.

"Nonsense," she said sharply as much to herself as to
Costello. "Listen."

Again came the sound, though it was choked off suddenly.
It seemed to come from the office. This time it was even less
human in its timbre. From behind them in the big room
somewhere there came an answer, a series of querulous, protesting squawks.

"The penguins!" gasped Costello. "Believe me, it gave
me a start for a minute. . . ."

The office door swung open, and a blaze of light struck
them in the face. "Who's that?"

The gray-clad form of Fink appeared, open-mouthed with
wonder. "How in the devil did you get in here?" he gasped
as he recognized Miss Withers. "Did I leave that door on the
latch again? Anyway, you can't come in here. . . ."

"We can so come in," Costello declared, shouldering his
way forward. Then the voice of Hemingway came from
within the long room.

"Fink! Get back here and hold this light. Never mind
who's there. . . ."

Miss Withers and Barry Costello pushed forward through
the doorway as Fink stepped aside. The office was a glare of
light, light that half-blinded the two who had come in through
the darkness. It was a moment before Miss Withers could
take in the picture.

Hemingway bent over a table, while Fink the guard held a
reflecting lamp at one side. On the table, its feet bound tight,
lay a fat black penguin, its bill opened wide, and its long
smooth belly shaken with gasps.

The Director of the New York Aquarium paid no more
attention to them than if they had been a thousand miles
away. Gently but with unshaking fingers he inserted a long
and curiously shaped instrument of gleaming nickel into the
maw of the rebellious bird.

"Steady, Nox old girl, steady there. I knew it's tough, but
we'll have it out in a jiffy. Hold fast. . . ."

His voice seemed to quiet the bird somewhat, and he bent
its head back so that the shining instrument slipped down,
almost out of sight.

Costello lunged forward. "Stop! What are you doing, you torturing fiend? Leave off crucifying that little bird, will you?"

Hemingway looked quickly, and his face was a mask of disgust. "Go away, you fool," he said swiftly. "I'm trying to save the penguin's life. . . ."

And showly, with infinite care, he lifted the gleaming nickel instrument from the gaping maw of the bird. Inch by inch . . . now it was almost out. . . .

There was a last resentful squawk from the penguin as it could draw the air into its throat again, and then the little bird was almost quiet under Hemingway's hand.

Miss Withers was staring at the shapeless black object which was caught firmly between the two jaws of the long tweezers.

## 15

# The Dumb Man Speaks

SLOWLY Miss Withers moved forward again, with Costello close behind her. The Director of the Aquarium was shaking his head.

"And a narrow squeak for you it was, Nox, old girl," he said to the bewildered penguin. Gently he loosed the bonds that held the short, webbed feet, and put the bird down on the floor. It stood uncertainly for a moment, staring at the newcomers.

Hemingway looked up defiantly. "I don't know how you people got in here, nor what you're snooping around for, but you've just seen one of the most delicate operations ever performed on an aquarium specimen. That bird would have died before morning if I hadn't taken the probe and the tweezers to remove the seat of the trouble. And you—" he whirled on Costello—"you tried to interfere, you meddling . . ."

"Gentlemen, gentlemen," interposed Miss Withers swiftly. But Costello bowed with a winning smile on his face.

"The Director is perfectly right," he said softly. "I had no business to meddle. But you see, I have always had what I realize is an exaggerated love for animals, and I thought for a moment that you were being cruel. I understand now, and I apologize."

"But that doesn't explain why you're here," Hemingway cut in swiftly. "Isn't it enough that my aquarium has to be turned into a mad-house of photographers and coroners and detectives and policemen without hounding me out at all hours of the night?"

"It's only seven o'clock," Miss Withers reminded him. "And you haven't explained why you're shut in this one office with the rest of the Aquarium lights out, working over the penguin. . . ."

"I had to put the other lights out so that there'd be current enough to light this room brilliantly," said Hemingway swiftly. "We have an old-fashioned dynamo in this building, because it's cheaper than city light. And it doesn't work so well. That's why I've been trying to argue my Board of Trustees into authorizing the installation of city light. But they maintain that we don't need it because the Aquarium is supposed to be closed at five in the evening. . . ."

He paused, as if angry that Miss Withers had tricked him into explaining himself instead of making her explain why she had come.

But she held up her hand arbitrarily. "Look at the penguin," she said.

The little black bird was moving uneasily across the floor, its ordeal on the operating table evidently already forgotten. It nibbled at Fink's finger.

"Poor old Nox," said Hemingway as the little bird squawked pipingly. From outside came an answer. "She wants to get back to Erebus. They're great pals, those two. And they've been through trying times these last few days. What with Nox getting this thing stuck in her gullet, and near starving to death. . . ."

Miss Withers strode forward. "Wait a minute! Just what sort of thing is it that was stuck in the penguin's gullet? That may be important!"

Hemingway barred her way as she reached for the waste-basket. "Listen to me," he protested. "I've stood for a whole lot from detectives, but I don't have to stand it from you. Besides, I tell you it's nothing . . . just a bit of cloth that must have fallen into the tank."

"Then it's important. Because the penguins were in that tank during the murder, and later that afternoon. And another thing—that looked like more than a bit of cloth to me. Besides, if it's nothing you shouldn't mind my seeing it."

"I'm the Director of this Aquarium, and I say . . ." Hemingway motioned to Fink. "If these people won't go, throw them out!"

Costello looked at the fat guard, and grinned. "Go on, throw me out," he invited. "I'm waiting."

Fink was waiting too. But Miss Withers acted. Before Hemingway could stop her she leaned over to the wastebasket in which the Director had dropped the wad of material taken from the penguin's throat, and snatched up the clammy mess in her fingers.

As the others watched, she laid it deftly on the very edge of the low table and picked at it with the tip of her black and red pencil. It was a toughly knotted mess, but slowly it loosened.

A bit of cloth, indeed! It was a twisted ribbon of fine black silk, its ends tied in the remains of a bow knot to form a circle perhaps ten inches in diameter.

Miss Withers looked up at Costello, and then they both turned toward Bertrand B. Hemingway.

"Do you know what it was that you took from the penguin's throat . . . and what you were about to throw away as of no consequence?" Her voice was deadly serious now. She tapped the silken band with her pencil to emphasize her remarks.

"I have every reason to believe that this is the band from the hat worn by the murderer of Gerald Lester!" Hemingway stepped back, his face white.

His eyes were focussed on the damp rag as if he saw something written there. "The hat-band . . . of . . . the murderer?"

"I told you we'd find out something if we came down here," Miss Withers reminded Barry Costello, who was still eyeing Fink belligerently. "Nobody touch that, now. I'm going to send for Inspector Piper. . . ."

The telephone was on the desk at the farther end of the room, out from under the glaring light of the one big reflecting lamp. But it only took Miss Hildegarde Withers a few seconds to reach it, and speak the magic words "Spring 3100."

If only Inspector Piper was in his office! At any rate, the man at the phone in Headquarters could find him . . . she waited impatiently, while the three men behind her glared at each other. The air in the room was tense, electric. . . .

Then the Inspector's familiar "Hello" came crisply over the wire. "Can you come to the Aquarium quickly?" she begged into the mouthpiece. "I've found some evidence on the Lester murder . . . evidence that will send someone to the electric chair. . . ."

Piper's voice changed, became shriller, almost eager. "I'll be there," he promised. "But what did you find?"

"I found . . ."

There was the sound of a movement behind her, a movement among the three men who had been standing like statues . . . and then the big reflecting light went out, plunging the room into absolute darkness.

Black, black night pressed against Miss Withers' face, blackness that she could taste and touch.

The telephone crashed to the floor, and there was the sound of a muffled oath behind her, followed by the scrape of a chair. Then Costello's triumphant voice rang out.

"No, you don't, my fine Mister Director. I've got you!"

Miss Withers whirled and then, her hand outstretched into the lowering darkness, she forced herself to move in the direction of the others.

"Get a light, somebody, quick," shouted Costello again. "Miss Withers, are you there? Get a light, I've got the spalpeen!"

Of course she had no match. "I'm here," she called out. "What . . . what happened, for God's sake? Where are you?"

"Here . . . by the table, with the little rat of a Hemingway in my grip and tight," said the Irishman. "I caught him trying for that hat-band when the lights went out. There's matches in my pocket, Miss Withers . . ."

"Not necessary at all," came the quiet voice of Hemingway, and suddenly the light went on again, half blinding them all.

Bertrand B. Hemingway knelt at the baseboard, with his fingers on the light plug which he had just shoved into its socket again.

Ten feet away from him, beside the table, Barry Costello held the struggling form of Fink, the guard!

Slowly the big Irishman released his prisoner, a look of honest amazement on his face. "I thought I had . . ." He rubbed his brow.

"Sure, when that villain over there kicked against the light cord, I knew that something was up, and I grabbed . . . and caught this. . . ."

Hemingway's face was a puzzle. "You know who kicked out that light cord, and you know it wasn't me," he said quickly.

"And as God is my witness it wasn't me," cried Fink. "I only made a try to save that hat-band there, because of your saying that it was important, and I heard somebody make a snatch for it. . . ."

Miss Withers paused for a second. She could not, for the life of her, remember who had been nearest that plug as she went to the phone. Even at that, it might have been any of them, for the thick twisted light cord curled all across the office, from plug to the lamp above the table.

Fink and Hemingway were defiant in their protests of innocence. They raised their voices . . . but Costello sat down quietly and relit his pipe.

"This is serious, mighty serious," Miss Withers announced. "It's not for me to settle, it's for the Inspector. Nobody move, please. This place will have to be searched, and everybody here. I suppose it will take some time for Inspector Piper to get here, but there'll be the dickens to pay when he does. Because . . ." she pointed toward the table top beneath which the black penguin named Nox was whimpering . . . "because the hat-band is gone!"

There was a little silence. This had come as no news to one of those here, at least. Miss Withers felt a positive wall of suspicion shut apart the four of them in that room.

Hemingway moved slowly to a chair, and sat down wea-ily. His dignity had vanished, somehow. His little eyes flashed from the one person to another, warily, but he kept his silence.

Fink, his neat gray uniform crumpled, was noisily protesting. "Arsk him what he was doing at the table," he kept saying, his grimy finger levelled at Costello. "Arsk him that. . . ."

"There'll be plenty of asking and answering to be done when the Inspector gets here," Costello warned him. "In the meantime, shut up."

He moved suddenly toward the door. "I don't suppose anyone could have come in from the main part of the building, and run off with the band? It's hard to believve that he could have come in and gone so quiet. . . ."

His hand touched the knob of the door, and he swung it open. It creaked noisily.

But Miss Withers was at his side. "I'm afraid you'd better come back inside this room and stay in the bright light," she warned him. "The Inspector will hold you with these others until he finds that hat-band."

"Of course! I hadn't thought . . ." Costello laughed shortly, and obediently seated himself in a chair near the table. He extended his fingers to the black penguin, who cast an inquisitive eye upon him, and waddled out of the protecting shadow of the table.

"Poor little Nox," said Costello. "Poor little penguin! Did he have a tough time with the stuffy old thing that caught in his throat?"

"Nox is not a *he*," Hemingway told him stiffly. "Nox is a female penguin, named after the Roman goddess of night. And your sympathy is wasted, because the silly birds eat everything that comes their way, from newspapers to shoe-laces. And usually they get by with it, having cast-iron stomachs. It was only because that hat-band made such a lump of itself that it caught in Nox's gullet. She could take your finger off without a bit of trouble, and I hope she does. . . ."

Costello drew his hand back quickly. "Beg pardon, ma'm," he said politely to the inquiring bird. "Stupid of me. . . ." He smoked contentedly.

And then a police siren rose above the noises of the city, a

screaming siren that rose to a shrill crescendo, and then died
away somewhere just outside. There came the sound of heavy
running footsteps, and a banging on the main door of the
Aquarium.

Miss Withers flung open the door of the office, so that the
way was illuminated. In a moment Inspector Piper, followed
by a quartet of sturdy policemen, burst into the room.

"Miss Withers! What happened! You dropped the phone
and I heard something happening, so I came down in a squad
car."

She told him what had happened. Oscar Piper did not
waste a moment. He faced Hemingway, Costello, and Fink
and his voice was stern.

"You realize that this business is deadly serious? Do you
know that by tampering with this evidence, some person here
has aided and abetted a murder, if not actually admitted his
complicity?"

He gave swift orders to his men. One stationed himself at
either door, and the other two waited for what was to follow.

"That hat-band is in this room," said the Inspector. "I've
every reason to believe that it is direct evidence against the
murderer of Gerald Lester. I have authority to arrest every
one of you and hold you over night, at least. But I don't want
to make the innocent suffer with the guilty. Will you all
submit to a search?"

Costello stepped forward, proudly. "I was just going to
suggest it myself, Inspector. I realize that no man's name is
clear here until that is done. Will you start with me?"

Piper nodded. "You bet we will. Miss Withers, will you
step out of the room a moment? The officer at the door will
wait for you, because I can't show any favorites here. You
may have the hat-band yourself."

"Yes, and so the penguin may have it under his wing, but
I doubt it," she said acidly. But she followed the officer out
of the room.

Then, as Barry Costello stood there, a faintly embarrassed
smile on his face, the two uniformed officers went over his
clothing and himself with a figurative fine tooth comb.

He had never dreamed that a search could be so absolute.
Every article was removed from his pockets and laid on the
table beneath the light for the Inspector's benefit.

There were some silver change, a pocket-knife with a folding blade, a ring with three keys on it, and two pocket handkerchiefs of fine linen.

There was a bank-book, which Piper opened and turned through rapidly, noting that the man had withdrawn two hundred dollars on his savings account that day, leaving only five dollars on deposit.

There was a bill-fold containing five hundred and forty dollars in bills, two checks made out to "B. M. Costello, Treasurer," one for one hundred and one for three hundred, a few engraved cards bearing the legend "Mr. Barry Costello, Attorney at Law, representing Be Kind to Animals Society . . ."

Piper looked at the man inquisitively. "That's my real life work," Costello told him. "I love all animals, and I love to work for their happiness. Those checks represent contributions toward a little society that I've formed . . ."

There was an address book, through which Piper necessarily skimmed, but in which the detective noticed that there were many names of prominent women, women of Fifth Avenue and Park Avenue circles. This fellow Costello had fine friends. Piper would have liked to make a few notes, but under the circumstances he could not. "Get your own phone numbers," Costello suggested with a bit of a smile as the Inspector lingered over the little book. "Most of those people are bridge pupils of mine."

There was the back of an empty envelope, which had been sent through the mail to Mr. Barry Costello at the Four Arts Club, with scribbles on it. Piper noticed the figure "$5000" written out several times, and beneath it a column of lesser numbers which had been added together to make a grand total of $940, with a notation "Pictures yet to come, approx $500. . . ."

Costello saw Piper's interest, and exploded. "I say, you can't find the hat-band thing in that envelope, you know. And that's all you're supposed to be looking for, Inspector. I don't mind telling you that those cryptic figures are simply a memo I made this afternoon of the money I'm raising for Gwen Lester's defense."

The man was right in objecting, and Piper laid the envelope aside. He watched his men probe into the linings of

Costello's clothes, into his shoes, even open the man's mouth and stare past his excellent set of teeth.

After half an hour of intense effort, they were forced to announce that Barry Costello possessed no hat-band in any way, shape, form, nor manner except for the narrow one sewed onto his derby, which lay on the shelf near the door. Even this was probed and inspected.

Even Nox, the little black lady penguin, came forward to peer up at the man who was being searched, as if she were aiding in the inquisition. She was growing more and more restless, but like the humans whom she so weirdly resembled, she was a prisoner in this stuffy office.

"Well, Inspector, you'll have to hand me a clean bill of health, I guess."

Piper nodded slowly. "No offense, Costello. But you walked into this mess, and you had to stand the search like everybody else who was here. Hemingway, you're the next."

There was considerable protesting here, but Piper stood by his guns, and the effects of Bertrand B. Hemingway were laid bare.

He was punched and prodded and worked over minutely, from the top of his baldish head to the soles of his feet, but he did not have the hat-band. He possessed a thin white-gold watch, five minutes before time, a bill-fold with eight dollars in it, a ring of some thirty keys, pocketful after pocketful of little pieces of paper marked with almost indistinguishable memoranda regarding fish and their habits, and a jack-knife with a complete set of tool blades.

But the Director proved as barren of hat-bands as had Costello. The Inspector impatiently motioned him to join the Irish lawyer against the wall.

"Well, Fink, it looks like you," said the detective threateningly. The two policemen moved forward to take the guard by the arms, but he threw himself back.

"You ain't got any business searching me," he protested. "I ain't done anything. I never even touched the hat-band. But I won't be searched."

"You won't what?" queried the biggest cop, reaching for his night stick. But the Inspector came forward.

"I know that I haven't legal authority to search you," he said. "But I can arrest you as an accessory after the fact, and if that's the only way to find the hat-band, don't think I won't do it. That bit of evidence will show us the approximate head size of the man who killed Gerald Lester. It will send somebody up the river, most likely. Now what about it? Will you be searched before or after arrest?"

Hemingway gave swift instructions to his employee. "Don't be a fool, Fink. You can't get out of it."

"You saw us go through it without whimpering, didn't you?" Costello took the big black pipe from his mouth. "Maybe you've got something to hide? You might as well hand it over to the Inspector, because he'll find it anyway. . . ."

Fink hesitated a moment, and then shrugged his shoulders hopelessly. "All right, you win," he said. He fished in an inside pocket and brought out a grimy packet. "I know I'll rot in jail for, this," he whined, "but I swear I . . ."

Inspector Piper snatched the packet from his fingers, and tore out its contents. Instead of what he had expected to find, here was a tattered set of colored "French" postcards, of a weakly pornographic character. Costello guffawed.

The detective gave Fink a glance of mingled pity and exasperation. He threw back the envelope of dirty postcards.

"Do you think I care one hoot in hell about this junk? Do you think the Homicide Squad has nothing to do but chase smut? I'm looking for elephants, not mice. Search him, boys, and give him a tight frisk."

But nothing of even moderate interest was discovered in the search. Fink's pockets ran to newspaper clippings of the Lester murder, bits of string, a square and marble-like hunk of eating tobacco, and some grimy one dollar bills.

Nothing was ignored. Even the man's shoes were given the eagle eye. Clothes linings, cuff of trousers . . . everywhere. Finally he allowed Fink to put on his clothes.

And at last Piper was forced to the conclusion that the guard was as innocent of hat-bands as the other two. He rubbed his nose reflectively, and then sent for Miss Withers.

She returned to the room in something of a huff at having been kept outside so long.

"I suppose you think you're going to search me, Inspector? Because . . ."

Piper hid a grin. "Nothing was farther from my mind, dear lady. In the first place, it would be against the ethics of the department to suggest such a thing, and I should have to send for a police matron. Again, I haven't the slightest suspicion that you would telephone me that you had found it, and then make away with it in the darkness."

He lit a cigar. "No, it's not on you, and none of these three have it. The window is closed, and you tell me that it has remained so. There wasn't time for anyone to get to the door, which squeaks terribly, and back before the lights went on. Therefore, the hat-band is still in this room."

"Wait one minute," said Miss Withers. "Mr. Costello here went to the door after the lights went on. It was he who found out how it squeaked. . . ."

"But he didn't go through the door?"

"No, not through the door. Just to it, and turned the knob. . . ."

"He didn't go far enough to throw or drop anything?"

Miss Withers shook her head.

Piper strode back and forth. "You didn't hear the sound of running water in the darkness?" He stood above the sink that was fastened against the farther wall. Its plug was in tight.

Miss Withers was sure that she hadn't. "All right, then," said the Piper conclusively. "The hat-band is here. One of you three snatched it up when the lights went out, after he had kicked the cord. Then he hid it somewhere, and it would hve to be somewhere close by. All right, boys, give the room the double O. Hunt till you find it."

He went over to the penguin, which had rested its sleek head on the rung of a chair and gone to sleep standing up.

"It would be just like this blasted little duck to have swallowed the hat-band for the second time," Piper said accusingly. "Only it couldn't hop up on the table, and it wouldn't be able to pull the light plug. . . ."

"Light plug!" Miss Withers had an idea. "He—" she pointed at Hemingway—"was down on the floor when the lights went on."

"Of course I was," snapped the Director. "I knew where the outlet was, and as soon as I found the plug, I made a connection."

"You did all that," said Miss Withers. "But maybe you did something more. Maybe you stuck that hat-band inside the fixture or somewhere before you pushed in the plug?"

Two policemen cast their flashlights on Miss Withers as once more she turned the room into darkness by jerking the light cord. Then she unscrewed the plug and took it out of the socket, but there was no wad of cloth behind it. And that was that. They put on the light again.

It was more than an hour later when at last the Inspector was forced to the conclusion that the missing hat-band was going to continue missing. "The thing didn't vanish in thin air, did it?" he demanded. "It's too big a thing for one of you to have swallowed, humans not having the distendible gullet of our penguin cousins. It didn't walk away, did it?"

"I suppose we're free to go now?" Hemingway asked acidly. "I'd like to put this poor little penguin back in her own pool, with her mate. Erebus has been whimpering out there from sheer loneliness."

Piper nodded. He surveyed the room again. There were few hiding places possible, and every one of them had been gone through with a fine tooth comb by the best brains of the uniformed division.

The glass tanks for specimens, both empty and full, had been taken down from the shelves. Tables, chairs, and shelves had been scrutinized from above and beneath. Every book had been turned through, the floor had been gone over for a loose board. Even the sink had been opened at the trap, and a hooked wire worked both ways to make sure that the band had not been so disposed of.

But it was all useless. "You can all go now," said Piper. "Beat it, and let me think. Yes, take your postcards, Fink. I'm sure I don't want them. Put the silly little bird back into its pool, and then clear out of here."

He turned to Miss Withers. "Well, we nearly got somewhere, anyway. But I don't think that hat-band is so important. After all, we don't know for sure that it was the murderer who dropped his hat in the pool, and who came back to get it that night. It might have been someone shielding the real murderer, some man shielding Gwen . . ."

"The worst part of the whole business," Miss Withers told him, "is the fact that it's all a mess of circumstantial evidence. You believe in it, and I don't. What we need in this case is an eye-witness."

Then the phone rang. Hemingway, who had preceded

Costello through the doorway, turned as if to come back and answer it, but Piper held up his hand.

"See who it is, Calloway." The biggest cop strode over to the desk, and lifted the receiver in one big red fist.

"Hello? Yes, sir, he is. Yes, sir. I'll tell him. Yes, Lieutenant." He replaced the instrument excitedly and faced his superior officer.

"That was Lieutenant Keller, sir, from your office. He just got a message from Warden Hyde over to the Tombs. He says that Chicago Lew, the dip, has written a note asking for you to come and see him tomorrow morning, and promising to spill something new on the Lester murder."

Barry Costello spoke from the doorway. "Well, ten to one there's your eye-witness you were talking about, if he'll only squeal. . . ."

"He'll squeal when the time comes," Inspector Piper promised.

# 16

# The Dumb Man is Silent

IT was bright and early when Inspector Piper sat down to the breakfast table next morning. Perhaps it was earlier than it was bright, since December mornings in New York City are not full blown at seven-thirty. But the Inspector was cheerful, unwontedly cheerful. He donned his best and brightest suit, and attacked the limp bacon and brittle toast which his housekeeper set before him with a definite feeling of optimism.

"Good mornin', Sergeant," said Mrs. McFeeters as she slopped a cup of coffee at his elbow. Mrs. McFeeters had been "doing" for the Inspector so many years that sometimes her none too active mind failed to grasp the extent of his rise in the world. She had come to work for him because it was the only way the Inspector could keep the dear old lady from getting into trouble via shop-lifting, and she stayed because he never had the heart to tell her to go.

"Good morning," said the Inspector. "Fine morning. Well, Mrs. McFeeters, this is a big day for your truly. Yes, ma'm. Today I settle a little business which has been on my mind a bit lately."

"Is it the Lester case, sir?"

"Nothing else. We've dug up a witness to the crime, Mrs. McFeeters, or at least a man who was in the neighborhood at the time it was committed. And that man has promised to talk, or at least to write his story, this very morning."

"Has he, now?"

"He has. And why not? The nasty little pickpocket will be getting his freedom for remembering in time. He'll be set loose from the jail, Mrs. McFeeters. Which is more than a couple of other people will have happen to them, I'm thinking. In spite of these smart amateur detectives. Bah!"

The Inspector stirred his coffee savagely and thought of Miss Withers. "I guess an eye-witness will settle any doubts in the matter. The Lester case was reopened last night, but today it closes again as far as my department is concerned. Bring me some more coffee, will you? I've got to get down to the Tombs, because it's after opening time down there."

"I suppose this pickpocket you've got in a cell down there will be just as eager to tell his story and get out as you are to hear it," observed the housekeeper. "Will you have the morning paper?"

"Bother the paper," said the Inspector. "What the devil is that?"

The telephone in the bedroom rang noisily. "Bother the telephone, too," he added.

"Now I wonder who that can be?" said Mrs. McFeeters, with detached interest.

"You'll never know by standing there," Piper observed. "Leap thither."

"It's a gentleman for you and he says it's on business and it's very important," he was told breathlessly in another moment. "Shall I tell him you've gone down to Headquarters?"

"Here," interrupted Piper. "Hello? What in the . . ." His voice changed. "Who? Costello? Well, what . . ."

"I'm down at the Tombs," came the voice of the Irish

lawyer. "Wait for me there at your place, I've got vital news for you."

"I'm coming down there . . ."

"It's about the Lester case," explained the voice at the other end of the wire. "I just had another interview with the pickpocket. Wanted to see him before the hue and cry, just for Gwen's protection, you know. And he's confessed to killing Lester!"

"Nonsense! Impossible!"

"I've got the written confession in my pocket," said Costello. "I'm bringing it up to you now, so wait for me." And he hung up.

Piper clicked the receiver angrily. "Damn his Mick impudence," he grumbled. "The nerve of his rushing down there as soon as the doors opened in the morning, so as to be the first to hear whatever it was that the dip was willing to say." He looked thoughtfully at his hat, across the room, and then sank into a chair. "If he's coming up here I suppose I might as well wait for him and see what sort of a confession he's dug up," Piper decided. He took up the morning paper.

"Mrs. McFeeters," he observed as he begun to read, "an Irishman is bad enough, and a lawyer is worse, but when the two are combined in one person there's positively hell to pay."

Eight o'clock struck, and eight thirty. The Inspector cast aside the scattered remains of his paper and reached for his hat. "That fresh Mick," he told the doorknob, "is worse to deal with than Miss Withers herself. At least she keeps her appointments."

He tore the door open savagely, and almost rammed into Barry Costello, who stood with his hand ready to knock. The Irishman was attired in full morning clothes, with gardenia, topper and all, and twirled a cane around his slender fingers.

"It's you, is it?" The Inspector's voice was icy. "Come in, my friend. You've got a lot of explaining to do, so talk fast. What do you mean sneaking down there and talking to that dummy before I could get there. . . ."

Costello placed his hat carefully on the table and lit a cigarette. "I'll explain," he said slowly. "You'll remember that you gave your permission, in front of the Warden, for me to talk with the pickpocket, some days ago? I was a little afraid that his testimony would incriminate Gwen, you see, so since I heard last night about his note to you, I rushed down and got in first across the line. Sorry, as it turned out. But the results are great. They speak for themselves. Here you are, Inspector.''

With a bow, Costello laid a folded note before his host. Piper snatched it, but hesitated before he opened it.

"You got this from the pickpocket?"

Costello nodded. "He asked me to give it to you, poor fellow. He's pretty well worn down, you know. Talks of ending it all and beating the noose that way.''

"Beating what noose? You mean the Chair?" Without waiting for an answer, the Inspector slowly opened the folded bit of coarse lined paper.

The message was printed in letters bold enough, and in itself was bolder still. "I KILLED THE BIG GUY BECAUSE HE CAME TO WHEN I GOT HIS WATCH BECAUSE I WAS AFRAYED HE WOULD SQUEAL AND MY NEXT OFFENSE MEANS LIFE UNDER BAUMES LAW I RATHER DIE.''

"No signature, huh?" Piper gave the note the closest scrutiny.

"He said he'd sign any confession you bring to him,'' Costello announced. "But he doesn't care whether he lives or dies, now. I guess this is a new slant on the case. Are you beginning to see eye to eye with me now?''

"About saving Gwen? I believe I am," said Piper heartily. "I don't like your methods, Costello, but somehow I feel that you do want to save Gwen Lester's life. You'd do pretty near anything to save her, wouldn't you?''

"Just about, yes," Costello confessed. "I'm crazy about her, Inspector, and I think she could learn to care for me. So it's not the usual case of lawyer and client. Our being thrown together like that, when I wandered into the Aquarium so calmly to while away an hour or two, and then stumbled on a beautiful woman in trouble . . . well, it appealed to the romantic in me.''

"Um," said Piper. He had little time for young love. "Wait a minute." From his pocket he took a thin bill-fold, and carefully folded the note from the pickpocket inside.

"And now do you think you can order Gwen's freedom?''

The Inspector laughed. "Freedom? Not until I get a better confession than this one. I've had confessions and confessions before, you know. Maybe, after Chicago Lew scribbles his signature at the bottom of a nice legal document, then we'll see. But I don't figure the dip as a murderer, somehow. Yet something happened to change him plenty in the time he was hidden behind the tanks with the penguins. I can tell more about it all when I see him, which will be pronto."

"Come on then, Inspector. I feel that we're nearing the end of this tangle, do you know? Gwen Lester is going to be out of that cell in a day or two. Maybe this afternoon. It was because I hoped you'd have her turned out today that I came rushing up here so early, calling you so you'd be sure and wait. But if getting to the Tombs will speed things up, let's go."

"Sure we'll go," said the Inspector. He stepped to the telephone and called a number.

"What's that for?" asked Costello.

"I'm going to let that school-teacher, Miss Withers, come in on this," said Piper above the mouthpiece. "Trafalgar three four three three—she's been pretty well mixed up in it so far, and I want her to be in at the death."

Costello looked up. "In at the *what*?"

"In at the death, like a fox hunt, you know. In case this business with the pickpocket turns out as you hope."

Costello was puzzled. "But why, Inspector? Why let an outsider in on this? It will only cause delay."

"Never fear," said Piper. "We won't have to wait for Miss Withers. And as for outsiders mixing in, I don't know but that would apply to you too. Remember, young man, I'm running this show. You're only a defense lawyer, and maybe you've dug up something to help your client and maybe you haven't. Besides, Miss Withers is a very good friend of mine. She has more sense than most men."

"She's a charming lady," said the Irishman. "Don't misunderstand me, Inspector. I'd be charmed to have her here."

The Inspector spoke briefly into the phone, and then dropped it. For the second time that morning he grabbed his hat, and then led the way out of the building and into a taxi. "Now you can tell me all about your interview with the dip," he told Costello. "And tell it all, from start to finish. You wanted to get there ahead of me, for fear the dip would spill something unfavorable to Gwen?''

"Not exactly that, Inspector. But I wanted to be forewarned, in case there was something in the situation which could hurt her. So I took pains to be the first visitor to the place, and went straight to call on Mr. Chicago Lew.''

"You didn't stop to talk with Seymour?"

Costello was thoughtful. "No, I didn't stop in front of his cell. I'd been in to see him yesterday, you know. And he was asleep in his bunk, or pretending to be asleep, as we passed. Schmaltz unlocked the door of the pickpocket's cell and left me there.''

"He stayed outside the door, on his chair there, as an extra witness, in case the dip should refuse to own this confession?"

"No, he didn't. Schmaltz grumbled about my coming in so early when he had a lot to do in the upstairs part of the prison. So he locked me in, and left me there. I started to talk to the dip . . .''

"But man, that's in defiance of regulations!"

"No, it isn't, Inspector. Remember that you vouched for me yourself a week or so ago. And of course he searched me thoroughly at the door.''

"Go on," said Piper. "Every rule of procedure seems to have been upset in this case, but go ahead.''

"I made the plea of my life to that pickpocket," said Costello. "I painted a picture for him of what might happen to an innocent woman, and of how he could save her. I knew he could hear me, and I knew that he could be touched. I don't like to praise myself, Inspector, but before I'd gotten really into the swing of my stride, I had that pickpocket almost in tears. And he broke down completely. He reached for the pad of paper and the pencil that you left in his cell in case he should want to make his wishes known, and wrote down this note, practically in the torments of the damned. I made him realize the enormity of his crime, Inspector, not so much in killing Lester as in letting someone else rot in prison for it. I knew all along that he was guilty, Inspector. And as soon as he had printed the last line of the note—printed I suppose because he's an illiterate sort—he toppled over onto his bunk and lay there sobbing, with his face in his hands. He was still carrying on when I shouted for the turnkey to come and let me out, as my time was up.

"Even then I stayed outside the cell door for awhile trying to cheer the man up a bit, you know. But even after I'd gone on to stop outside Seymour's cell and tell him the good news, I could hear the pickpocket making a fuss. I believe he'd kill himself if he had the means, Inspector."

"Quite possibly," said Piper. "Chicago Lew is the suicide type, not the murder type. He might kill himself, but I doubt if he could ever come to killing another man. That takes more guts than Chicago Lew McGirr ever had."

"Even if the man to be killed were lying helpless and unconscious in his power?"

"Maybe that would make a difference, at that. Well, here we are at the Tombs. And there, if I'm not mistaken, is Miss Withers standing on the steps waiting for us. I told you we wouldn't have to wait for that lady, Costello. But she looks upset . . ."

Miss Withers was upset, plenty. She came running down the flight of stone steps and threw herself at the taxi.

"I thought you'd never get here, Inspector," she cried. "Why didn't you tell me what had happened here? I walked in, all unsuspecting . . ."

"So what, my dear lady? I thought you might like to be in the last act of our little playlet. I figured that you might like to see Chicago Lew sign his name at the bottom of another of our famous confessions, that's all."

"Confessions?" Miss Withers drew back. "Then you don't know?"

"I don't know what?" queried Piper testily, as he stepped out onto the sidewalk.

"And I thought that was why you called me to come down, because of what happened in the pickpocket's cell. Chicago Lew isn't going to sign any confession . . ."

"And why not, pray?" put in Barry Costello.

"Because the pickpocket is hanging in the middle of his cell at the end of a wire, stone cold," announced the school-teacher.

Inspector Piper stroked his chin thoughtfully. "We have bad luck with our confessions in this case, don't we?" He led the way swiftly up the steps.

# 17

# The Happy Dispatch

"YES, it was me that found him," declared Schmaltz, the turnkey of the Tombs. "I was the only guard on duty in that wing this morning. I got through my regular chores and started down to my usual post at the end of the corridor, figuring to read the paper and rest a bit. Then I saw him, hanging there like a Christmas turkey."

"You hadn't heard anything, anything at all?" The Inspector fumbled for a cigar.

"Look here," burst in Warden Hyde, "what's the use of questioning this man now? Why aren't you going to the cell, where the prisoner killed himself?"

"Shut up," said Piper. "You may be number one around the Tombs, but the death of a material witness in my business, see? And I do it the way I like, and if you don't see why, you can go tell Tom Roche." He whirled on the worried turnkey, who stood twisting his fingers. Miss Withers and Costello stood a little out of the center of things, waiting and watching.

"Go on, tell me everything that happened this morning, in your own words," ordered the Inspector. "Start at the beginning . . ."

"I hadn't heard anything, no, sir. Not since I'd let Mr. Costello out of the cell-block."

"Go on, tell us about Mr. Costello's visit. Rather early, wasn't it?"

"Yes, sir, it was. I didn't have my morning chores finished. But you and the Warden told me it was all right for him to come in, and I passed him through. He said he had to see the pickpocket, McGirr, and I led him to the cell and unlocked it for him. He said he wanted to try to make the man come clean, so I locked him in and went on with my work in the other part of the building."

"Mr. Costello didn't stop anywhere else, at Seymour's cell, for instance?"

"He did not. When we passed Seymour's cell he was asleep, or seemed to be so. Anyway he was lying down, sir. So was the pickpocket, for that matter, though he looked up when I let Mr. Costello in to see him."

"And then?"

"And then I heard Mr. Costello call out, and I came back to let him out of the cell, as his twenty minutes was up."

"Notice anything then? Was the prisoner any different?"

The man was thoughtful. "I wouldn't say he was different. He was laying in his bunk, sort of sobbing. I let Mr. Costello out and locked the door. The prisoner looked down and out. Mr. Costello said he's stay outside the cell awhile, if it was all right, to try and cheer the fellow up. I could see McGirr in the dark cell, hunching his shoulders like he was weeping, and the bunk creaked. I said I guessed it was all right, and went back to my work of giving breakfast to the prisoners in the other ward."

"That was the last you saw of Mr. Costello?"

"Until he came to the cell-block door to be let out, yes sir. He told me to sort of keep an eye on the pickpocket, sir, because he was afraid the man might try to destroy himself. I said more likely it would be Mr. Seymour that would destroy himself, sir. Because Mr. Seymour, since he quit asking for news about Mrs. Lester, hasn't hardly showed any signs of life at all."

"All right, go on. You went back to block of cells called Murderer's Row, where Seymour and the pickpocket were confined?"

"Not right away, sir. Maybe half an hour. You see, I hadn't finished my sweeping. When I finally got done, I took my morning News and went down to my usual chair at the end of the corridor. It's where I'm on duty except in the early morning and at mealtimes. And when I walked past the pickpocket's cell, I noticed that something was wrong. I stopped . . ."

"Tell us what you saw." Piper was eager.

"I saw what looked like a man walking on air. Because the place hasn't got much of a window, and the wire didn't show. All I could see was the pickpocket there in mid-air, with a chair kicked out from under him where he'd dropped off from, I figure.''

"The door of the cell . . . was it locked?'' put in Miss Withers?''

"It was that, ma'm. I had to fumble through my keys before I found the right one. And I swung the door open, and then I saw what had happened. I cut him down, but there wasn't the bit of a breath of life in him at all. And I called the Warden.''

Piper nodded. "I suppose you might as well show us around, Schmaltz. Miss Withers, would you like to have a look-see? Better not, a man hanged isn't the nicest sight.''

"I guess I can stand it,'' Miss Withers told him. "Come on, young man.'' But Costello hung back.

"Do you mind?'' he asked. "You know where to reach me if you need me. I don't like to go in there and see him, now. It's only a couple of hours since I forced him and bullied him into confessing the crime that made his life forfeit, and I feel a bit guilty of it, you see. Unless there's something you need me for . . .''

"Nothing at all,'' said Piper. "See you later. This may mean something to your client, and it may not. We can't tell yet.'' And he led the way toward the massive iron doors of the cell-block, followed by Schmaltz, the Warden, and Miss Withers.

Murderer's Row was a dank and gloomy place, with a concrete floor that never seemed completely dry, and a light that even now, at mid-day, was pale and feeble.

They passed the cell where Philip Seymour sat, brooding in his bunk. He did not look up as they passed, nor did he seem to wonder why all this excitement was going on. There were no other occupied cells in that block, except the one where, around the corner and at the far end of the passage, a little frightened man had gained the freedom denied him so long.

Piper paused at the door of the cell, and peered into the obscurity. He had no eyes for the blanket-covered bundle on the bunk, at least, not as yet.

"And that's the wire he used,'' pointed out Schmaltz. From a roughly caught knot on the iron grill-work of the door, a tough braided wire of copper ran up, over a steam-pipe that curved from above the door to the center of the ceiling, and then down to dangle in a loose end a little above the height of a man.

"That's where I cut it," said Schmaltz. "The noose is still around his neck."

Piper nodded. Miss Withers noticed the rough chair, which lay on its side in a corner. She shivered a little at the thought of those trembling but resolute feet that had had the courage to kick it aside and then tread air . . .

Piper moved to the bunk and threw back the blanket. He had seen men hung before, suicides and executed prisoners, and he had learned not to show his feelings. But at the sight of the pickpocket's face he almost drew back with an exclamation.

Whatever had impelled Chicago Lew to take his own life, his thoughts at the last moment had not been pleasant, for his face was contorted most evilly. Piper touched the noose gingerly. It had cut deeply into the flesh of the man's throat.

He drew back the blanket, and Miss Withers breathed more easily. "Notify the Coroner's office and get the medical examiner here," said the Inspector. "Tell Doc Bloom that I want particularly an autopsy on this man's throat and vocal cords."

Miss Withers looked up swiftly. "Then you think, too, that he wasn't dumb at all?"

"How do I know? That's what we'll find out," said Piper. "And there's another thing that we've got to find out," he announced accusingly, glaring meanwhile at the Warden. "How did this wire get into the cell?"

"How should I know?" asked Hyde.

"You'd better know. You're responsible for the safety of this prisoner. Did that wire come from inside the Prison?"

The Warden shook his head. "We don't use that type here, even for wiring."

"Then it came from outside. Somebody smuggled it in to the prisoner. You're supposed to search all visitors, aren't you?"

"We are, and we do. Now Inspector, I won't have this . . ."

"Shut up," said Piper again. "Schmaltz, have you searched evvery visitor to this place lately, without exception?"

Schmaltz insisted that he had.

"Why was it you forgot to search Mr. Costello this morning? Were you in a hurry?" This was a shot in the dark, and it got nowhere.

"But I *did* search Mr. Costello."

"Certainly. Do you mind showing me, Schmaltz, just how you search a person who is coming in here? Suppose I were the person . . ."

Schmalz moved ponderously over to the Inspector and moved his hands swiftly over the larger man's lapels, down to his coat and vest pockets, snatching at a bulky army revolver and a pair of steel handcuffs as they passed.

Schmaltz patted the hip and trouser pockets, and stood back. "You could go in now. That search always shows up weapons, or saws either."

"Sure, it would," said the Inspector, as he pocketed the implements of his trade again. "But suppose a man wound fifteen feet of wire around his trouser leg, or around his waist under his belt, he could get it in, couldn't he?"

Schmaltz was forced to admit that possibly a man could. "We aren't on the lookout for fountain pens or matches or bits of wire," said the Warden testily. "All we search for are things that might be made into weapons of attack or escape. We hadn't thought of wire."

"Well, you'd better think of wire, and think of it plenty," said the Inspector. "Prisoners aren't supposed to get the means of dispatching themselves from this earthly plane. It's due to somebody's stupidity or negligence that this man is dead. Somebody smuggled in to him the means of escaping the consequences of his crime."

"Good heavens, man," interrupted Miss Withers, "you don't really think that the pickpocket killed Gerald Lester, do you?"

Inspector Piper hesitated. "Well, why not? Why else would a man leave a note of confession, hinting at suicide, and then take his own life. Unless he was crazy . . ."

"Exactly," said Miss Withers. "Has it occurred to you that the only explanation of the way this pickpocket acted all the way through was that he was a little touched, maybe from the crack he got when he tripped over my umbrella?"

"Maybe you're right," said Piper. "But meanwhile, what do you think I ought to do? If you were me, would you advise the D.A. to hold Gwen Lester for trial? The grand jury found against her the other day."

They were leaving the death cell. "Since you're asking me," Miss Withers announced, "I'll tell you what I'd do."

"You'd free them both, Seymour and the girl . . ."

"I would have, but not now. If I had the authority, I'd put Gwen Lester and Philip Seymour under so many bars and locks that not even dynamite could get to them. Until the trial, I mean. That's what I'd do."

"Wait a minute," said Piper. They were in the corridor outside Philip Seymour's cell. "I'd better ask a few questions here, too."

Warden Hyde unlocked the door, and Piper entered. Miss Withers and the others waited outside.

"Can't you even leave me alone in here?" Seymour wanted to know.

"I'm afraid not," Piper admitted. "I just wanted to find out what you know about the events of this morning, Seymour. You were the nearest one to the scene, you know."

Seymour showed no interest. "I don't know anything about any events," he said.

"Not even about the pickpocket's suicide?"

"So the little man cast off his mortal coil, did he? No, I don't know anything about it. I was trying to sleep this morning."

"You didn't hear anything? The drumming of a man's feet on the cement, for instance?"

Seymour shook his head. "I tell you, I heard nothing," he insisted. "And I don't want to be bothered, do you hear? Don't come here again until you come to let me out, Inspector."

"That might just possibly be a long wait," Piper reminded him. "Can I take any message from you to Mrs. Lester up in the women's ward?"

For the first time Philip Seymour showed some interest. "You can tell her for me," he said slowly, "that her name should have been Cressida." And he turned his back to the Inspector, who left the cell shaking his head.

"I don't remember my Latin so well," he admitted to Miss Withers. "Who in the devil was Cressida?"

"She wasn't Latin, she was Greek," Miss Withers informed him. "I don't know quite how to say it, but she was a

Trojan girl whom Homer painted as a prime extra-fancy variety of prehistoric slut. But you're not going to tell poor Gwen that, are you?"

"Maybe I am," said Piper. "Maybe she is."

# 18

# The Plots Thicken

MISS WITHERS was not due at Jefferson School that afternoon. Her participation in the Lester murder case, both as sleuth and as witness, had made a leave-of-absence necessary, and a paid substitute was in charge of Grade Number Three. All the same, Miss Withers appeared before her class that afternoon, just as the pupils were beginning to fidget in their seats with an eye on the clock.

She was greeted with hearty cheers. Her activities on the memorable afternoon in the Aquarium had completely captured the blood-thirsty little savages of Grade Number Three. And when she had explained what she wanted of them now they volunteered in a body, from Isidore Marx to Abraham Lincoln Washington, from Becky Arons to Nola McGann.

Fifteen minutes later a little army swarmed towards street cars and subways, each childish fist gripped around a quarter for carfare and incidental sodas, and a precious half-inch of copper wire.

The children of Grade Three at Jefferson were playing detective in deadly earnest. Miss Withers watched them go with pride in her heart.

Then she took the subway north to her own apartment. Before she had taken off her hat the telephone rang.

It was the Inspector. "I thought you might like to know," he began. "Just got a report from Doc Bloom on the autopsy. He's had an expert in nose and throat diseases to consult with him, too, and they both agree that Chicago Lew McGirr had as good a set of vocal cords as any of us. There was nothing structurally wrong with his speech mechanism at all!''

''Now what do you know about that? Do you think the pickpocket was malingering?''

''Either that or he was nuts,'' said Piper unfeelingly. ''And another thing that's worrying me is what to do about this confession from the dip. The D.A. says that with that in existence, there isn't a chance of pinning the rap on Gwen Lester. It would be all right if only Costello hadn't seen it, but now he can insist on its being introduced as evidence, and no jury will bring in a conviction against her with that hanging fire. Even if it can't be proved absolutely that he wrote it, although both sides will dig up handwriting experts, I suppose.''

''Where do I come in on all this?'' Miss Withers wanted to know.

Piper hesitated. ''I don't know. But you've been acting all along as if you had some ideas or suspicions that you weren't talking about. Tell me frankly, have you got anything that will tend to clear Gwen Lester? Because if you have, I'll be forced to release her when Costello comes down tomorrow morning to make his plea.''

''Costello is coming to your office in the morning?''

''He is. He just called up, and said he knew I'd be wanting to question him on the pickpocket affair, and when did I want to see him. An obliging chap, Costello. And smart, too. He's going to free Gwen Lester, whether she did the murder or not.''

''Maybe,'' said Miss Withers. ''Anyway, I'd like to drop in at that little conference tomorrow morning, if you don't mind. And I'll bring a friend, if I'm lucky.''

Then she hung up without further explanation. All the same, she was pleased that the Inspector had called on her for help. Before she was through with this business she would show that man that a woman could play sleuth just as well as a member of the so-called stronger sex.

Miss Withers was sitting in Inspector Piper's office the next morning, with a smile on her face reminiscent of the cat that ate the canary.

''But I don't see . . . .'' the Inspector was saying.

"You let me handle this," Miss Withers insisted. "Here he comes now!"

Lieutenant Keller opened the door and ushered in Barry Costello.

"Good morning, Miss Withers! And the top of the morning to you, Inspector." He took in the Inspector's new suit, a roughish tweed shot with blobs of red and orange brown, donned in honor of the unseasonably sunny December day. "Well, you certainly are a *Pied Piper* today, Inspector . . . Ha, ha . . ."

Miss Withers cocked her head thoughtfully on one side. She detested puns, and people who made them.

Costello seated himself, and leaned back against a case of gruesome exhibits. "What I wanted to see you about, Inspector, is this . . ."

"Wait a moment, please," cut in Miss Withers. "Mr. Costello, do you happen to know how the pickpocket met his death yesterday morning?"

"He was hanging at the end of some wire, wasn't he?"

"Right. It was thick, strong, braided copper wire. There isn't much of it used, and right away I figured that it could be traced. Naturally it didn't grow there in the Tombs."

"Naturally, Madam."

Miss Withers raised her voice. "Becky! Come in now."

The door opened, and in from the anteroom came a small, freckle-faced girl towing a tallish, near-sighted man in a well-worn serge suit.

"This is Becky, one of my best pupils," Miss Withers announced. "I sent out my entire class yesterday afternoon to do a little errand for me, and Becky was the lucky girl to make good."

Miss Withers was watching Costello's face, but he gave no sign of perturbation. "I gave each of my children a little piece of that copper wire, bits of a length that I cut off the roll when it lay on the Warden's table, with his shears. I assigned them each a certain section of the city, and between three and six o'clock last night they covered every hardware store in Manhattan. And Becky has brought this gentleman down here because he remembers selling a length of this braided wire a day or two ago, in his hardware and paint store on Third Avenue!"

Piper was eager. "Quick, man. Do you remember the person who bought that wire? Can you describe him . . . or her?"

The hardware man hesitated, and chewed a bit of gum reflectively. "I can do that, officer," he said slowly. "It was a gentleman in gray striped trousers, and he carried a crooked topped stick and wore a posie in his buttonhole."

Costello was smiling. But Miss Withers pointed an accusing finger at him. "Was it this man here?"

The gentleman from the Third Avenue hardware store was not one to rush into anything. "It might have been," he said. "And then again, it might not. Seems like he was a little taller, kind of. And then this fellow had on a top hat, like they wear in the movies. No, I wouldn't go to swear as to that, though they're mighty alike . . ."

"Naturally," said Barry Costello. "Miss Withers, let me congratulate you. But if you'd given me a chance to explain why I wanted this interview with the Inspector, you might have saved yourself some breath. I bought that wire, and I smuggled it into the Tombs."

Piper leaped to his feet. "Why didn't you tell us this yesterday?"

"Nobody asked me yesterday. And besides, I was hoping to keep out of it if I could. I realize that it's illegal to smuggle anything into the City Prison. But I took stock of the risks before I did it, and I'm perfectly willing to admit everything I did. The wire was wrapped around my waist, under my vest, and Schmaltz never came near it when he gave me the usual search."

"I don't get this," boomed Piper. "Why did you do it?"

"To achieve what I've been working for since I interested myself in this case," explained Costello patiently. "To save Gwen Lester."

"But how did you think that giving the pickpocket means of committing suicide was going to help Gwen?"

"I don't think the pickpocket committed suicide," explained Costello gently. "And I didn't mean to help him. I brought that wire into the Tombs because Philip Seymour begged me to do it. He wanted the means of ending his life. And I figured that a suicide in Seymour's position was tantamount to a confession of guilt, and that a jury would take it that way. So I broke the rules and helped him."

"Good God, man, what are you trying to make us believe? You smuggled in a wire to Philip Seymour, and a man down the corridor in another cell committed suicide with it?"

Barry Costello smiled. "I just told you that I don't think the pickpocket did commit suicide. It's a tangled mess, but I'm forced to believe that I was wrong in thinking the pickpocket committed the murder. He must have been out of his head, I'm thinking, and confessed to it just the way that a lot of queer people do after every crime. Yesterday this case was straightening itself out nicely. The pickpocket was the murderer and he had given me a confession note. But when I heard you say, Miss Withers, that the pickpocket hung at the end of a wire . . . and I knew that the only wire in the Tombs was the one I'd taken to Philip Seymour at his own request . . . well, it looks as if Seymour killed the pickpocket."

"Seymour! What are you saying, man? Do you think that Seymour could walk through walls and bars? If the pickpocket didn't commit suicide, how could Seymour have killed him?"

"I'm no detective, Inspector. All I know is that I slipped the wire into Seymour's cell when the turnkey was leading me out of the place yesterday morning."

"Young man, I don't believe you! People don't do such things. You expect us to believe that you actually handed that poor boy a length of wire and told him to hang himself?" Miss Withers was wroth. Somehow the wind had been taken out of her sails.

Costello nodded. "In a way, I did just that. Because I believe that every man has a right to put an end to his existence if it becomes unbearable. What was there ahead for Philip Seymour? Disgrace, long months of torture in a cell, and then the public murder in the chair up at Sing Sing which the prisoners call the 'Hot Squat.' Can you blame a man for wanting to escape all that? Why shouldn't I help him?"

"But he didn't kill himself with the wire," Miss Withers reminded them. "I suppose he sent the wire by Western Union messenger to the cell around the corner, and with it a message 'hang yourself, please'?"

"I'm not explaining what happened," said Costello patiently. "I'm telling you what I did, and why. I realize that I'm liable for what I did, but it isn't a very serious offense as long as I took in neither tools of escape nor a lethal weapon, although the wire may have indirectly proved to be both. Arrest me if you care to, although it would certainly be bad psychology to arrest the defense attorney in a murder case of this magnitude, a week before the trial. The public would think you were persecuting Gwen, you see . . ."

"But how could a wire get from Seymour's cell to the pickpocket's neck?" Piper had chewed up three cigars in this interview.

"I'm not the detective," Costello reminded him. "I'm telling you the facts and you can figure it out for yourself. All I'm trying to do is to protect Gwen Lester's interests, and to make the greatest advantage of every change in the situation for her. My cards are on the table."

"Well, there's something screwy somewhere," Piper said slowly. "That wire didn't walk down the corridor. And you and the turnkey were the only two people loose in the cell-block yesterday morning."

"Were we?" asked Costello. Just then the phone rang, and Piper snatched it up.

"Good morning, Warden. Yes, I left word for you to call me. Did you search the cells as I suggested, empty and full ones both. You did?"

There was a long pause, and then the Inspector put down the telephone without saying good-bye.

He looked out of the window, and then leaned back wearily in his chair. There was, for the first time since he had entered this case, a slump to his wide shoulders.

"I just got word," he remarked to nobody in particular, "that Hyde found a file and the broken pieces of a homemade key in Seymour's slop-bucket. The key is rough, but at least it was *planned* to fit the old-fashioned lock to Philip Seymour's cell!"

# 19

# Nor Iron Bars a Cage

MISS WITHERS looked at the Inspector, and the Inspector looked at Barry Costello, and the Irishman grinned back at both of them.

"Now maybe I wasn't the only person besides the turnkey to be loose in that cell-block yesterday morning!"

Miss Withers shook her head. "I don't see how Seymour could have killed the pickpocket, even if he was loose in the corridor. Nor do I see any reason for his killing the little man."

"Not even if he knew of the pickpocket's message to me on the previous evening, promising to spill the beans on the Lester murder?" Piper rose slowly to his feet. "Seymour must have made a key to the pickpocket's cell, too, and gone there to kill him for fear the pickpocket would implicate him. Either Chicago Lew was a witness to the killing of Gerald Lester or else Seymour thought he was, which is the same thing. He was bumped off in his cell by the murderer of Gerald Lester!"

Costello nodded in agreement. "It certainly looks that way, Inspector. Though it's hard to believe that a prisoner in the Tombs could kill another prisoner there. I'm blaming myself, of course, for being an innocent accessory before the fact. But I took the wire to Philip Seymour because he had me fooled with his suicide story, and because I felt that if he did bump himself off he'd be making a confession that would free Gwen. And what he really wanted was the means of killing the man he was afraid would squeal on him."

"What did Seymour say when they found the file and the scraps of broken key in his slop-bucket?" Miss Withers was thoughtfully pleating the hem of her skirt.

"Denied any knowledge of it, of course," said Piper.

"They always do. I suppose he figured that they'd be thrown out, and nothing could ever pin the murder of the pickpocket on him. But that foxy lad has been a little too foxy. If we can't pin the murder of Gerald Lester on him, we'll get him anyway for the killing of Chicago Lew McGirr. All that's necesary to do now is for us to reconstruct the crime. I'm going over to the Tombs. You people better come along."

Costello hesitated. "I *did* have an appointment," he ventured. "But it can wait. I have a feeling that we're getting closer and closer to the end of this snipe-hunt."

"Do you know, I have that same feeling," said Miss Withers confidentially as they followed Inspector Piper out of the building.

They found Warden Hyde waiting for them at the Tombs, an exhibit lying before him on his desk. It consisted of a tiny file, not more than two inches long, but of finely hardened steel, and three broken bits of metal which when fitted together made the crude outline of a key.

"Here's what we took from the cell of your prisoner, Seymour," the Warden said. "That key was to fit the old-fashioned lock of Seymour's cell."

Piper stared down. "You're sure it could have opened the cell door?"

"Of course I'm not sure. All I know is that it is of the same type of indentation as the genuine key that Schmaltz carries, with the same notches. Broken as it is, of course we can't test it. But I'll stake my professional reputation that if this key didn't unlock Seymour's cell door yesterday morning, then the man had made another and a better second version that did!"

"Let me get this straight," said Piper. "Would this key have unlocked the pickpocket's cell door also? Are both keys alike?"

"Not at all," said the Warden. "There is only one row of cells in the place that opens with these old-fashioned keys at all, and while Seymour's cell happened to be in that row, the pickpocket's wasn't. Chicago Lew McGirr was locked in with a special new device that nobody but the turnkey could have opened. We're putting them on all the doors in the Tombs as soon as the appropriation permits."

"That doesn't make sense," said Miss Withers. "What

good would it have done for Seymour to make a key to his own cell, when he couldn't make one to fit the pickpocket's? You didn't find another key anywhere in the man's cell, did you?''

Warden Hyde looked dubiously at Miss Withers, but the Inspector nodded his head. "She's a sort of unofficial assistant of mine," he told Hyde. "Answer the question."

"We searched this place from ceiling to floor," said Hyde testily. "Naturally the honor of myself and my men has been implicated when a suicide or a murder takes place within these walls. And we found nothing out of the way but this file and the bits of a key."

"Maybe Seymour didn't kill the pickpocket after all," said Miss Withers thoughtfully. "Maybe he only took the wire to the man and poked it through the bars, telling him to go ahead and commit suicide with it. Only it doesn't sound so plausible . . ."

"Men don't make keys and go to all that trouble just to help another prisoner commit hari-kari," Piper pointed out. "But we're wasting time here. You had Seymour transferred to another cell-block, Warden?"

Hyde nodded. "As it happens, there's no prisoners in Murderer's Row right now. Want to go back there?"

"I certainly do." And again Piper led the way, carrying in one hand the broken key that had been taken from Seymour's cell.

As the others watched, he took a fine pair of tweezers from his pocket, and attempted to turn the lock of the cell door with the fragment of the business end of the key. It fitted, but he could not secure purchase enough to turn it.

"That doesn't prove anything anyway." Costello suggested. "If Seymour could make a key as good as that one, he could make a better one in case he needed it."

"Right you are," said Piper. "Now let's try to reconstruct the crime. You say you tossed the wire into Seymour's cell as you followed the turnkey out of the place yesterday morning?"

Costello nodded. "All right, then," said Piper. "Let's suppose that Seymour is in this cell, waiting eagerly for the wire. He knows that he has perhaps half an hour during which time the turnkey will be working elsewhere in the prison. And he knows that the pickpocket has promised to make disclosures which he fears will fix the Lester murder on himself. He has made his key, and he unlocks his cell door as soon as the turnkey and Costello here are out of sight. He knows that the other cells in the block are empty, so he goes swiftly to the pickpocket's cell."

"And there he stops," said Miss Withers, "because he hasn't got any way of getting into that cell, if what the Warden says about the new patent locks is true. Schmaltz is certain that the pickpocket's door was locked after he let Mr. Costello out."

They were once more before the cell where Chicago Lew had given up the ghost. "With a gun or even a sword, a murderer might do damage from the corridor, through the bars," Miss Withers pointed out. "But I don't see how a strangler could get in his work, and then leave the body hanging in the middle of the cell."

"Wait a minute," cried Piper excitedly. "Quick, Hyde, unlock this door for me. I want to get in that cell."

The place was dark and gloomy as usual, but Piper cast his pocket flash into every corner, and even toward the ceiling. When the blinding flood of light touched the steam-pipe at the ceiling, the Inspector held it steady.

"Miss Withers, Costello . . . notice anything? See there on the pipe where the wire was drawn? Stand on the chair."

They both did see. Something had cut into the soft iron pipe, making an indentation a quarter of an inch deep, as if a saw had been drawn across the top.

"I don't understand why a wire would cut so deeply into the iron pipe with only a man's weight dropping at the end of it," said Piper. "This is a little detail that is going to get us somewhere . . ."

"You bet it is," said Barry Costello slowly. "Now I know how the thing was done, and made to look like suicide. I'll show you . . . send for that wire, will you?"

Piper stared at the man for a moment, and then sent Schmaltz speeding toward his office, with a note to Lieutenant Keller.

"Seymour never got inside that cell!" insisted Costello. "He managed the business from the corridor, and I'll show you how. I'm no detective, but I see this thing like a book. Somehow, he persuaded the pickpocket to come over to the door, perhaps by promising him freedom, and then he slipped a noose around the fellow's neck and throttled him. It was the best way to kill him, he figured, because it was silent and it could be *made* to look like suicide."

"So far it's possible," said Piper gravely. "Though there wasn't much room to spare through those bars. Anyway, suppose that Seymour did all this, and held the noose tight until his victim collapsed on the floor inside the door. How did Seymour manage to suspend his victim in the air?"

By this time the wire had arrived, less the foot or so of its length that Miss Withers had purloined.

"Watch me," said Barry Costello. "Notice that the steam-pipe at the ceiling makes a curve and comes out near the door?"

Letting one end of the wire remain where the dead man had theoretically lain, Barry Costello worked the other up and over the steam-pipe remaining outside the door all the time. By making a little jump he succeeded in catching the end again and drawing it down.

"All right," said Miss Withers. "But this looks fishy to me. Your wire isn't anywhere near the place on the steam-pipe where the scratch was made, and from which the dead man hung."

"Wait patiently," said Costello. "Couldn't the man have worked the wire along the pipe, away from him? Wire is stiffer than rope, you know. Maybe he used the turnkey's broom which you'll see over there under the window. Anyway . . . there it is!"

The loop of wire slipped into the notch. And now Barry Costello held the free end in his hands, outside the cell, from which the wire ran up, over the steam-pipe in the middle of the ceiling and then back down to where the murdered pickpocket had lain.

"All there was left for Philip Seymour to do," said Costello, "was to make a loop of the wire around his hands and pull like the very devil. The pickpocket was a little fellow, you know. He couldn't have weighed more than a hundred pounds. Seymour was a college athlete, you remember, and he's still in good enough condition to knock out a man with one blow, as he admits doing to Lester. He pulled the dying man up in the air by sheer force, and then when he got him there, he made the end of the wire fast around the bars of the door, with the knot inside so that it would look as if the suicide had simply chosen that very natural place to fasten it before climbing on the chair and jumping off."

"Hell's bells, man," Piper said wonderingly. "I believe you're right. It's not half as impossible as it sounded when you first claimed it. But why are you so interested in pinning this crime on Seymour?"

"I'm not interested in pinning any crime on anybody," said Costello. "But I realize that it was my fault that this wire got into the prison in the first place, and for that reason I want to square myself. Besides, if Philip Seymour killed the pickpocket, he killed Gerald Lester too. Which means that he's a double murderer, an enemy of society, and every man's hand ought to be turned against him. Again, as I said in your office, Gwen Lester can go free now . . ."

"Not necessarily," Miss Withers reminded him unpleasantly. "She might still have been mixed up in the killing of her husband, as an accessory anyway. Besides, there's one thing you haven't made clear. How did the murderer arrange to have the chair so conveniently tipped over in the corner to suggest that it had been jumped from?"

Barry Costello shrugged his shoulders. "I don't know. Maybe it was that way when he came to kill McGirr. It's a minor detail. The main thing is that Philip Seymour had both the motive, the means, and the opportunity of killing the pickpocket."

"Do you know, you've been a great help to me," said Piper. "A very great help. That's a most ingenious suggestion as to the means of committing the murder, and you've convinced me that it was a murder, and done that way, too."

Costello lit his black pipe. "Then you won't be holding that business of bringing in the wire against me?"

"No, I guess we'll forget about the wire," Piper promised him. "Anyway, that is the least important phase of this case."

"The most important phase of it," Barry Costello announced, "is that now I've got a sure-fire defense for Gwen Lester, even if you do insist on going ahead and bringing her to trial next week. No jury in the world will convict her in the face of what has happened here in the Tombs yesterday and today.''

''You're very probably right,'' said Oscar Piper. ''But I don't think Tom Roche will see it that way. He likes the publicity that comes from trying a beautiful woman for murder. And even if he fails to get a conviction on the woman, the public always thinks that the jury was influenced by her looks.''

''The jury will be,'' said Costello. ''Anybody would be. Let me tell you, I was and am. And will be, too, for the rest of my life, if the Gods are good to me.''

Miss Withers looked at her wrist watch. ''Gentlemen, it's two o'clock in the afternoon, and I had breakfast at seven-thirty. I'm hungry.''

''Heavens,'' said Costello. ''I had a lunch appointment for twelve, with Launcelot Billings, Seymour's lawyer. We're to discuss handling the cases as one, but now I won't consent to it. You'll excuse me?''

''I certainly will,'' said the Inspector. ''But don't bring any more wires and things into the Tombs, if you should feel inclined to visit your client or one of the other material witnesses. If you do we won't have anybody to try when the case comes up next week.'' He turned to Miss Withers. ''Wait for me at my office, will you? I'd like to buy you lunch, but I have a little errand to do first. You'll wait?''

''Sure I'll wait,'' agreed Miss Withers. She didn't have to wait long among the knives, sash-weights and guns of Piper's office. He was with her in ten minutes, and shortly afterward the detective faced the school-teacher across a lunch-room table.

''You went up to grill Seymour about this business?'' she hazarded.

Piper grinned. ''Yes, I went to see Seymour in the cell where they moved him. But not to grill him. He won't talk anyway, except about Gwen, for whom his heavy passion seems to have curdled. No, I didn't grill him. I just looked at his hands.''

''His hands?'' Miss Withers attacked her omelet.

''Yeah, his hands.''

''And what did you find out of the ordinary about his hands?''

The Inspector let fall a veritable snowstorm of salt above his steak. "That's the remarkable part about the whole thing," he said. "There was nothing out of the ordinary about his hands."

20

# Whom the Gods Destroy

THERE was a jury in the box, and Judge Maxwell Thayer on the bench, and the case of the People of the State of New York versus Philip Seymour and Gwen Lester was beginning to show every sign of dragging itself through until the Ides of March.

"If it took them two days to pick a jury, only God himself knows how long it will take to pick a murderer," said Piper to Miss Withers. They sat together on the first row of benches.

Miss Withers did not answer. Her eyes were glued on the litttle door on the right of the dais. Finally it opened, and Gwen Lester came through.

It was the first time Miss Withers had seen the young widow since the memorable evening of the flashlight photos and the green silk pajamas. Gwen was not dressed in green pajamas now. She was wearing black, with a frilly lace collar and a simple cameo pin at her throat. The dress was low, but it gave the air of being accidentally low, and suggested that if the wearer had known of the shadow of breast it revealed she would at once have pulled it around her throat.

"Smart girl, Gwen Lester," said the Inspector.

Behind her came Philip Seymour. He was wearing a dark double-breasted suit, a blue tie, and his hair was combed neatly, which was more than Miss Withers could say for him when she had seen him in the Tombs. At least it was a good thing he had given over the idea of being his own lawyer, and let Launcelot Billings, his partner, handle the case. Miss Withers noticed that the two defendants avoided each other's eyes. She was sorry for that. She would have liked to see them smile comfortingly across the space between them.

Suddenly the bustling figure of Tom Roche had arisen, and was giving tongue. He had an air of efficiency, an evident desire to make up for the long bickering that had delayed the picking of the jury. His air of ease suggested that after all this trial was a mere matter of form, and that all that was really necessary would be to send the man and the woman who faced him up the river and through a little green door into Eternity.

"Plese Your Honor and gentlemen of the jury," he began, "we are gathered here for a stern and necessary purpose. At noon on the fourteenth day of last November a particularly bloody and cruel murder was perpetrated in this metropolis of ours. A successful young business man, gentlemen, a former college athlete, was struck down in a dastardly fashion and under particularly unusual circumstances. The body of Gerald Lester, whom his friends and business associates knew as Jerry, was found floating in a tank in the New York Aquarium. He was not drowned, as was first thought. He had not met his death through a good clean blow on the chin, though he was bruised there. Gerald Lester, gentlemen, had been killed by the insertion of a hatpin in his ear, piercing the bone and entering the brain."

Tom Roche paused for effect, and then continued. "The State will demonstrate to you, during the course of this trial, that Gerald Lester had come to the Aquarium because some friend had warned him by telephone that his young and beautiful wife was having an assignation there with a former lover. We shall prove in the proper time the purposes of that assignation between the defendants you see before you.

"The State will prove to you, gentlemen, that Gwen Lester was tired of her husband. The State will bring you evidence to prove that her fancy had turned once more toward her former lover, particularly since the collapse of the Wall Street market that hit her husband in his pocketbook, and Philip Seymour was rapidly becoming a success in his chosen vocation.

"The State will show you the movements of the young broker on the fatal day. We are prepared to prove how he went to the Aquarium in defense of the honor of his home, armed with a heavy walking stick, which he was forced to leave at the door, and how he accosted his faithless wife and her lover. We shall continue by showing how the man in the case . . .'' Roche let his eyes linger on the impassive face of Philip Seymour for a moment, and then got back into the swing of his discourse . . . ''how the man in the case met the accusations of the wronged husband with physical combat, how he knocked Gerald Lester into unconsciousness, carried his body behind the tanks into a hidden and secret place, and there completed his job, on a homicidal impulse, with a weapon ready to hand.

"The State will prove, gentlemen, that the wife of the wronged man was a willing accomplice in this murder, if not an actual participant. We shall show that her stockings were stained with the slime of the penguin tank, although her story maintains that she never passed through the door that led to the murder scene. We shall show that she connived in the attack on her husband by her lover, instead of taking her rightful place in defense at her husband's side. We shall show you, gentlemen, that before and after the fact, if not during the actual crime, she and Philip Seymour were partners in murder. We shall show that this young and undeniably beautiful woman before you, gentlemen, was the actual one to stumble upon and suggest the weapon with which this murder was committed. The crime itself was womanishly planned, gentlemen. I shall not presume upon your patience further. The State is prepared to demonstrate beyond the possibility of a doubt every point that I have outlined to you above.

"You have received your instructions from His Honor. You know your duty, gentlemen, and I know as I gaze into your eager and intelligent faces that you will not hesitate to bring in a verdict, when you have heard the evidence, in accordance with that duty."

Mr. Tom Roche took a glass of water, and turned his profile so that if a newspaper artist were sketching him, the best angle would be shown.

"First State witness is Miss Hildegarde Withers!"

"Miss Hildegarde Withers!" The voice of the court crier boomed through the long room, jammed with people.

For a moment Miss Withers sat in her place as if turned to stone. Then at a nudge from the Inspector, she rose and went forward. Through the gate, past the table where Launcelot Billings, Seymour's nervous partner, sat beside Barry Costello, and on, on, practically under the nose of Judge Thayer, who sat in his heavy robes of black silk and appeared to doze. She had not thought to be the first.

The words of the clerk, who popped up so suddenly that Miss Withers almost screamed, came like the jumbled litany of a mass. "Youdosolemnlyswearthatthetestimonyyougiveto thecourtandjuryinthiscasenowontrialshallbethetruththewhole truthandnothingbutthetruthsohelpyouGod?"

Miss Withers gave her solemn oath that this should be so. Then she mounted the stand, made sure that her skirt hung neatly, and leaned back. Down in the front row she could see the Inspector's face, and a look of understanding passed swiftly between them.

Tom Roche pushed aside the heap of papers that littered his wide mahogany table, and cleared his throat. His tone was so matter of fact that Miss Withers had to remind herself that this was a murder trial, that two human lives were at stake for the taking of another human life, and that her words might strike the balance between life and death for the boy and girl who watched her.

"Miss Withers, you are a school-teacher?"

"I am. Jefferson Public School, Grade Number Three . . ."

"Will you tell the court what you were doing during the noon hour on the fourteenth day of last November?"

"Certainly. I was conducting my class of some twenty pupils through the New York Aquarium, located at the Battery."

"And what were you doing at approximately one o'clock on that same afternoon?"

"I was hunting for my garnet hatpin, which I had lost somehow during the preceding hour. And my pupils were helping me."

"You found the hatpin?"

"I did, or rather one of my pupils did. It was on the lower step of the Aquarium stair that leads to the upper level."

Tom Roche nodded approvingly. "Do you recognize this article, Miss Withers?" He took a tissue-wrapped bundle from his brief-case and opened it. Between his fingers he rolled a six-inch length of shining steel, with a dark red stone at the end.

"I do," said Miss Withers. "That is my hatpin."

"May I ask to have this introduced as evidence?" asked Tom Roche. There was no objection, and the hatpin was marked for identification.

This was not what Miss Withers had expected of a murder trial. She had visualized it as a battle between the opposing lawyers, a long and bitter contest of objections and clashes. And now everyone simply sat still and fiddled with bits of paper while the prosecuting Attorney built up his case against the two defendants.

"You will go on and tell us exactly what happened after one of your pupils found the hatpin?" said Tom Roche.

"I found that one of my pupils, Isidore Marx by name, was missing," said Miss Withers. "I looked for him, and finally found him underneath the stairs staring into the penguin tank. He was engrossed in watching the peculiar movements of the birds, which were leaping and biting at something over their heads, out of sight. As I watched, I saw something fall into the tank. It was a dead body."

"Just a minute, Miss Withers. How did you know it was a dead body?"

"I've got eyes, haven't I? A dead man looks different from a live man. So I sent one of my pupils for the guard, who was at the door, and another for a policeman."

"Who got there first?"

"First? Some of the bystanders, I guess. I must have screamed a little. The guard came, took one look, and ran for the Director. He came running, bringing the two people who had been in his office . . ."

"And who were the two people?" Tom Roche's voice was oily.

"You know who they were. The defendants in this case, of course." Miss Withers was annoyed.

"Please answer the State's questions without comment, Miss Withers," said His Honor dreamily, and went back to his doze.

"By that time there was a big crowd around the tank," Miss Withers continued. "The Director forced his way through the crush, and the others followed him. Then Gwen Lester said . . . " 'Philip, what have we—' " Miss Withers hesitated.

"Go on, tell the court what the defendant said!" Roche was urgent.

Barry Costello was on his feet. "I object, Your Honor. That is hearsay evidence, and absolutely inadmissable." His voice rang through the overheated courtroom, and suddenly everybody was wide awake.

Tom Roche was also awake. "But Your Honor, I invoke the right of . . ."

The gavel pounded sharply on the Judge's bench. "Objection sustained," said His Honor. "You may strike that out of the testimony. Go on."

"Then the officer came, and took charge. He insisted that the man in the tank might not be dead, and chose one of the bystanders . . ."

"Who did he choose?"

"It was Mr. Costello, the defense lawyer," said Miss Withers. "He was trying to help Gwen Lester, who had fainted, and the officer saw his flask. I guess he thought liquor might revive the man in the tank . . ."

"Never mind the guessing, Miss Withers. Mr. Costello and the officer went behind the tank, and removed the body from the water?"

"They did. And we all followed after, and watched. They tried artificial respiration without any results, as I could have told them . . ."

"Why could you have told them? Did you see any evidences of murder?"

"As a matter of fact, I did. When I first saw the face in the water, through the glass of the tank, I noticed a reddish tinge of dissolving blood around the ear. That must have suggested something more than drowning to me, though I didn't reason it out then."

"You didn't, of course, connect your hatpin, which had been lost and found, with the dead body? You didn't suspect that you had furnished the weapon?"

"Mercy sakes, no!"

"All right, go on from there. What happened?"

"That was all that happened. In a few minutes an Inspector of Police arrived and took charge."

Tom Roche nodded. "Very good, Miss Withers. I may want to call on you later, but that will be all for now. Will the defense cross-examine?"

Miss Withers looked anxiously at Launcelot Billings. He was pulling nervously at a little moustache, already losing its waxed smartness. This being a witness was more wearing on the spirit than she had dreamed it would be. Only an occasional glimpse of Piper's honest and homely face strengthened her.

Billings whispered briefly with his client, and then shrugged his shoulders. "No questions now," he said shortly.

But Barry Costello thought differently. He stood erect, drawing himself up to his full five feet eleven inches, and threw a look of reassuring comfort at Gwen. Then he faced Miss Withers.

His air was that of a stage manager of some amateur production. It was understood that this was all among friends, that it was only a farce, and that the serious overtones of Mr. Roche were to be dismissed as the natural lines of a stage villain. Barry Costello might have been drawing Miss Withers out at a very charming dinner party in regard to some amusing adventures of her own. His personal charm took in judge, jury, witnesses, defendants . . . yes, and even the prosecutor.

"Miss Withers," began Barry Costello, "I am going to ask you to tell the Court a few more details about the case before us. I am going . . ."

But Miss Withers was not listening. She was staring down into the courtroom, into the faces of the people who waited there. She saw the strained face of Bertrand B. Hemingway, nervously nibbling at his fingernails. There was a guilty face if ever a man had one. She remembered little details, countless little details, as Costello's pleasant booming voice with its faint touch of the brogue rolled on and over her. She remembered how Hemingway had concealed his stock deals with Lester. She remembered the dark interlude behind the tanks, when Hemingway had left her alone with the Inspector to fetch a flashlight, and how somehow dallied searching for it while the Unknown came back to beat down the officer on guard and carry away an incriminating hat.

She remembered the incident of the operation on the little

black penguin named Nox, and the hat-band that Hemingway
had so unwillingly allowed her to identify, and that had
disappeared in a flash of darkness.

Other little incidents, oddly assorted, flitted through her
mind, contrary to her early ideas on the matter, but pointed
now, and sharp. The cigarette butts that had disappeared from
the glass tray on Hemingway's desk, and the cigarette butts
that had appeared in the Men's Room of the Aquarium . . .
had that been a blind, too?

Beyond Hemingway she could see Marian Templeton, Lester's secretary, the "office-wife" already picked as fair game
by the tabloids. Whatever happened here in this courtroom
Marian Templeton's life was going to be ruined, and every
unsavory bit of soiled laundry would have to be hung out to
dry. Before this case was over, even if the guilty were
punished, Marian Templeton would be a real sufferer. Hemingway could only lose his Directorship and his life's work.
She herself had only lost a month's pay at Jefferson School.
The Inspector had lost his sleep for many a night. Everyone
lost, nobody gained. Even the State of New York, even if it
succeeded in gaining a conviction, would pay out some thousands of dollars of taxpayers' money for every day the trial
held forth, and more for the execution if that should ever
happen.

A hush brought her back to herself, and Miss Withers
realized that she had been asked a question. Costello repeated
it sharply.

"Miss Withers, I'd like to ask if it is your habit to wear a
hatpin?"

"It's not a habit, exactly."

"Yet you were wearing one on the day in question?"

"'I was. I always wear my mother's hatpin with that hat,
because it doesn't stay on very well. Hats nowadays are made
for bobbed hair, and mine is long. I . . .'"

"Quite so. An unlucky chance for Gerald Lester that you
wore it that day, Miss Withers."

That didn't seem to require an answer. Costello went on.
"Where is your home, Miss Withers?"

"In New York City, on 76th Street . . ."

"I beg your pardon. I mean, where were you born and
brought up?"

"In the city of Dubuque, Iowa."

"You are aware that the murdered man was a native of Cedar Rapids, in the same state—that he was practically a neighbor of yours until he left to come East?"

"I am so informed, yes."

"You did not know him back home?"

"Young man, we don't consider people across the width of a state neighbors out in Iowa. I never . . ."

"Answer the question, please."

"The answer is no." Miss Withers was getting hot under the collar.

"You did not ever have a love affair with Gerald Lester?"

"I did not! And I'll thank . . ."

The judge rapped his gavel.

Costello smiled knowingly. He ostentatiously referred to some entries in a little notebook, and then plunged on. "On the night of September first, fifteen years ago, you did not meet Gerald Lester on the eve of his departure for an eastern college and beg him to marry you?"

Miss Withers was speechless. She mantled a flaming red, and then realized that the jury would take this as the flush of guilt. She gulped.

"I did not!" she said. "Do you think I would ask a man some ten years my junior . . ."

"Answer the questions, Miss Withers. Did you not threaten Gerald Lester with personal injury, which was overheard by other young lovers in that Iowa park, in case he went away without taking you?"

"I did not!"

The Judge interrupted. "Really, I do not see where this is getting the defense in cross-examination. The witness is not on trial for the murder of Gerald Lester."

Barry Costello was instantly apologetic. "Your Honor, I beg the Court's pardon for my delay. But I assure the Court that I have a definite plan in mind, and one that will contribute to the case of my client. May I go on?"

Judge Thayer nodded slowly, and stared at his gavel.

"Miss Withers, did you not write letter after letter to Gerald Lester while he was at college in the East, begging him to come back to you?"

"I tell you, I never saw the man until I came on him in the Aquarium tank . . ."

"Miss Withers, you are under oath. Was it not true that you came to New York, giving up a better position in the Iowa school you left, in order to try and find Gerald Lester?"

"I refuse to answer!" Miss Withers was on her feet. "The questions all have one answer, No!"

"Very good." Barry Costello bowed most politely, and Miss Withers swiftly realized the weight that his daring fabrications had carried. Already the jury was gazing at her with a speculative leer.

"You have told the Court, Miss Withers, that you dispatched your pupils on a hunt for your hatpin, there in the Aquarium?"

"That's what I did." Miss Withers was trying to regain her temper. But Barry Costello was warming up to his work.

"You lagged behind them in the search, Miss Withers? So that no one knows exactly where you were during that twenty minutes or so, and no one could be brought forward to testify as to your innocent participation in the search?"

Miss Withers thought carefully. "Yes, I did lag behind. I don't know whether anyone saw me or not. But you'd lag behind, too, if you were riding herd on a bunch of scampering little outlaws . . ."

Costello nodded. "You are willing to swear that you did not have the missing hatpin tucked away in your dress or concealed in your hand at the time?"

"What? I certainly did not!"

"You had not noticed the defendant in this case, Mr. Seymour, carry the unconscious body of the man you had once loved—and then hated—in behind the tanks, and then come out and disappear toward the door? You did not seize your opportunity, send your little innocent charges on a wild-goose chase, and then dart into the runway behind the tanks to draw forth your deadly, if improvised, stiletto of a hatpin and drive it more foully and cruelly home in the right ear of the unconscious man?"

Before Barry Costello had finished, the courtroom was in an uproar, with Judge Thayer wielding his gavel right willingly, Tom Roche on his feet thundering objections, and Miss Withers tottering to her feet.

But Costello had made his point. He did not even wait for a denial of his last whirlwind, but turned and smiled triumphantly at Gwen Lester.

"Finished with the witness," he said.

Miss Withers rose to her feet. The world stopped whirling around her, and suddenly she realized that the one tiny gap left in the Lester murder puzzle was complete.

She found her voice, and it was a strong voice, a voice used to command. It rang out above the demands of Tom Roche to have the questions stricken from the record. It rang above the murmurings of the people in the courtroom.

"You may be finished with the witness, Mr. Barry Costello," she cried. "But the witness isn't finished with you. So Gerald Lester was stabbed in the *right* ear, was he? Let them strike the rest of your question out of the record, but leave that in. Because it's going to send you to the Chair, Barry Costello!"

Judge Thayer had his gavel poised to strike, but he did not let it fall. Perhaps the old man was weary of a Justice that wore bandages across her eyes.

Miss Withers caught her breath, and plunged on. "Only four people knew that Lester was stabbed in the right ear, young man. The medical examiner, who will testify to that when he's called as the next witness . . . he's one. Inspector Piper and I, who agreed to giving the story out to the newspapers and the public as the left ear, are number two and three."

Miss Withers pointed her finger at the amazed lawyer, whose mouth was open. "The fourth person who knew is the murderer, and there he stands, branded by his own tongue!"

For a moment she stood there, a flaming, triumphant Brunnhilde in a serge suit. Then the scandalized courtroom rose in waves about her, but not before she saw Inspector Piper vault the rail and fling himself on Barry Costello whose face was a twisted mask of hate and horror, and who was fumbling in the brief-case before him.

She had a glimpse of light on burnished metal, and saw the muzzle of a stubby gun press against Costello's forehead, and then twist away under the Inspector's strong grip. There was the click of handcuffs.

Then, for the first time since the whole affair had begun, Miss Withers allowed herself the luxury of a good, old fashioned fainting spell.

# 21

# And So to Bed

Iᴛ seemed several centuries later, though it could not have
been more than ten minutes or so, when Miss Withers saw
daylight again. She was lying on a davenport in a room she
guessed to be one of the judge's chambers, and Oscar Piper,
Inspector of Detectives, was clumsily putting wet cloths on
her forehead. She sat up suddenly.

"Don't bother with me, man." She pushed him away.
"Get your prisoner. Get Costello."

"You're not to worry yourself any more about Costello,"
said the Inspector with a grave smile. "He's safely *got*. Mr.
Barry Costello is hard and fast behind the bars by this time,
and he'll stay there until he comes out to stand trial himself
for the murder of Gerald Lester, thanks to you."

"Poor man," said Miss Withers. "Though I suppose he
deserves whatever he gets. He certainly handed me an unpleasant half hour on the witness stand. The idea of his nasty
insinuations . . ."

"He found you a bad person to monkey with," said Piper
soothingly. "I don't suppose you'd mind telling me how you
got wise to him? They've given me credit, outside, for being
in with you on this because we ran around together such a lot,
and because I was the first one to light into Costello when he
tried suicide."

"Sure I'll tell you," said Miss Withers. "I started suspecting Costello when I saw he had a book on collecting butterflies. A man who'd spent his boyhood sticking pins through
the heads of lovely insects would quite possibly think of
skewering somebody to death. But that was only suspecting."

"Go on," said Piper.

"And then he was so anxious to promote himself with
Gwen Lester," Miss Withers explained. "He told me, and

you too, about how another girl had turned him down because he lost his money. I didn't see at the time just how the dramatic justice of killing the man who had wronged him, and then marrying the widow and inheriting the insurance, would appeal to an adventurer like Costello. But the idea remained in the back of my mind. And then after that, you must have noticed that whatever happened to incriminate Gwen, or Seymour, or Hemingway, or anybody was also incriminating to Costello, too. He was there in the Aquarium for some reason he never explained. He was supposed to have gone home with Gwen that first afternoon, but he didn't get there, the maid admitted to your policeman. He could easily have returned to the place, or else have never even left it. He hid himself in the Men's Room, and smoked the cigarettes that we found on the floor."

"Sure," said Piper. "I was figuring along those lines. But I didn't see the ghost of a motive."

"I'll come to the motive in a minute," Miss Withers told him. "Costello was just the type of man to realize that he was safest right in the limelight, where he could keep tabs on the development of the case. The main difficulties he was up against were the two accidents. He'd dropped his hat in the pool during the murder, and he had to take the dead man's hat in order to mingle with the crowd outside. You didn't notice that he was extra polite during the questioning in Hemingway's office, and kept his hat always in his hand?"

"I didn't notice," admitted Piper.

"Well, he returned that night to get the hat out of the tank, where it had sunk among the rocks. A felt hat doesn't sink by itself for hours, Inspector. I tried it last week for an experiment. Well, it floated in our bathtub all night. So I reasoned that if the hat was floating in the pool when the officer and Costello drew out the dead man, somebody pushed it under then. And again Costello had a chance which no one else had."

Miss Withers was feeling much better now. She walked up and down the room.

"The other accident in what he figured to be the perfect murder was the fact that he'd been discovered behind the tanks by the pickpocket. Probably he was standing in the corner space behind the door when the little man ducked inside to escape the chase. Costello took no chances, and scared the little man out of his wits and his threats of what would happen if he talked . . . so much so that the pickpocket pretended to be dumb.

"Anyway, that night, while we were up on the upper level behind the tanks, Costello slipped out of the Men's Room and after laying out Rollins, snatched his own hat out of the tank. But the band was gone, only he didn't notice it then, or if he did it didn't matter, because it was beyond his reach. The penguin had swallowed it.

"So far, so good. But the pickpocket—after he got safe in jail, as he thought—lost his fear of Costello, and began blackmailing him. Remember how the Irishman was trying to raise money there for a few days? That wasn't for Gwen's defense; that was to pay off the pickpocket! But he couldn't get enough together to quiet the man, so he had to try something else."

"That would explain Costello's strange interest in the man called Chicago Lew," agreed Piper. "I wondered if it was simply because he thought the man had information that would free Gwen. Though, as a matter of fact, he had."

"Certainly. Then again, at the Aquarium. I brought Costello down there with me before I really suspected him. And we happened to walk in right when Hemingway was operating on the sick penguin . . . and Costello realized as soon as I did what that wad of silk was. He knew that it would give the head size of the murderer, and so he contrived to kick out the light plug and snatch it up."

"I don't see what he did with it," objected Piper.

"Did you think of his pipe? Neither did I, at the time. But it was going furiously, and smelling even worse than most pipes smell. It was a big briar, you remember. Couldn't the man have stuffed the hat-band, damp as it was, into his pipe and tamped it down with tobacco? That evidence did disappear into thin air, Inspector. It went up in smoke, literally."

"I take off my hat," said Piper.

"And then the business of the pickpocket suicide, Inspector. It struck us both funny that Costello made such a point of getting in to see the pickpocket first that morning, didn't it? He covered himself well by claiming he was protecting Gwen's interests. And then, when the net was closing around him, he very neatly turned our suspicions toward Seymour. He'd arranged for that by making a key that seemed to fit the cell door, and tossing it through the bars that morning as Seymour slept. The murder of Chicago Lew was done almost as Costello described it to us, except that he probably killed the man while he was inside the cell, and then after the guard had let him out into the corridor and established his alibi, he dragged on the wire and jerked the dead body into the air, to make it look like suicide.''

''And while he was inside the cell he tipped over the chair, too,'' suggested Piper. ''But how about the turnkey's statement that he saw the pickpocket sobbing and heard the bunk creak after he had locked Costello out of the cell?''

''Simple,'' Miss Withers pronounced. ''Costello was holding the end of the wire in his hand, though the turnkey didn't see it on account of the darkness and his own shortsightedness. And Costello simply jerked the wire and pulled the neck of the dead man from outside, to convince the guard!

''Did you ever see anything in your life as convincing as the way he demonstrated to us how Seymour must have killed the pickpocket?'' she went on. ''It didn't occur to me for hours that it might have been somebody besides the accused man who did the job, for the reason suggested. And when we sprung the business of the traced copper wire on him wasn't he glib with the admission that he'd bought it? A less smart man would have denied it, but Costello never denied anything that we could prove.''

''I noticed, myself, that Costello, for all his full morning dress when he came to tell me about the pickpocket's confession, which he had undoubtedly forged, hadn't his gloves with him,'' said Piper. ''When I went up to have a look at Seymour's hands, I saw that they were unmarked. And the man who dragged the body of the pickpocket up in the air by tugging on a wire must have either worn gloves or cut through his hands.''

''I didn't get that point,'' admitted Miss Withers. ''But didn't need it. You see, the whole case was complete for me when Costello made that little pun in your office. Remember He looked at your brightly spotted tweed suit and said that you were a regular *Pied* Piper?''

''That didn't strike me as so funny,'' said Piper.

"It wouldn't. But I've always hated puns. They're the lowest known form of humor. And it was then that I discovered the motive for the murder of Gerald Lester, only it was so far-fetched that I couldn't believe it myself for some time. Remember the mysterious client of Gerald Lester's, a Mr. Parson? That was the man who got sold out——yes, ruined—— on the market, though the transactions showed his stock was sold out before it hit bottom. In other words, a Mr. Parson had a real grudge against Lester, for it was a shady deal. Much more of a motive there than Hemingway had. A man who will pun once will pun again. He punned about your name, and when he chose a phoney name to use in undercover stock transactions some months ago, Costello punned again. He called himself Parson . . . Mr. Parson, or, in French, 'personne' meaning nobody! Mr. Nobody!"

"Then Costello was a client of Lester's? But why the undercover business?"

"Because he was gambling with money paid in to him as Treasurer of a non-existent Be Kind to Animals Society, mostly by the rich and silly women to whom he gave bridge lessons. And that is why he couldn't make a squawk about the undoubtedly sharp practice that Lester put over on him. Lester sold out Mr. Parson's stocks before they dropped five points, as the quotations in the paper of that day showed, but he charged up the account with a complete fifteen point drop, which wiped it out. See?"

"I'm beginning to," said Piper. "There *is* a motive."

"Sure there is. Lester feared Costello. That's why the broker hired a private detective to protect him for a while. That's why the man carried a loaded stick and had a gun in his desk. And Costello didn't confine himself to threats. He hung around Lester's home, undoubtedly. He followed Gwen Lester to the Aquarium that day, God knows why, and then when he saw what she was up to, he called her husband out of pure maliciousness. Only I don't see why Lester didn't recognize his voice."

"There's where I can help," said Piper humbly. "Remember the drinking tumbler in the booth?"

Miss Withers remembered it well. "That's an old trick," Piper told her. "In speaking over the phone, if you hold a tumbler up to the mouthpiece and speak into that, nobody on earth can recognize your voice. Remember how the switch-board girl said that the voice came from very far away, like a long distance call?''

"That fits in," said Miss Withers. "Anyhow, up to then Costello had only meant to cause trouble to the man he hated. Then he saw Lester and Seymour fight, and saw the broker go down, and then be carried behind the tank. Seymour and Gwen made for the door by their devious ways, and Costello saw his chance. He grabbed up my hatpin which was lying there on the steps or nearby, and with it in his hand he stepped through into the runway. There lay his enemy, and he did what he had come to do. As soon as he could get out, he mingled with the crowd, but it was too late to make a getaway because I had given the alarm, and he was forced to stand by. In that event, he was egotistic enough to enjoy worming his way into the spot-light as Gwen's rescuer, and then like a flash came the idea to him that he could get his fingers on the situation, free her and convict Seymour, and then marry her and live happily on the money. Of course, he's a madman, but you've said most murderers are. Neat, eh?''

"Neater than neat," said Piper. "You're a grand sleuth, Miss Withers. You had the right track all along. And I was digging for evidence that would convict somebody, not for the underlying motives. Now that we know all this, we can sweat the truth out of Costello. Probably they'll try him on the charge of murdering the pickpocket first, because that is plain premeditated murder, and the other might come under the second-degree charge. How do you feel?''

"Sort of sick," admitted Miss Withers. "Did I break up the murder trial?''

"You certainly did. Tom Roche had to ask for a dismissal under the circumstances. They'll be freeing Gwen and Philip Seymour in a little while. Want to see it?''

"More than anything in the world," said Miss Withers. "I've laid awake at night and thought of that young couple. They still have a chance at happiness now. They've won through it all, and maybe life will make up to them for what it did to them years ago when Gwen was forced to marry someone else, and these last few terrible weeks when they faced death together . . .''

"You are romantic, aren't you?" grinned the Inspector.

"Well, I'm old-fashioned," admitted Miss Withers. "I like my stories to finish up with a good happy love match. I like the last scene to be a fadeout, like a moving picture, with the suggestion at least that the young couple live happy ever after."

"You'll have to hurry if you want to see it," Piper told her. "They'll be releasing Gwen Lester and Philip Seymour in the next few minutes. Probably they'll send them out the back way to avoid the crowds and publicity. Tom Roche won't want the newspaper boys in on this. Come on, I know the place . . ."

He led Miss Withers out of the chamber and down a long hall. There was a high window at the end of the hall, which looked down on a narrow courtyard that opened into an alley.

"This is the back entrance to the Tombs," he told her. "Watch that little door down there if you want to see your last scene."

They waited there, it seemed interminably. Finally the little door opened, and someone looked out quickly. Then Philip Seymour came out, and paused on the steps. He was holding his shoulders square and erect again, and taking deep breaths of comparatively fresh air for the first time in weeks.

"He's waiting for her," said Miss Withers in a hushed voice. They watched Seymour light a cigarette.

Then the door opened again, and Gwen Lester came out. She looked at the man who waited there.

"We did it," whispered Miss Withers. She groped for the Inspector's rough hand. "Those kids are happy now because we . . ." She stopped suddenly.

Philip Seymour had held out his hand to Gwen, and she ignored it. Her nose was tilted into the wintry air, and a chill vibrated from her that even the two watchers on the third floor could sense.

She started to walk away, toward the distant street and the stream of taxicabs. And then Philip Seymour made a gesture that left Miss Withers gasping.

With his left hand he caught the beautiful, faithless cheek of Gwen Lester a resounding slap!

Then he turned on his heel and walked away. "Attaboy!" said Piper joyfully. "She led him a devil of a chase, but at least he had the good old-fashioned guts to hand her that one!"

Miss Withers was nearly crying. "But I thought they'd forget everything and start new," she said. "I wanted to see them kiss and go out arm in arm, taking up life where they were when she left him to marry Lester. I thought that the suffering they've been through would bring them together."

Piper folded his arms and glared at Miss Withers. "You've simply got to have the happy ending, haven't you? And so they married and lived happily ever after! Well, I don't see how you're going to get it, unless you can make up your mind to marry me."

His voice was light, but his gray-green eyes were serious. He was chewing a cigar very fast.

"Are you serious? You don't think it's too sudden?" Miss Withers blinked swiftly.

"I'm perfectly serious. I can't let as good a sleuth as you've shown yourself get out of the family. Come on, the License Bureau closes in fifteen minutes."

So they dashed madly toward City Hall.